"What the hell do you think you're doing?"

Spencer's deep voice bellowed with outrage.

Keeli snorted. "Saving your ass." She lay sprawled across him, his body hard and warm beneath hers. Too warm...

Too hard...

He was six feet of pure muscle and male indignation.

"You knocked me down!" he shouted.

A smirk tugged at her lips. He probably hadn't thought she could, since the first thing he'd done when she'd been assigned his bodyguard at the Payne Protection Agency meeting moments before was to call her his Bodyguard Barbie. Well, she'd had no problem knocking him down. She'd done it quickly and easily—just as the first shots had rung out. "To keep you from getting your head blown off."

* * *

Be sure to check out the previous books in the exciting Bachelor Bodyguards miniseries.

P9-CPZ-191

Dear Reader,

This book is the conclusion of my latest miniseries, Bachelor Bodyguards, from Harlequin Romantic Suspense. I hope you've all enjoyed the Payne Protection Agency and the Payne family as much as I've enjoyed writing this series. This particular series, featuring one main villain, has been extra fun for me to write, and Luther Mills has been a formidable and interesting foe for the Payne family.

As a member of a large family myself, I love how family always pulls together in tough times. Unfortunately the Paynes have more tough times than most, and so this series has gone on, picking up new "family" members along the way with the Payne Protection bodyguards. Keeli Abbott has been one of my favorite heroines to write, and I felt like she and Detective Spencer Dubridge were stealing the first four books in this series even though they were secondary characters in those books. Now they are the leads, locked in an exciting showdown with the supervillain. I hope you enjoy this conclusion to the series, although I suspect this won't be the last time we see the Payne family!

Happy reading!

Lisa Childs

BODYGUARD UNDER SIEGE

Lisa Childs

PAPL
DISCARDED

HARLEQUIN
ROMANTIC
SUSPENSE

If you purchased this book without a cover you should be aware
that this book is stolen property. It was reported as "unsold and
destroyed" to the publisher, and neither the author nor the
publisher has received any payment for this "stripped book."

HARLEQUIN®

ROMANTIC SUSPENSE™

Recycling programs
for this product may
not exist in your area.

ISBN-13: 978-1-335-75967-2

Bodyguard Under Siege

Copyright © 2022 by Lisa Childs

All rights reserved. No part of this book may be used or reproduced in
any manner whatsoever without written permission except in the case of
brief quotations embodied in critical articles and reviews.

This is a work of fiction. Names, characters, places and incidents
are either the product of the author's imagination or are used fictitiously.
Any resemblance to actual persons, living or dead, businesses,
companies, events or locales is entirely coincidental.

This edition published by arrangement with Harlequin Books S.A.

For questions and comments about the quality of this book,
please contact us at CustomerService@Harlequin.com.

Harlequin Enterprises ULC
22 Adelaide St. West, 41st Floor
Toronto, Ontario M5H 4E3, Canada
www.Harlequin.com

Printed in U.S.A.

Ever since **Lisa Childs** read her first romance novel—a Harlequin story, of course—at age eleven, all she wanted was to be a romance writer. With over seventy novels published with Harlequin, Lisa is living her dream. She is an award-winning, bestselling romance author. She loves to hear from readers, who can contact her on Facebook or through her website, lisachilds.com.

Books by Lisa Childs

Harlequin Romantic Suspense

Bachelor Bodyguards

His Christmas Assignment
Bodyguard Daddy
Bodyguard's Baby Surprise
Beauty and the Bodyguard
Nanny Bodyguard
Single Mom's Bodyguard
In the Bodyguard's Arms
Close Quarters with the Bodyguard

Colton 911: Chicago

Colton 911: Unlikely Alibi

The Coltons of Kansas

Colton Christmas Conspiracy

Visit the Author Profile page at Harlequin.com for more titles.

In loving memory of the very special people in my life that I've lost over the past two years: my father-in-law, John Ahearne; my sisters-in-law, Barbara Childs and Julia Scalici; my almost brother-in-law, Rick Coots; and my uncles Frank Childs and Leonard Wisniewski.

Chapter 1

Keeli's hand shook as she stared down at the pregnancy stick she was holding. Despite the shaking, she could, unfortunately, still read it. The little plus sign stared back at her, almost mockingly. It could not be right.

Sure, she'd been sick for the past several weeks, but she'd thought it was Spencer Dubridge who'd been making her ill with his chauvinistic comments and attitudes. But if this test was accurate, he had actually made her sick another way—that night so many weeks ago.

The night she'd lost her damn mind...

Her skin tingled, and she shivered as she remembered the heat—the passion. But then she quickly pushed thoughts of that encounter from her head. Keeli needed to get back into the courtroom. She was supposed to be serving as backup to her fellow bodyguards if infamous drug lord Luther Mills tried anything during his trial.

And of course he would try something. That was why she'd been protecting Spencer Dubridge, because the detective had been threatened along with everyone else associated with Luther Mills's arrest and prosecution for first-degree murder. Despite Luther's best efforts over the past nine weeks, everybody had survived.

Although Keeli felt like dying…

She tucked the test into a clear plastic bag and dropped it into her purse. Then she pulled open the door to the bathroom stall and stepped out. She was all alone in the ladies' room with only her reflection staring back at her from the wall of mirrors behind the row of sinks. Her face was pale, and it wasn't just in contrast to the black sweater and pants she wore. The pallor of her skin made her eyes look even bluer and brighter than they usually appeared. After washing her hands, she ran her fingers through her long blond hair, pushing it back into place.

Dubridge was out there—probably waiting in the hall since he had yet to testify against Luther. Despite how incredibly handsome he looked in his dark suit with his crisp white shirt, or maybe *because* of it, she dreaded seeing him. But the chief of police had hired the Payne Protection Agency to guard everyone associated with the trial, so it was her job—as a bodyguard—to keep him safe.

He hadn't made it easy for her—with his insulting, chauvinistic attitude or with that damn unfortunate attraction she felt for him. Her stomach churned, and feeling sick again, she nearly returned to the bathroom stall. How could she be drawn to such a chauvinist? He had been nothing but rude to her back when they'd worked together in the River City Police Department Vice Unit. And that certainly hadn't changed when she'd been assigned as his bodyguard.

Bodyguard Barbie—that was what he called her.

She grimaced as she headed toward the doorway. As she pushed opened the door and stepped into the corridor, gunfire blasted, rattling the windows. People shrieked and dropped to the floor.

Keeli didn't wonder from where the shots were coming. The shooting had to be taking place in Judge Holmes's courtroom, where Luther Mills was being tried for murder.

How many more murders had he just committed?

Her heart raced with fear and dread. So many of her friends were in that courtroom. And maybe Spencer had already been called inside to testify.

She reached for her purse to pull out her weapon, just as Luther Mills appeared. He was dressed in a suit, his dark hair clipped short and his jaw clean-shaven. But with a gun in his hand, he still looked like the thug he was. He laughed when he saw her and grabbed her arm with his free hand, his grasp painfully tight.

She could have dropped him with an elbow or her knee. But she wouldn't have been able to escape the armed men with him. They had their backs turned toward her, their guns blasting as they fired down the hallway. But if she overpowered Luther, they would see her.

Then she noticed something else—*someone* else— in the doorway next to the ladies' room. A dark-haired head peeked around the men's room door. Spencer...

She wasn't the only one who spotted him, unfortunately. The men fired at Spencer, splintering the doorjamb near his head while Luther pressed his gun against her temple.

"Stay back, Detective," Luther warned, "or your bodyguard's brains are going to get blown all over this courthouse!"

Keeli was more worried about Spencer's brains because of how close some of those bullets had come to his handsome face. "Stay back!" she told him. It was her job to protect him; she couldn't let him get hurt because he was trying to rescue her.

But before she could say anything else, Luther jerked her away from the restroom doorways and dragged her down the hall. Using his back, he pushed open a door and pulled her inside a stairwell with him. Every instinct screamed at her to struggle, to stumble on the steps or fall to try to escape from him. But that barrel was pressed so tightly against her temple and his finger was nearly squeezing the trigger, so the gun could easily go off.

And now, if the test she'd taken was accurate, it wasn't just her life she was risking if she tried to get away. And she wasn't even sure that she *should* get away. If Luther made it out of the courthouse, she wanted to know where the hell he was going.

And there was no easier or more surefire way for her to do that than to go with him. She would have to be careful to escape—just as he had—before getting killed.

They didn't make it easily out of the courthouse, though. Once they opened the door to the stairwell on the main level, more gunfire rang out. Courthouse security and other bodyguards fired at them. Luther ducked down, but he didn't press on his trigger.

Instead, he let the men with them fire back at the guards, allowing them to take the bullets meant for him, as he pulled Keeli along with him. They were headed toward a back door that opened onto an alley. It should have been secured, but the guard manning it held the door for Luther and for her.

The guard must have been on the drug dealer's payroll as so many other people had been. Police officers and assistant district attorneys and crime scene technicians… And now apparently courthouse security guards, too. Maybe that was how he and his men had gotten weapons past the ordinarily high security of the courthouse.

A van was parked in the alley, its side door standing open to the cargo area in the back. The colors identified it as a police van, but it wasn't a police officer driving it. Or if it was, he worked for Luther because he shouted, "Get in! Get in!"

Gunfire continued to blast, echoing through the alley. The guard holding open the door suddenly fell back against it, and as his body slid down the metal, he left a thick trail of blood behind and pooling beneath him.

As Luther headed toward the van, he dragged Keeli along with him but kept her between him and that open back door to the building—the door the guard's body propped open now. Spencer suddenly appeared in that doorway, his gun raised toward Luther—toward her.

Over the past several weeks, he had probably felt like shooting her once or twice. She'd certainly felt like killing him a time or four or ten. He was so damn infuriating.

But instead of firing, he shouted, "Let her go!"

Luther chuckled in amusement as he pressed the gun barrel even more tightly against her temple.

She flinched, and a curse slipped from Spencer's lips as he noticed her pain. Hopefully Luther hadn't because she knew better than to reveal any weakness to him.

Mills stepped through the open side door of that van. "Don't try to follow me," he warned the detective as he dragged her up into the vehicle with him. "Or you'll be picking up pieces of her off the road behind me."

He had a gun—not a knife. But she wasn't about to point that out to him. She wasn't about to say anything until she found out where the hell he was going and who all was helping him.

He pulled the door closed, and the driver pressed hard on the accelerator, tires squealing as he sped out of the alley. She and Luther fell against the side of the van. Keeli could have broken away from him then. She also probably could have jerked open that door and jumped out. It looked as though Luther hadn't closed it tightly. If he had, it would be locked on the inside—since it looked like the jail transport vehicle with a cage between the front and the back. But instead of testing the lock, she just sat down on the floor.

Luther narrowed his dark eyes and studied her face as if trying to figure her out. They'd met before—back when she'd worked vice. Of course he hadn't known she was a cop at the time, or she probably wouldn't have survived her undercover assignment. Unlike most everybody else in the vice unit who'd been after him, she'd focused more on sex trafficking, which was the one major crime Luther Mills had not committed.

"You better not be playing me," he warned her. "Or I really will cut you up in pieces."

Panic pressed heavily on Spencer's heart as he watched the van race away with Keeli locked inside—with that animal Luther Mills. How the hell had that happened?

He cursed as he ran toward the parking garage and the unmarked detective's vehicle Keeli had parked there when they'd arrived at the courthouse. Footsteps echoed his and he turned, with his weapon drawn, to make sure none of Luther's crew was trying to stop him.

Parker Payne was at his heels. "Where the hell are you going?" Keeli's boss asked him.

"I have to try to catch them!" Spencer said. He was not about to lose Keeli—not that he actually had her. Except for that one night…

But he was beginning to believe that had all been just a dream, that it had never really happened. That they had never actually been together like that—out of control with desire for each other.

"You can't!" Parker snapped. "Didn't you hear Luther's threats?"

Keeli's boss must have caught up with them just as they'd been heading out that back door to the alley. Spencer hadn't noticed Parker or anyone else, though. He'd been too focused on her, too focused on that damn gun pressed to her head.

Should he have tried to take the shot? But that would have meant risking Luther squeezing the trigger as he went down, taking Keeli with him.

"I'm damn sick of Luther's threats," Spencer said. Luther's reign of terror was why Keeli was in danger in the first place—because she had been assigned to protect him from the crime boss.

Now Spencer needed to protect *her*. Keeli was in far more danger than he had ever been. She was the one who had been kidnapped. Why had Luther taken her? Just to make sure he got away? Or to kill her?

"Luther's making good on some of those threats," Parker said.

Spencer stopped running as dread gripped him. He hadn't been in the courtroom when the shooting started. He'd been in the men's restroom while Keeli had been using the ladies'. And once the shooting had started, he'd thought only of finding her but, unfortunately, Luther had found her first. Now he wondered what had happened to everyone else.

"Who's dead?" he asked anxiously. Spencer knew that, since his arrest nine weeks ago, Luther Mills had threatened to eliminate everyone associated with his trial: the eyewitness, the crime scene tech, even the judge's daughter, the assistant district attorney prosecuting his case and Spencer. Some of these people were Spencer's colleagues, some of them friends as well. "Or hurt?"

Parker flinched. "The chief."

Woodrow Lynch wasn't just the man who'd hired Parker's security agency for extra protection for everyone associated with the trial. Lynch was also Parker's stepfather. Parker had already lost one father—years ago.

Spencer reached out and gripped his former co-worker's shoulder. "Is he…?"

"Not dead," Parker said with a shake of his head. But Spencer didn't release the breath he held until the man added, "Just a shoulder wound."

Now he sighed. But then the breath jammed up again in his lungs when he thought of Keeli—alone with a killer. She could be the next one getting injured or even killed. Suddenly, that sense of urgency gripped him again, making his heart pound furiously and his pulse race hard and fast.

"We have to try to follow them," Spencer insisted as he began to run toward his vehicle again. "We can't let him get her too far away from us."

From *him*…

But he'd been the one pushing her away for years. When they'd worked together in the River City PD Vice Unit, she'd requested the most dangerous assignments, and it drove him crazy how she always rushed in without waiting for backup. Either she'd been trying to prove herself or she'd had a death wish. He'd never been able to figure that one out. All Spencer knew for sure was that he'd already lost someone he'd known— someone like her who'd been too headstrong to accept any help. Keeli probably thought that was why he didn't want her as his bodyguard—that he was too proud and stubborn to admit he needed protection. He just didn't want her taking those unnecessary risks for him. So he'd been obnoxious to her for years—at first to get her to leave her job in the vice unit and then to get her to quit her assignment protecting him.

"Keeli can take care of herself," Parker said.

Everybody had been telling him that—for years. No one more vehemently than she had. But he wanted to be the one to take care of her. Just like he'd wanted to take care of Rebecca. He'd lost his chance with Rebecca. Now he might have lost Keeli, too.

Forever...

Luther glanced in the side mirror, watching for anyone following them. He couldn't believe he'd gotten away from the courthouse as easily as he had. Sure, he'd lost most of the special talent he'd hired to help with his escape. Several had gotten shot in the courtroom.

Thanks to Parker Payne and his damn bodyguards.

He glanced back at Keeli—to where she sat in the back of the van. A safe distance from the courthouse, Luther had had the driver stop and let him out of the locked cargo area, so he could ride up front—separated from her by that protective glass.

She was one of those damn bodyguards. So even after taking her weapon, he didn't trust her.

Maybe he should cut her up and leave pieces of her like bread crumbs along the road. That would send a message to Parker Payne to mind his own damn business and stay the hell out of Luther's.

But it wasn't just Parker that Luther had to worry about. Detective Dubridge had arrested him once, so he would be even more determined to arrest him again.

For escaping.

And kidnapping his bodyguard.

Why hadn't Keeli fought him harder—either at the courthouse or when he'd had the cargo area opened so he could move to the front? She could have tried to escape then, too. But she hadn't...

Luther knew the former undercover vice cop pretty well. She was usually feisty. A fighter...

But she hadn't fought him at all. He glanced back at her again. Her face was pale. With fear?

She'd never shown any before.

Before he'd had the driver open the back of the van, Luther had frisked her for weapons and grabbed her purse. The red leather bag was heavy, so her gun was probably in it. He unclasped the flap on the front of it and looked inside the deep bag. Sure enough her Glock lay on the bottom of it in a holster. But that wasn't what caught his attention.

He noticed the test in the plastic baggie. And he laughed. "Congratulations, Mama," he said.

And her face got even paler.

Maybe that was why she hadn't fought him—because she was pregnant.

"Who's the daddy?" he wondered aloud. The last he'd heard about her, she was single. Maybe being a bodyguard left no more time for a relationship than it had when she'd been an undercover cop. So who had she hooked up with?

She pressed her lips together as if to hold in the answer. Was that just because she didn't want to tell him? Or because she was disgusted with the answer herself?

And he knew.

He laughed harder. "Detective Dubridge…"

It seemed as if every damn one of Parker Payne's bodyguards had crossed the line with the person they'd been assigned to protect. He could understand the guys with the women. But he couldn't understand Keeli Abbott. She was the kind of beauty who could have any man she wanted.

He snorted then. "Why Dubridge?"

She shook her head, looking as befuddled as Luther was. Maybe she hadn't fought him because she'd wanted to get away from Dubridge.

"It was a mistake," she murmured.

For a moment Luther had thought bringing her along might have been a mistake—that she was playing him. But now, seeing this pregnancy test, he realized how important a hostage she was. The Payne Protection Agency would back off to keep her alive. And now so would Dubridge—because if he lost Keeli, he wasn't just losing his bodyguard, he'd be losing his kid, too.

Chapter 2

Keeli's stomach lurched with every turn of the van. But she forced down the nausea and focused on the ride, trying to keep track of every one of those turns— even after Luther had pulled a privacy curtain across the other side of the protective glass separating the front from the back. She had been especially cognizant then, of the rights and lefts and of the possible distances between each of those turns.

During her years with the River City PD and even before that, she'd spent a lot of time on the streets, so she knew this Michigan city well. She hadn't spent much time in a patrol car, though.

Shortly after graduating from the police academy, she'd been assigned to the vice unit. Due to her youthful appearance and small stature, she'd looked more like a kid than a cop, so she'd been perfect for undercover work. She'd only had one problem...

Spencer Dubridge.

He'd been in the vice unit then and had been adamantly opposed to her going undercover. Hell, he'd been adamantly opposed to her being a cop. He'd given her such a damn hard time.

Telling her she didn't belong...

That she should choose a desk job over an undercover assignment. That she wasn't strong enough to survive the streets...

Little did he know that she already had.

Fortunately nobody else she'd worked with had shared his chauvinistic beliefs. And she'd made damn certain his opinions and the man himself hadn't gotten to her. His doubts about her abilities had not only chased away whatever misgivings of her own she might have had, but he'd made her even more determined to be the best damn cop she could be.

And she *had* been a good cop for the five years she'd been on the force. She was an even better bodyguard. Or she had been until she'd been assigned to protect Spencer Dubridge.

Of course he'd survived. She wasn't so certain she would, though. And that had nothing to do with Luther Mills abducting her from the courthouse and everything to do with that positive test result.

She was pregnant.

That was mostly why she hadn't fought Luther back at the courthouse. Even though she was surprised about the pregnancy, she didn't want to risk causing harm to her unborn baby. That was why she hadn't wrestled Luther for his gun or tumbled down the stairs with him. It was also why she couldn't jump out of the van—even if she could unlock the door from the inside. After he'd switched to the front, Luther had made damn certain it had closed tightly, and since this was the jail transport van, there was no way for her to open that door from the inside. So now she had to wait until someone opened it for her.

The driver...

She couldn't believe Luther had another police officer helping him. But then she shouldn't have been surprised. They'd already known he had moles in the police department and the district attorney's office. And he had to have been getting help *in* jail. So of course he'd been able to get help to get *out* of jail.

What had it taken for these people to betray their morals—their positions—their coworkers...?

Had Luther threatened the lives of people they cared about—like he'd tried using the judge's daughter to sway him into ruling how he'd wanted in court? Or had he simply thrown a ton of money at them like he had at the leak in the district attorney's office?

While she had enough money to pay her bills, Keeli didn't have any extra to throw around. She couldn't outbid Luther for the driver's loyalty. So she had no doubt that if Luther ordered the guy to kill her, he would.

She had to figure out how to get away from them— just as soon as she ascertained where they'd taken her. She was counting in her head, still keeping track of those turns. Then the van rumbled over something that felt like tracks, and she heard a shrill whistle and the telltale beeping of a gate lowering over those train tracks. They'd already crossed over them, so the van continued on a short distance before making another right turn. Then it braked momentarily. Metal cranked and clattered as an overhead door shuddered open. The van moved forward—just a few yards—before braking again. Then the engine shut off.

They had arrived at their destination. But where the hell *were* they?

A garage of some sort? Was it attached to a house? Or was it part of a building? Not as many train tracks ran through residential areas as through the industrial part of the city.

The front doors of the van opened, and the vehicle rose a bit higher after the two big men stepped out. Then the doors slammed shut again. Were they going to leave her locked in the back of the van?

Maybe that wouldn't be a bad thing. She could be safer in here than anywhere with Luther. But then the sliding door rolled open, and he stared inside at her.

"We're here, Keeli."

"Where's here?" she asked.

He grinned. "Wouldn't you love to know?"

She would. But if he told her, she knew she had no hope of surviving her abduction. Luther wouldn't let her live if she could lead authorities to where he was hiding.

"No," she said. "I don't want to know."

"What *do* you want?" he asked, and he narrowed his dark eyes at her, as if he was trying to figure it out himself. "Detective Dubridge?"

She'd wanted Spencer once. Hell, she'd wanted him more than that. But she'd only given in to that temptation one night. Apparently once—they'd actually done it several times that night, though—had been enough for her to get pregnant.

She shook her head. "No." She shook her head more vehemently. "Hell, no."

And Luther laughed. "I always wondered what people were talking about with that protesting too much saying…" He grinned. "Now I get it."

She kept shaking her head. "No…"

"It would be better if you were telling the truth, " he said. "Because Spencer Dubridge isn't going to be alive much longer."

She gasped at the twinge of pain striking her heart. She couldn't stand the man, but she certainly didn't want him dead. In fact, she couldn't imagine her life without his infuriatingly handsome face in it…

"What are you talking about?" she asked.

Luther grinned. "Revenge, sweet Keeli. I'm talking about revenge on everybody who tried to bring me down."

She felt another twinge in her heart, but the fear wasn't just for Spencer but for all of her friends. And herself…

And the baby she'd just learned she was carrying. Maybe it was because she'd been so stunned that she had stumbled out of the restroom and so easily into Luther's clutches.

But if she hadn't been thinking about her child, she might already be dead—because she would have fought Luther in the courthouse and caused the gun to go off. And then she would have had no chance of escaping him alive.

She might not have a chance now—if she didn't start working on it. "Luther, you don't have time for revenge," she advised him. "Everybody—police, FBI, US Marshals—is out looking for you. If you want to get away, you need to leave River City as soon as you possibly can."

She knew that they hadn't left town. They hadn't driven far enough or long enough to escape the Michigan city that was even bigger than Detroit. So they were somewhere within the city limits. But where?

Beyond the open side door of the van, the garage was dark with no windows to let in light. If not for the dome light inside the van, she probably wouldn't have seen Luther's face. She couldn't see much beyond it but the dark shadow of a vehicle parked next to the van.

The big black SUV looked quite similar to those driven by Payne Protection bodyguards. A chill chased down Keeli's spine as she realized that was probably not an accident. Luther had a plan—for that SUV and for the agency.

"Don't worry about me," he told her. "I have plenty of time to take care of my business before I need to get out of here."

Of course Luther wouldn't retire and go into hiding somewhere, keeping low. Instead, he would take over another city, probably in another country, with his crime and corruption once again endangering everyone.

She shook her head. "You might have time…if it was only the FBI, Marshals and police coming after you. But the Payne Protection Agency is coming for you, too. And they're going to come hard."

He reached out then and grabbed her arms, jerking her toward him. "Because of you…"

"You shouldn't have taken me," she told him.

His mouth curved into that evil grin of his. "I can remedy that right now…" And he slid his hands up her arms to her shoulders and then her throat.

She could have broken his hold and pushed him back. But she doubted the guard would let her slip past both of them. And she wasn't sure where they were, so she had no idea if they'd joined other gunmen.

So instead of fighting him physically, she fought him mentally. "You know I'm of more use to you alive than dead…"

He tilted his head and his grin tilted, too, sliding into a crooked one. "Really? How so?"

"Parker will work with you—to make sure you don't hurt me," she explained. Not long after she'd joined the River City PD, Parker had left it to start the bodyguard business with his twin brother, Logan, but during the time they'd worked together, he'd treated her like a kid sister. Not *his* sister, though. According to his actual sister, Nikki Payne-Ecklund, Parker had treated Keeli with more respect than he had her. He'd been too protective of Nikki to let her become a bodyguard in his branch of the family business, so she'd gone to work for one of her other brothers, Cooper. The former Marine had his own branch of the family business, just like Parker did now, while Logan ran the original one.

"Dubridge has more to lose," Luther said.

"No…" She shook her head, tumbling her hair around her face. "We hate each other."

Her abductor held up the plastic bag he'd taken from her purse. "That whole thing about protesting too much…"

"Sure, I'm pregnant," she said, and the announcement sucked the breath from her lungs for a moment. She felt as if she'd punched herself. "But that doesn't mean Spencer Dubridge is the father."

How she wished he wasn't...

But she hadn't been involved with anyone else for a while before she'd been assigned the job of protecting him. If only she'd protected herself...

That night had been so crazy, though. They'd been crazy—for each other. They'd used protection... Until they'd run out of condoms. But then it had been too late and they hadn't wanted to stop. Hell, they'd been so out of control that they hadn't been *able* to stop.

"You're right that my time is limited," Luther said. "Too limited to play games with you." He jerked her out of the van then and pulled her toward a door.

She remained silent as he dragged her into a small kitchen. They were in a house. But all the blinds and curtains were drawn. She couldn't see outside, couldn't tell where the house was...just that it was dated.

The appliances were green, the countertops yellow and the cabinets were dark-stained plywood—like the spool-like tabletop in the eat-in area of the kitchen. But at least it was all clean, the counters and appliances shiny and the wooden tabletop polished so it looked smooth. Someone had cleaned it up and gotten it ready for Luther. Who the hell all was helping him?

While the bodyguard agency had found the leak in the district attorney's office, they weren't sure who'd been helping Luther within the River City Police Department. They'd found a complicit crime scene tech, and a young officer had died trying to take out the witness for him. But the chief and Parker Payne suspected there were others—higher-ranking officers—

helping Luther. That there almost had to be, otherwise Luther wouldn't have come so close to taking out all the people he'd threatened.

But close wasn't good enough for this criminal mastermind. He was determined to finish what he'd started. And she was the only one who could figure out a way to stop him.

But she couldn't even get him to linger in the kitchen. He pulled her down a short hall, pushed open a door and shoved her inside it. "Don't waste your time screaming," he advised her. "The houses around here are all vacant."

So it was a residential area—not industrial. And if the other houses were vacant, it was a bad area of the city. Or one where Luther owned enough of the homes to empty them for his plan.

He continued, "So nobody will hear you but me. And that'll just piss me off." He lowered his voice to a growl. "And, Keeli, you don't want to piss me off any more than you already have."

"What did I do, Luther?" she asked.

"You kept Dubridge alive," Luther said.

She wasn't certain what he was talking about. Sure, there had been a couple of attempts on Spencer's life, but they'd seemed almost half-hearted tries. There hadn't been the number of attempts and the sheer onslaught on Spencer that there had been on the other people Luther had threatened.

"But you're not going to be around to do that anymore," Luther assured her. "And Detective Dubridge won't be around much longer either."

A chill coursed down her spine. Was he intending to kill them both?

Before she could ask, Luther pulled the door closed—leaving her in the dark. Figuratively.

And literally…

Keeli could see nothing of the room in which he'd locked her. She'd heard the lock slide; there was a dead bolt on the outside of the door.

Luther had thought of everything when he'd set up his escape and his hideout. Maybe he'd even planned to take a hostage when he'd fled from the courthouse.

But when he'd taken her, he'd taken the wrong damn one. Keeli wasn't going to be used as leverage to control her boss or the chief of police. She was going to be the weapon taking Luther down again.

She just had to figure out where the hell they were. She walked forward carefully, her hands outstretched so she didn't fall. Her foot hit the edge of something low to the ground, and she knelt down and touched the softness of a mattress lying on the floor.

Weariness tugged at her. But she pushed it aside to focus on the room. Using her hands, she blindly explored every inch of it—which didn't take long. The place wasn't big. The only door, besides the locked one, was to an empty closet. And the one window had been boarded over with plywood—the nails driven too deep for her to pry out—even if she'd found a tool for that job.

Maybe she could make a tool. But from what…?

The only thing in the room was the mattress on the floor. Keeli dropped onto it. She would sit down for a moment—just a moment—to think.

And listen…

She could hear the rumble of Luther's deep voice outside the door. He was talking to someone. But she couldn't hear the other person talking back. The guard hadn't come inside the house with them, and she hadn't heard the door between the garage and the kitchen open since Luther had locked her in the room. He must have been on a phone. But it sounded as if he was the one doing all the talking. He must have been giving orders to someone who didn't dare question or comment on anything their boss said.

He expected blind obedience. That was why he'd killed that kid, Javier Mendez, for whose murder he'd been standing trial today—because Javier had turned into a police informant. The boy had been working with the vice unit, Clint Quarters specifically, to try to bring Luther down. And he'd wound up shot dead in front of his sister...

Luther didn't tolerate what he saw as betrayal. Anybody who crossed him died—some far more painfully than Javier Mendez had died.

Keeli and her Payne Protection colleagues had crossed him. But Spencer—he was the one who'd tracked Luther down and, in front of his crew, had slapped the handcuffs on him, had put the drug lord in the back of a police car and hauled him off to jail.

Luther probably wanted Spencer dead more than anyone else. But he'd sent more of his crew after the eyewitness, Javier Mendez's sister, and the crime scene technician than he had Spencer. He'd even managed to have the judge's daughter abducted—though it hadn't taken her bodyguard, Tyce Jackson, very long to find and rescue her. Even the assistant district attorney prosecuting Luther had had more attempts on her life. But most of those had been from her coworker, who'd been Luther's leak in the DA's office.

The attempts on Spencer's life might not have even been because of Luther. Anyone could want revenge against Detective Dubridge—for his arresting them or hassling them like he'd hassled her.

For how difficult he'd made her job in vice, she could want revenge against him. But when those attempts had happened, she'd knocked him to the ground; she'd saved his life. And instead of being grateful, he'd yelled at her for putting herself in danger. He had to be furious with her now—for not fighting Luther—for letting him take her.

She remembered the last time he'd been that furious with her...

Chapter 3

Eight weeks earlier...

"What the hell do you think you're doing?" Spencer yelled, his deep voice cracking with outrage.

Keeli snorted. "Saving your ass." She lay sprawled across him, his body hard and warm beneath hers. Too warm...

Too hard.

He was six feet of pure muscle and male indignation.

"You knocked me down!" he shouted.

A smirk tugged at her lips. He probably hadn't thought she could, since the first thing he'd done when she'd been assigned his bodyguard at the Payne Protection Agency meeting moments before was to call her his Bodyguard Barbie. Well, she'd had no problem knocking him down. She'd done it quickly and easily—just as the first shots had rung out. "To keep you from getting your head blown off."

The bullets had whizzed over them as she'd slammed them to the ground. They were lucky they hadn't been hit.

Spencer's big hands gripped her hips, easing her away from him. But it was too late; she'd already felt his body's reaction to her closeness. Her skin heated and tingled from the contact, too, from the fiery attraction that she always tried so hard to ignore.

How could she be drawn to such a chauvinistic pig? She couldn't; it wasn't possible.

But then he effortlessly lifted her as he got to his feet, and more heat streaked through her, from where his hands gripped her hips to the tips of her breasts to her very core. Anger, with herself as well as with him, pushed aside that attraction, though, as she pushed his hands off her.

Undeterred, he grabbed her again, by the elbow, and tugged her along behind him into his house. He'd just unlocked the door of the little brick ranch when the gunfire had first rung out.

"It's not safe to stay here," she told him.

"The shooter is gone now," he said. But he didn't even glance at the street as he closed the door behind them.

"He could come back." And probably would…if he was working for Luther.

Spencer shrugged off her concerns. "I doubt it."

"We need to call the police," she said.

"I *am* the police."

"You can't investigate an attempt on your own life," she pointed out.

"I don't need to," he said as he walked into his living room. Despite all the years she'd known him, this was the first time she'd been to his house. It was like him—dark and masculine—with deep chocolate walls and leather furniture. "I'm fine."

"Thanks to me," she retorted as she trailed him across the hardwood floors.

Mahogany California shutters were closed at the front windows. She couldn't see out, but nobody could see inside either. That didn't mean he was safe. She certainly didn't feel safe—not with this damn attraction she felt for Spencer Dubridge. Why the hell did he have to be so good-looking? It wasn't fair.

But she pushed her unwanted desire aside and focused on the anger instead. "You're welcome."

"I didn't thank you."

"I know." And she hadn't expected him to—he was too proud to admit a woman had saved his life. Especially her...

Spencer had treated her so badly back when they'd been in the vice unit together. He'd told her and whoever else would listen that she would wind up dead—that there was no way she could survive going undercover on the streets of River City.

Not only had she survived undercover, she'd shut down several sex trafficking rings—not that he had ever acknowledged her success. Nor had he ever found out why she was so successful—because she'd grown up on those streets. She knew well how to survive on them.

"I don't need you," he said, reminding her of all

the times he'd told her she didn't belong on the police force and most especially in the vice unit.

"I'm not any happier about this than you are," she assured him. "You're the last person I want to protect."

His mouth curved into a slight grin. "You'd rather hurt me yourself."

Not wanting him to think that he actually got to her, she shook her head. "I wouldn't waste my time."

He snorted. "You just know that you couldn't."

A growl of anger slipped through her lips. "I just dropped you outside." That had been to save his life, though. "Why the hell can't you admit that I can do my job?"

He snorted again.

And she snapped, kicking his legs out from under him to topple him down to his couch. Instinctively, he'd reached out and caught her arms, jerking her down with him—on top of him like before when she'd knocked him to the ground. She felt the hardness of his body beneath her, his immediate reaction to her closeness.

And she had a reaction of her own. Heat flowed through her, making her skin tingle and her heart race. "Why…?" she murmured, but she was asking herself that question.

Spencer stared up at her, his brown eyes going even darker as his pupils dilated. "I don't need you," he gritted out, but instead of releasing her, he moved his hand to the back of her head. "But I damn well want you."

She wanted him, too. "Damn you," she murmured as she closed the distance between them and pressed her mouth to his.

And he kissed her.

Deeply.

Passionately...

So passionately that Keeli's control snapped, and she kissed him back, giving in to the attraction she felt for him—that she'd *always* felt for him.

If only all she'd done was kiss him... But they'd done more. So much more...

Spencer couldn't forget that night all those weeks ago—no matter how much he'd tried. But maybe he hadn't tried that hard. He'd never felt like that before, had never felt that zealous with desire, had never experienced that much pleasure.

But it had been a mistake. One they had been careful not to repeat. Maybe giving in to their attraction hadn't been the mistake. Maybe not doing it again had been.

No. Having Keeli as his bodyguard had been the mistake. One that would probably get her killed—just like he'd been worried would happen. Maybe it already had.

Spencer shook his head to forget that horrific thought as well as the memories of that night—that incredible night. He forced himself to focus on the people in the hospital room with him instead.

Chief Lynch lay on the bed, one shoulder heavily bandaged. His wife, Penny Payne-Lynch, lay next to him, her curly-haired head pressed against his other shoulder, her arm around his waist. She clung to him like she never intended to let him go. Woodrow Lynch leaned down and kissed her forehead.

And a pang of envy struck Spencer's heart. The

chief and his wife had something special—something rare—a love that was deep and true.

Spencer had once thought he was in love, but he realized now that those feelings had been the shallow feelings of infatuation and friendship. It had still hurt when it ended, though.

Or maybe what had hurt more was not so much that it had ended but *how* it had ended. Spencer had felt so helpless then. But it was nothing in comparison to how helpless he felt now.

"We have to find her!" He pushed his fingers through his mussed-up hair. "I never should have let him get her into that van. Damn it!"

Parker, who was also in the room with his mom and stepfather, snorted. "Keeli wouldn't have let him take her—if she hadn't wanted to go."

"Why the hell would she want to go with a killer?" Spencer demanded.

"To make sure he didn't get away," Parker said.

It sounded like Keeli—like the determined young cop she'd been. But it was that determination to prove herself that kept putting her life in danger, just like it had now. His harping on what he called her recklessness might have been another reason for her to go with Luther. She probably hadn't minded getting away from Spencer for a while.

He had been such an ass to her—pretty much since the moment he'd met her at the River City PD and had learned she'd been assigned to the vice unit. Seeing her in disguise, knowing how much danger she was putting herself in undercover—especially when she'd insisted on going alone, with no backup. And the assignments she'd taken, the risks, had reminded him too much of Rebecca. Of the risk she'd taken…

Of his inability to protect her.

It had infuriated him, making him feel helpless all over again.

Just like he felt now. Just like he'd felt with Rebecca. Sure, Keeli had survived all her assignments but not without some scrapes and bruises, not without some way-too-close calls. And he'd worried that she would eventually wind up like Rebecca had.

Dead.

Spencer squared his jaw. He couldn't let himself think about that now, that it could already be too late to save her.

"But Luther did get away," he pointed out. "And he took Keeli with him, and now we don't know where either one of them is."

"We'll find them," Parker said.

"How?" He realized why his former coworker had wanted to check on the chief; the guy was his stepfather. But they were wasting valuable time here. "You know that if we don't find Keeli within forty-eight hours that we probably won't find her alive."

Parker flinched, probably because he was also well aware of the statistics and how they were not in Keeli's favor. "It's only been a few hours," he pointed out. "We'll figure out where he took her."

"How?" Spencer asked again. "If you would've let me follow that damn van…" His voice cracked.

"If we'd tried to follow him, Luther would have killed her just like he'd threatened," Parker said, "to make sure he could get away."

If he'd tossed her out like he'd threatened, they would have stopped for Keeli's body.

Spencer shuddered at the thought—at the horrific threat Luther had made about what he would do to her. "But because we let him get away, he doesn't need her anymore. He might have already killed her."

Penny Payne-Lynch reached out and grasped Spencer's arm, then squeezed it reassuringly. "She's alive," she said, and she sounded so damn certain.

But Spencer shook his head in denial. "I know all about your sixth sense," he told her. It was the stuff of River City legend. "I know that it only works the other way—that you know when bad stuff's going to happen—not good..."

That was probably how Penny had wound up at the courthouse even before the ambulance had arrived to take her husband to the hospital. Her legendary clairvoyance must have warned her that something bad was about to happen to the chief, and that was how she'd made it to the scene so quickly.

"But that's the point," she said. "I don't feel like anything bad is about to happen."

Spencer resisted the urge to laugh at her naivete. Luther Mills was on the loose; of *course* bad things were going to happen. A lot of bad things...

"Are you close enough to Keeli to even have your sixth sense about her?" Spencer asked, out of curiosity about their relationship.

The young bodyguard wasn't related to Penny. Now that Spencer thought about it—about Keeli—he wondered if she even had any family. While they hadn't been close while they worked together at the River City PD, he didn't remember her ever mentioning any of her family to him or to anyone else. In fact, over the past several weeks that they'd spent together, she hadn't talked to him about anyone but her coworkers.

Maybe they *were* her family, which probably made Parker about as close to a big brother as she had, so perhaps Penny was her mother by default.

She spoke of her with a mother's pride when she said, "Keeli is a very special young woman. She reminds me so much of my daughter, Nikki. She's beautiful."

He couldn't argue that. Keeli Abbott was so damn beautiful that he struggled to think whenever she was close to him. No wonder he hadn't figured out yet who the leak in the police department was. He hadn't been able to focus on anything but her and how damn much he wanted her.

"And she's so smart," Penny continued. "And strong. And fearless…"

Spencer groaned. He couldn't disagree with any of what she'd said. Unfortunately. Parker was probably right; she had willingly—and recklessly—gone with Luther with the intent of bringing him back into custody. Just like when she'd been a cop, she was willing to risk her life for her job.

That wasn't her job anymore, though. She was supposed to be protecting him. He hadn't wanted a bodyguard at all—let alone her. But now he wanted her close. So *he* could protect her.

"Yeah," he murmured in agreement, "and it's that fearlessness that's going to get her killed." If it hadn't already.

Maybe that was why Penny didn't feel as if something bad was about to happen—because it already had. Because Keeli was already gone…

* * *

Parker saw the resignation and fear cross Spencer Dubridge's face. But he refused to entertain any of that trepidation or doubt. "No," he said. "She's not dead."

Not Keeli… She was too tough, too resourceful.

Spencer tensed, then turned toward Parker, and his dark eyes were wide with surprise.

"I didn't read your mind," Parker assured him. He'd read his face. All the panic and dread on it had been very easy to recognize.

Spencer shuddered and murmured, "You just did it again…"

Parker's mom squeezed the detective's arm again. She was like that—always so warm and supportive. Unfortunately Spencer was nothing like Penny. He had always been so cold and sarcastic—especially to Keeli.

Maybe that was why he was so upset now—because he blamed himself for her being in danger. But that was Parker's fault. He was the one who'd hired her to be a bodyguard. She hadn't quit the police department to work for him, though; she'd quit the police department to get away from working with chauvinists like Spencer Dubridge.

Then Parker had assigned her to protect him. Yeah, if anything happened to her, it was Parker's fault. But he had hired her and assigned her dangerous jobs because *he* was not a chauvinist—despite what his sister, Nikki, might have said about him.

His wanting to protect Nikki was what had made her choose to work for their brother Cooper instead of him or their brother Logan. Parker hadn't wanted to make that same mistake with Keeli. He'd also wanted to show her that he supported and respected her. He knew that, no matter Keeli's size and appearance, she was tough.

Hell, she'd had to be tough to survive growing up like and where she had. She would survive this, too. She wouldn't let Luther take her out—not without one hell of a fight.

Chapter 4

"We both know you're not going to pull that trigger," Keeli bluffed. "So you might as well put the gun away."

For a moment the barrel pushed even harder against her temple. But Keeli refused to react. She didn't flinch. Hell, she didn't even dare to blink.

Light from the open door dimly illuminated the room. But her eyes had adjusted, so she could see Luther clearly—as he knelt on the mattress next to her, leaning over her.

She didn't move. She couldn't—not without risking that gun going off. Just like she hadn't been able to fight him off at the courthouse because of that damn gun—and her fear for the child she'd just found out she was carrying.

Well, she'd had her suspicions or she wouldn't have

bought the test. Pretty much since that night, she'd felt sick. But she'd thought that was just because she'd had sex with a man she despised.

Finally Luther pulled the barrel away from her head and chuckled. "You're awful damn cocky for a captive."

She wasn't. But she knew not to show an animal like Luther any fear. He would attack for certain if he saw any sign of weakness. She'd always been careful to conceal her weaknesses from Spencer Dubridge, too, until that night. Now he knew *he* was her weakness.

Through the bubble of fear choking her throat, she managed a chuckle, too. "I know you would have killed me already if you didn't have some plan for me."

He laughed loudly now. "Maybe I'm just keeping you alive because you're so damn entertaining, Keeli." He rubbed the gun barrel along her cheek now in a sick sort of caress.

And Keeli tensed. She didn't care if the damn gun went off. If Luther tried to touch her *that* way, she was going to fight like hell. Just like she'd had to fight as a kid. And just like then, she had nobody around to help her. She could rely only on herself. Trust only herself...

"Relax," he told her. "I don't want Spencer Dubridge's sloppy seconds."

She cursed.

And he chuckled. "I have eyes and ears everywhere, Keeli. I knew who you were even when you were working undercover. Someone inside River City PD told me all about you and spilled how Dubridge never wanted to work with you. That's why your whole act of being his girlfriend when you were really his bodyguard didn't go over with anyone else. But I figured there was always something between the two of you..."

"Loathing," she spat, but she probably should have kept the remark to herself since Spencer was apparently the reason Luther wasn't going to mess with her.

He just chuckled again. "No wonder you're not happy about being pregnant with his kid."

"I never said that I was——"

"You forget I have the test you took," he said.

"That test doesn't say that Spencer is the father," she pointed out. "And neither have I." The only thing she'd confirmed was that it had been a mistake but not with whom.

He snorted. "You didn't have to say it. It's all over your face."

She wasn't thrilled that Spencer was the father, and that feeling probably showed. Her shock probably did as well—since she had yet to get used to the idea that she was going to be a mother.

A single mother.

Even if Spencer wanted to be a father, she didn't want him as a husband. Or anything else...

Liar.

She wanted him as a lover. Even more so now that she knew just how damn good a lover he was. No. He was more than good—a hell of a lot more.

Heat rushed to her face as she thought of him—of that night. But she sucked in a breath and forced those thoughts from her mind. She told Luther, "It's none of your business who the father of my baby is."

"So you want me to stay out of your business?" he asked. Luther moved the gun barrel back to her temple.

"Then you should have stayed out of mine—you and the rest of the damn Payne Protection Agency."

"The chief hired us," Keeli reminded him. Not that she wanted to throw the police chief under the bus, but she didn't want to lose her baby or her life before she had a chance to even figure out how to be a mother.

Luther's grin flashed in the dim light. "Lynch paid for that back at the courthouse."

She gasped. "You killed the chief?" Woodrow Lynch had been in that courtroom, watching the trial, with Parker and some of the other bodyguards.

"I can only hope," Luther murmured. "But he definitely took a bullet. That's how he paid. Your agency and Spencer Dubridge are going to pay another way."

Keeli shivered because she had a horrible feeling that she somehow played into his sick plan for vengeance. "How?"

He snorted. "You don't need to know the specifics, Keeli. Just know that whatever happens to them will be partially your fault as well."

She was right; he definitely intended to use her to get back at them. "Luther, come on, you know we were all just doing our jobs."

He shook his head. "No. If that was really the case, you would have backed off. You wouldn't have kept interfering in my business. It got personal, Keeli— just like whatever the hell happened between you and Dubridge."

She couldn't argue that. It had gotten personal when Luther had hired gunmen to try to take out people she and the other bodyguards cared about. And it had gotten too damn personal with Spencer. "Using me is not going to work with Detective Dubridge," she advised him. "He doesn't care about me any more than I do him."

Luther chuckled, obviously amused at her claim. "Then I'd say that's probably just enough to get him to do what I want him to do."

She shook her head. Spencer was too smart to fall for whatever trap Luther was setting—with her as the bait. "No. He won't."

Luther snorted. "Then you don't know him very well. He can't help himself and he can't handle seeing a female in danger. If there's a chick in trouble, he's got to try to save her."

"You think Spencer Dubridge is chivalrous?" She snorted now. "Far from it."

"How so?" he murmured.

"He's a chauvinist."

"Then you really don't know him very well," Luther said. "You have no idea why he acts so overly protective, do you?"

"I thought it was because he was a dick," she admitted.

Luther chuckled. "Maybe that, too, but the love of his life died on the streets. That's why he became a cop, you know, so he could try to save little runaway girls like his high school sweetheart."

"What the hell are you talking about?" Keeli asked. "And how in the world do you know any of this?"

He leaned back on the mattress and flashed another big grin. "I know everything, Keeli. I own these streets."

"Did you kill her?" And who was the love of Spencer Dubridge's life—and why was it bothering Keeli so much to learn he had one?

Luther shook his head. "Nope. Not me. But I think Dubridge blames me. He thinks I got her hooked on the drugs. But she came to me looking for them. And you know I have nothing to do with prostitution."

She'd tried to prove that he'd been behind prostitution—back in her undercover days. But the only link she'd found between Luther and sex trafficking was the fact that many of the prostitutes she'd met had bought their drugs from him. Rumor had it that Luther's mother had been one, and that was why he'd wanted nothing to do with that business. He'd witnessed too much of it growing up, had seen what it had done to his mother. But his dad had been a drug dealer and that hadn't stopped him from getting involved in that business.

Keeli didn't care to know any more about Luther than how to get him back to jail. She hadn't realized until now how little she'd known about Spencer, though.

"You're saying the love of Detective Dubridge's life was a prostitute?" she asked as her head began to pound with confusion. Keeli had never even heard anything about Spencer dating—until she'd posed as his girlfriend in order to be his bodyguard. She didn't believe many people in the police department had fallen for their ruse, though. But maybe that was why he hadn't dated much; he'd never gotten over the love of his life.

"Yeah, that's how most little runaways wind up," he said. Then he stared at her for a long moment before adding, "Except for you."

She shivered. "How the hell do you know that?" So few people knew about her past. Just Parker and a couple of the other guys she'd worked with; she'd never told Spencer. She hadn't wanted him knowing anything about her that she suspected would have only made him doubt her abilities more than he already did.

Luther's evil grin flashed again. "Because I know everything. River City is mine. And you're all going to learn that."

"Is that why you haven't left the city? Because you're planning to stay?" If he'd been smart, he would have fled to an airport and a country with no extradition the minute he'd escaped the courthouse.

"Why so interested in my plans, Keeli?" Luther asked. "You think you're going to be able to stop them?"

She could have pointed out that they'd stopped one of his plans—his scheme to take out everyone associated with his case so that it got thrown out before ever going to trial had backfired. *Big-time.* But this time she held the words back, not wanting to enrage him.

He cocked his head and studied her, and as if he'd read her mind, he said, "Nobody's going to stop me this time."

"How do you intend to prevent that?" she asked, although she didn't expect him to actually answer her.

He grinned and replied, "Let's just say that if I'm leaving River City, I won't be the only one no longer living here." Then he stood up and headed toward the door.

Keeli resisted the instincts that screamed at her to jump up and try to rush out the door with him. He still had the gun in his hand. And it would only take him seconds to pull that trigger and end her life and that of her unborn child. She couldn't risk it.

Yet.

But she knew she had to get away from him soon.

Not only did he intend to use her against Parker and Spencer but, it appeared, he also planned to make sure they all left River City. And she didn't think he meant on a plane. He intended to kill them all.

His cell phone pressed to his ear, Spencer paced the corridor outside the conference room of the Payne Protection Agency.

"Where are you?" Detective Robertson asked. "All of River City PD is out looking for Luther Mills but you."

Frustration tied Spencer's stomach in knots. He wanted to be out looking, too, but he wasn't as interested in finding Luther as he was Keeli. Sure, he wanted to bring Luther back to jail—for the rest of his miserable life. But he needed to find Keeli—to make sure she was still alive.

Over three hours had passed since Luther had abducted her. So less than forty-five hours of the statistical forty-eight left. But Spencer doubted that Luther would follow that forty-eight-hour rule. No. Spencer knew that he had to find Keeli soon to have any chance of finding her alive.

"I'll be back at headquarters soon," Dubridge promised his coworker. But Detective Robertson was more than his coworker. The older detective was Spencer's mentor and had been long before Spencer had even joined the force. Spencer had grown up just a few houses down the block from Robertson, who'd paid him to mow his yard and do other odd jobs around the bachelor's house.

"Just be careful," Robertson advised him. "Nobody's safe with Luther Mills on the loose."

"Nobody was safe when he was in jail either," Spencer reminded him.

"Yeah, but those attempts on the lives of the eyewitness and evidence tech and the abduction of the judge's daughter haven't been officially traced back to Luther," Robertson said.

The veteran detective had to be as frustrated as everyone else was that there had been no way to link Luther to any of those crimes. The members of his crew who'd been arrested from those attempts had refused to turn against him.

Too damn many people were either afraid of him or on his payroll. Who was helping him now? Helping him hold Keeli?

"We don't need to link him to those other crimes," Spencer told him. "Not now. Not since he escaped custody. He's going down for that and for murder."

The detective's gasp crackled in the cell phone. "Did he kill that girl he abducted from the courthouse?"

"No!" Spencer shouted.

"So she was found?"

"No..." he had to admit in a defeated murmur. "Not yet..." But they would. They had to.

"Then what were you talking about? What murder?"

Spencer's brow furrowed with frustration. "The one I arrested him for," he reminded his mentor. "Javier Mendez. Luther was losing his trial. I'm sure that's why he escaped." Because he knew he was going to prison soon and probably for the rest of his life.

"Oh, yes, of course," Robertson said. "It's just that so much else has happened since then..."

"Too much," Spencer agreed. He wasn't so naive that when he'd arrested Luther, he'd believed the man's crime spree was over, but he hadn't suspected that Luther would prove almost as dangerous behind bars.

Hell, maybe more so because now he had nothing to lose. That was why it was imperative that they find Keeli right away. "I have to go, Frank," he said. "I'll talk to you when I get down to the station."

"Where are—"

Spencer clicked off his cell before his friend could even finish his question. He needed to get back into that conference room. And his first order of business? He needed to know if Nikki Payne had managed to track down the location of Keeli's cell phone. Hopefully it was in the same place she was.

But Luther was always at least one step ahead of them, so he'd probably already thrown it out along with her gun. What about her? What had he done with Keeli?

As he reached for the handle of the conference room door, his cell rang. Probably Frank Robertson again.

The older man worried about Spencer as if Frank was one of his parents. But then he'd known Spencer nearly as long as they had, and he'd always looked out for him. That was probably why he wanted to know where he was—to make sure he was someplace safe with Luther on the loose.

Despite wanting to just ignore the call, Spencer pulled out his phone again. But when he glanced down at the screen, it wasn't Robertson's contact information that came up; it was Keeli's.

If Luther had thrown out her cell, someone had found it. But why call the person she'd listed as Detective Dick in her contacts? She'd shown him that weeks ago, and he'd had to fight to keep from smiling over it. His finger shook as he pressed the screen to accept the call. "Hello?"

"Detective Dubridge or should I say Dick?" A male voice greeted him.

And Spencer shuddered with revulsion. Luther definitely had Keeli's phone, but he hadn't thrown it out. "Mills…" he bit out.

Luther chuckled. "You don't sound particularly happy to hear from me."

"I'd rather be hearing from Keeli," he admitted tersely. "Where is she?"

"You really expect me to just tell you that?" Luther asked him, as if disappointed that Spencer wasn't eager to play his sick game.

"Why did you call me if that's not the reason?" Spencer knew the scumbag hadn't called to tell him anything; he probably only wanted to taunt him.

Luther chuckled again. "Oh, Detective Dubridge, I was sorry you and I had to cut our conversation short at the courthouse. We have so many things to talk about."

That knot of frustration in Spencer's stomach tightened even more. "Like what?"

"Like my demands."

"Demands?" Hope quickened his pulse. Keeli had to still be alive for Luther to think he had leverage for making demands.

"Yes, the list of things I need," Luther replied. "Like a passport for me—a clean one for a new identity. And a plane with a pilot that has clearance to fly to a country with no extradition."

Spencer chuckled now. "I think you called the wrong damn person. I'm not a negotiator."

"No. I called the right person," Luther countered. "You're the one with the most incentive to help me."

Keeli…

But Spencer couldn't betray to Luther how much he cared about her—which shouldn't be too hard since Keeli herself had no idea.

Of course how could she when Spencer had always been such an ass to her? But that had been because he'd been worried that something like this would happen, that her rashness would put her in too much danger for even her to escape.

Unwilling to admit to Luther just how much incentive Spencer had, he snorted derisively. "Yeah, right. You took my bodyguard. I never wanted one anyways."

But he *had* wanted Keeli. He'd wanted her from the first moment he'd met her. She was so damn beautiful and feisty and stubborn.

Luther snorted now. "We both know Keeli Abbott is more than your bodyguard."

Spencer knew that. But how the hell did Luther know? What had Keeli told him?

"You want me to read you that list again, Detective?" Luther prompted him.

Spencer forced out a weary-sounding sigh. "How do you think I can get you any of these things? I'm just a detective. But even if I could, *why* would I?"

"Because I don't just have your bodyguard," Luther said, his voice rising with wicked glee. "I got your baby mama, Detective."

Spencer's heart slammed against his ribs. "What the hell...?"

Could Keeli be pregnant?

Luther chuckled. "Along with her cell phone and her gun, I've got the pregnancy test that proves it. You're going to be a daddy, Detective." Luther laughed harder. "Or is that Detective Daddy?"

Spencer cursed.

"So you're not any happier about this than she is, huh?" Luther asked. "Oops..."

Spencer cursed again. Maybe Luther was just messing with him. But Spencer doubted he could have come up with this twisted plan on his own. There was also a damn good possibility the man spoke the truth. Keeli had been sick recently. He'd thought she had the flu. But by noon she'd always felt better; she'd only been sick in the morning.

Could she really be pregnant?

With his baby?

Panic surged through him, but he forced it down. He had to stay focused. He couldn't give in to the urge to lose it like he wanted to. It was bad enough that Keeli was in such danger. But now...

"Let me talk to her, Luther," Spencer said.

But the man just chuckled. "You'll get the chance," he said, "once you get me everything I asked for..." Instead of repeating his list of demands, Luther ended the call.

Did he really expect Spencer to get him anything? Or was he only messing with him?

And why not let him talk to Keeli?

Spencer had a sick feeling that he knew why. She was already dead.

* * *

Luther laughed so hard his stomach ached a little. Or maybe that was the greasy takeout he'd just consumed. No. He'd had the prison guards smuggle him in far greasier crap than what he'd just eaten. It was the laughter making him ache.

He'd rattled the hell out of Spencer Dubridge during that phone call. "Damn, that was fun," he murmured.

Detective Dubridge was probably scrambling right now to meet his demands. He would have done it for Keeli alone but knowing now that she was pregnant...

That had to have gotten every one of Dubridge's protective instincts screaming. He would want to save her even more than he already had—now that he knew she carried his kid.

Of course Luther didn't need a damn thing he'd demanded. He already had all of that and then some. He didn't need anything from Spencer Dubridge but his life. Luther was going to take his and the life of every single damn person who'd crossed him.

Starting with Keeli Abbott...

Yeah, no matter what the detective managed to get together for Luther, it wasn't going to be enough to save her. It was time—past time—for her to die.

Once she was gone, Luther would finish off the others. Either one by one or all together. If he stuck around for a couple more days, he could take out most of the Payne family in one place—their legendary Sunday dinner at their mama's house.

He felt a twinge of resentment over the perfect family they were—and that he had never had. But they wouldn't have it much longer. And Spencer would never get the family he'd just learned he'd started with Keeli.

He laughed again and just ignored that ache in his gut. He was too damn happy to let it bother him. It thrilled him to no end knowing just how miserable Spencer Dubridge would be... Until Luther put him out of his misery.

Hell, maybe he would save Spencer for last—to draw out that misery as long as possible.

Chapter 5

The knob rattled, the sound making goose bumps rise on Keeli's skin as it reminded her of the nightmare of her past, of her childhood. Someone was unlocking the door to the room where Keeli was being held in the dark. But she'd grown accustomed to the dark. And she'd managed to stay awake this time so she would not be taken by surprise again.

Instead she was going to be the one to do the surprising. She hurried to the other side of the door, so when it opened, it provided her with a hiding place. But she didn't intend to hide and cower in the darkness.

As the light from the hall fell across the mattress lying on the floor, a gasp escaped from whoever had opened the door. It didn't sound like Luther. But Keeli couldn't be sure from just that brief noise. Whoever it was entered cautiously, with the barrel of his gun leading the way. So Keeli grabbed that gun, snapping it easily from the person's grasp. Then she whirled around the door, pointing the gun barrel at him.

It wasn't Luther.

This man was in uniform. He was the driver of the jail escort van. His eyes widened with surprise and he raised his hands. "Don't shoot," he told her.

"What the hell were you intending to do with this?" she asked him. "Weren't you going to use it to shoot me?"

A gun cocked, drawing Keeli's attention to the man who appeared suddenly behind the guard. "No. I'm the one who's going to shoot you."

She cocked the gun she'd grabbed as well and raised the barrel. But the guard was bigger than Luther, and she couldn't see much of the escaped killer beyond the weapon he pointed at her.

"You going to shoot an innocent man, Keeli?" Luther asked her. "That's not like you."

"It's not like he's innocent," Keeli scoffed. "He helped you escape."

Sweat beaded on the guard's upper lip and brow. "He gave me no choice—"

Luther smacked the back of the guard's head with his hand. "Don't tell her anything!"

"Why not?" Keeli asked. "Don't you intend to kill me?"

"That's the plan," he admitted.

"Then I might as well go down shooting," she said. She wouldn't be able to hit Luther, though, until she shot the guard first. And he was unarmed...

No matter what he'd done or why, she couldn't shoot an unarmed man. And Luther knew it.

He chuckled at her predicament. "You just can't do it, can you, Keeli?"

Tears of frustration stung her eyes, but she blinked them back. Again—she knew better than to show Luther any sign of weakness.

But she was weak now—with that gun pointed at her. Nobody stood in front of her. Nobody would block a bullet from hitting her body. And even if she ducked and dodged, she wouldn't be able to avoid getting hit. She had no place to hide. And with Luther and the guard blocking the door, she had no way of escaping.

She should have fought back at the courthouse—when she'd had Spencer to back her up. Because now she had a feeling that she might never see Spencer again...

And she would never get to carry their child to term, to deliver the baby they'd made together. She hadn't been sure how she'd felt when she'd read the positive result on the test Luther had taken from her purse. But now she knew without a doubt that she wanted this baby. She wanted to be a mother. Now she wouldn't have the chance.

Luther pulled the trigger. Instinctively she covered her stomach with her hands, as if they would protect her baby. And she flinched as she braced herself for the bullet to strike.

The chief ignored the pain throbbing in his shoulder and focused on the people crowding his office. Of course it didn't take many people to crowd the small space—just these four. The doctor had advised him to stay in the hospital. But Woodrow hadn't wanted to take these meetings while lying on his back in bed. And fortunately his amazing wife had understood and helped him dress.

Penny had been there, during the chaos after the shooting in the courthouse, so she knew how scared people were that Luther Mills had escaped custody. But that wasn't all the felon had done; he'd also taken Keeli Abbott hostage.

Or so he claimed, because a hostage situation gave him the chance to negotiate with them if they wanted to gain the release of the hostage. They wanted Keeli back. But they had to get Luther back, too, behind bars where he belonged.

The assistant district attorney, Jocelyn Gerber, shook her head, and her black hair moved like a curtain around her shoulders. "This list of demands is ridiculous," she told Detective Dubridge after he'd read them off to her.

"We have to do our best to meet them," Dubridge insisted. "Or he'll kill Keeli for certain." The detective's hand shook as he dropped the list onto Woodrow's desk. It wasn't just his hand that was shaking; he looked like he was shaken to his soul. What exactly did Keeli mean to him?

More than his bodyguard?

Jocelyn Gerber shot a significant glance at Woodrow; her blue eyes were full of skepticism and regret. She didn't believe Keeli was still alive. Like everyone else, the ADA knew what a monster Mills was.

While Penny had assured Spencer that Keeli was still alive, Woodrow wasn't as convinced. Like Spencer had pointed out, his wife's sixth sense only predicted when something bad was about to happen. Not good things...

Landon Myers stood close to Jocelyn as if her bodyguard boyfriend expected Luther Mills and his crew to storm the police department at any moment. Maybe Landon was right to worry about that since no one had predicted Luther shooting up the courthouse.

Well, Penny had predicted it, but she hadn't reached Woodrow until it was too late—until he'd already been shot. He moved his shoulder and flinched at the stab of pain the movement caused. His beautiful bride had insisted on filling the prescription for painkillers that the doctor had given him. But the bottle sat unopened on Woodrow's desk. He needed to keep a clear head until Luther Mills was apprehended and, hopefully, Keeli found alive.

"C'mon, Landon," Spencer urged his former coworker. "Tell the ADA that Keeli's still alive." Apparently he hadn't missed the look Jocelyn had given the chief.

Like Keeli, Landon Myers had also once worked for the River City Police Department Vice Unit. They'd both worked for the PD for at least five years. Unfortunately Parker had talked Landon, Keeli and a few other good cops into becoming bodyguards for the Payne Protection Agency before Woodrow had taken the position of chief of police a couple of years ago. At least Spencer Dubridge had stayed with River City PD.

"You know Keeli," Spencer continued. "You know how tough she is."

"*I* know," Landon said, his deep voice rumbling with resentment. "I know she's smart and resourceful, and she's probably already working on a way to get herself out of this situation and Luther back behind bars. I know what a good cop she was. I didn't think *you* did."

"She was a good cop, and she's an even better bodyguard." Parker chimed in with his support of his friend and employee. "She's always managed to take care of herself and her fellow officers or whoever she's protecting. You're alive, Dubridge, and she is, too."

Woodrow wasn't as convinced as Parker and Landon were that she was all right, but then he didn't know Keeli as well as they did. She'd already been gone when he'd taken his job with River City PD.

Spencer's face flushed with embarrassment. Even the chief had heard the things the detective had said about his female bodyguard. "She's alive," the detective said, "but she won't stay that way unless we get Luther the things he wants."

"Luther can get all of those things himself," Jocelyn Gerber remarked. "And probably already has."

Woodrow nodded in agreement. "He got himself out of a heavily guarded courthouse," he pointed out. "He planned that. He had to have plans for what to do once he escaped."

"So you're not going to help?" Spencer asked, his dark eyes wide with shock.

"If he calls again, tell him we need more time," the chief advised.

His stepdaughter, Nikki, had put a trace on Keeli's phone. It was off now, but once it was turned on again, she would be able to track down the location of it. Nikki had also put a trace on Spencer's phone; she'd done all that before he'd even left the Payne Protection Agency.

Nikki had stayed back at Parker's office while Parker and Dubridge had come here to fill in the chief and the assistant district attorney on Luther making contact with Spencer.

Why had he done that? What the hell was Luther's plan now? He seemed to always have one.

Spencer shook his head. "Keeli doesn't have time. We need to get Luther what he wants."

Parker, who must have replaced Keeli as the detective's bodyguard, glanced down at the list Spencer had written out. It sat on Woodrow's desk next to that unopened prescription bottle. "That isn't what Luther wants."

"What does he want?" Spencer asked.

But Woodrow suspected the detective knew—that they all knew. He pointed to his shoulder anyway. "He wants this." Luther wanted them all to feel pain. "Revenge. He wants to get back at all of us."

At everyone who'd helped put him in jail and had worked to keep him there.

And he had probably already started with Keeli Abbott. No matter what Woodrow's wife believed, he feared that Keeli was already dead. He also suspected that Spencer Dubridge knew that, and that was why he was so upset.

Or had Luther given him more than just that list of demands? Had he told Spencer something that the detective hadn't shared with them?

Before he could ask, Spencer pushed through his friends and headed toward the office door. "I'm not going to stand around here doing nothing! I'm going to do everything I can to get Keeli back."

The door slammed behind him as he exited. And nobody said anything. But Woodrow suspected that at least some of them were thinking what he was: that it was probably already too late.

Spencer couldn't stop shaking. He was so damn furious—and frustrated. He couldn't believe that nobody was helping him find Keeli.

Sure, Nikki Payne-Ecklund had a trace on his phone and on Keeli's. But that was it. Nobody had even considered trying to meet Luther's demands.

That was why he'd stormed out of the chief's office. He'd hated how they'd all been looking at each other and him—like he was losing his damn mind. Hell, he would gladly give that up to get Keeli back. His life, too—that was why he'd hustled out of the police department before Parker had had a chance to catch up with him.

Spencer didn't need a bodyguard. He didn't need anyone distracting him from finding Keeli. She was the bodyguard he needed.

Was he the only one who wanted Keeli back?

The other Payne Protection bodyguards were supposed to be her friends. When they'd worked vice together, they had all supported her. They had even defended her—to him—saying that she was tough and smart and strong. And sure, Parker and Landon had defended her again, but it was as if they expected her to free herself. As if they didn't think she needed anyone to help her...

And the chief and the ADA, they clearly believed she was already dead. Spencer couldn't let himself consider that possibility. His chest already ached with fear; if something had happened to her, the pain would be unbearable. If she was actually gone... Then so was the baby Luther claimed she was carrying.

Spencer's baby. Was Luther telling the truth or was he only messing with Spencer? He had to just be messing with him. She couldn't really be pregnant.

But that night...

That night they'd both totally lost control. In each

other's arms. He'd never wanted anyone the way he'd wanted her then. The way he wanted her now...

Spencer's hand shook again as he pushed the key into the lock of his house. That had happened here, after they'd nearly been shot.

After Keeli had saved his life...

He'd never really thanked her for that, but he'd showed his appreciation in other ways that night. So many times—and in so many ways.

There had been that one time without protection—after they'd run out of condoms and had both been more asleep than awake. He'd thought he might have only dreamed that—that he might have dreamed that whole night. Especially when the next morning Keeli had acted as though nothing had happened between them—like she still couldn't even stand the sight of him, let alone his touch.

So he'd thought he must have imagined her moaning when he caressed her, when he'd kissed her...

His body tensed, but not just because of those memories. When he pushed open the door to his house, a strange sensation rushed over him like a cold breeze, chilling his flesh. And he knew, even before he heard the gun cock, that he was not alone...

Someone had broken into his house. Someone was waiting for him.

He reached for his holster, but he knew he was already too late. Even if he drew his gun, he would never have a chance to pull the trigger before the first bullet struck him.

Chapter 6

It was too late by the time it dawned on Parker that Spencer hadn't stopped at his desk in the detectives' bullpen but had walked right out of the police department. He hadn't been able to catch up with him. Spencer was long gone.

Parker drove up and down the streets of River City looking for him.

Where the hell could he be?

Was he actually going to try to negotiate with Luther Mills?

Parker wanted to believe, like Spencer did, that Keeli was still alive, but as well as he knew Keeli, he knew Luther, too. Just as the chief had pointed out, Mills wanted to make them all suffer.

Killing Keeli would cause that.

Especially for Spencer. Despite how difficult he'd

made things for his bodyguard, he seemed to really care about her. And maybe that was why he'd given her such a hard time—just like Parker had tried to keep his sister out of the bodyguard business. He and his brothers would have preferred her working with their mother at the chapel where Penny operated her full-service wedding planning business.

Thinking of his sister had Parker pulling into a parking lot while reaching for his cell phone. He hit her contact.

"Nothing yet," she said as she answered his call.

"What?" he asked, confused, since he hadn't actually asked her anything. But that was Nikki—always one step ahead of the rest of them.

"Keeli's phone must be turned off. Or dead…" She sounded as if she thought Keeli probably was as well.

He didn't want to believe that, but she'd been alone too long with Luther Mills. And no matter how tough a fighter Keeli was, Luther was a monster.

Parker's stomach churned, and he tightened his hands around the steering wheel of his SUV. The downtown parking lot he pulled into was nearly deserted. The day was over for the surrounding office buildings, the sun dropping from the sky. Streetlamps flickered on, dimly illuminating the asphalt.

He had to focus on Dubridge right now. "What about Spencer's phone?" he asked.

"He's not taken any more calls," she said.

"No," Parker said. "I need you to track down where he is."

"He gave you the slip?" Nikki asked, and there was a slight taunt in her voice. She'd proven him and Logan wrong once she'd gone to work for their brother Cooper. His sister had turned out to be a damn good body-guard—maybe even better than him and Logan.

Parker groaned. "I didn't realize he was going to take off from the police department like he did."

"Where did he go?" she asked.

"That's what I need you to help me find out," Parker said.

"Do you think he's meeting with Luther somewhere?"

He winced, knowing that Luther could have lured Spencer into a meeting, using Keeli as the bait. Then he would hurt Dubridge like he wanted to hurt all of them.

"Put a trace on his phone," Parker said. "Tell me where he is."

"Okay, okay," Nikki murmured. "I'm tracking him…"

Parker shifted the SUV into Drive, ready to speed off to wherever she told him. He only hoped that he would get there in time.

He might have already lost one friend—Keeli. He could not lose another.

Keeli uncocked the gun and dropped her arm back to her side. "Don't worry," she told Spencer as she stepped out of the shadows of his dark living room. "It's not loaded. I just wasn't sure who you were…"

His breath shuddered out in a ragged sigh of relief. But she didn't know if he was relieved that she wasn't going to kill him or that she was alive.

And his next words revealed nothing of what he was thinking or feeling when he snidely remarked, "It's my place. Who else would I be?"

Despite a brief flash of disappointment that he

didn't seem happy to see her, her lips curved into a slight smile. Keeli probably would have been more disappointed had he reacted any other way than how they usually did to each other—with snark and sarcasm and the passion that always simmered just beneath the surface of their terse exchanges. She felt it—in the tingling of her skin and the tenseness of his body as he stalked toward her.

He looked at her so intently, as if he was checking her for any marks. But he was also looking deeper, as if he trying to see inside her. Strangely, though, his gaze had dropped to her stomach—which flipped with nerves over his sudden interest.

"I thought you might be Luther," she admitted, and she trembled with the fear that had gripped her since the killer had abducted her from the courthouse.

"How the hell did you escape from him?" Spencer asked, and his gaze moved back to her face—his stare still so damn intense.

She shook her head. "I didn't." She was furious that she hadn't fought harder—that she'd just stood there waiting for the bullet to hit her.

But it had hit the wall of the house behind her instead. And Luther hadn't fired another shot. Instead he'd cursed.

"Then how the hell did you get here?" Spencer asked.

"Luther brought me here," she said.

Spencer reached for his weapon again and peered around the dark living room. "Is he...?"

"He left," she said. "Just a few minutes ago. That's why when you opened the door—" she shuddered "—I thought you were him coming back."

Spencer touched the weapon she held at her side. "And you were going to shoot him with an unloaded gun?"

"He wouldn't know that I didn't have time to find the ammo you keep in the house," she said. "He gave me back my gun when he dropped me here. But he took the magazine from it."

"What about the one in the chamber?" Spencer asked.

She shook her head. "He fired it…" It was the bullet that had struck the wall behind her—instead of her. He'd had the magazine, so he could have fired more. For some reason, maybe unbeknownst even to him, he'd chosen to let her live.

For the moment…

He'd warned her that he was coming back. And not just for her. "We need to get out of here," she told Spencer as she reached out and grasped his arm.

He tensed beneath her touch. "Why? Do you think he's coming back for you?"

"For *us*," she said. "For all of us. You need to call Parker to warn everybody."

"Everybody already knows they're not safe," Spencer told her. "Not with Luther on the loose. And now you've told him where I live."

She shook her head. "Hell, no. I had no idea where he was bringing me."

He'd loaded her into the back of that SUV that had looked so much like a Payne Protection Agency vehicle. But he'd forced her to lie on the floor between the front and back seats, so she hadn't been able to see where they were going. And even when the SUV had stopped, she hadn't been able to see because Luther had pulled a pillowcase over her head. She'd thought for certain he was going to kill her then, and she'd struggled, but he and the guard had easily over-powered her, then carried her into another house. She hadn't known which house until he'd pulled the case off her head.

She shuddered. "He must have a key, too, because he opened the door too quickly to have been picking the lock."

"Maybe he took the key from you," he suggested.

"You never gave me a key," she reminded him. Because she'd only been his bodyguard, a bodyguard he'd made clear he'd never wanted.

Was he disappointed she was free?

Had he not wanted her back? A twinge struck her heart. She'd wanted so badly to see him again, and while he was looking at her, it wasn't with relief. It was with...

Suspicion?

Did he think she had helped Luther escape? Maybe that was why Luther had let her live, so people would suspect she was one of his many moles. He had to know that having her integrity questioned would kill her almost as much as that bullet would have. She'd had someone close to her—someone who should have loved her—refuse to believe her in the past, and it had nearly destroyed her.

Spencer shrugged. "Then I don't know how he got in. Maybe he knows where I keep the hide-a-key. He seems to know a hell of a lot..."

Keeli couldn't argue that; it creeped her out how much Luther knew about Spencer, and especially about her. Just who else were his moles that enabled him to know so damn much?

The person had to be someone close to both her and Spencer. And now she was suddenly not so eager to call the others. Like Spencer had said, they were all well aware that they were in danger. Luther Mills had been a threat from behind bars. He was an even bigger threat now.

"He knows more than I do," Spencer said. "Like that I'm going to be a father..."

She sucked in a breath, feeling like she'd been slapped. She'd known Luther had called some people while he'd had her locked in that room, and she'd listened at the door, trying to overhear his conversations. But she'd only made out bits and pieces, and she'd never realized he might have had one of those conversations with Spencer.

"Wh-what are you talking about?" she stammered, hoping to buy some time to recover from the shock of his knowing. She hadn't intended to tell him—at least not yet, not until she knew for certain. That little drugstore test could have been wrong.

She might not be pregnant. But if she was... The baby was definitely Spencer's. She hadn't been involved with anyone else for a long time. Not that she was involved with Spencer. She'd just had that one little slip—of her control.

And she *never* lost control. That was why even the relationships she'd had had never become serious. She hadn't wanted to fall for anyone. Hadn't trusted any other person enough to fall for them. After what she'd been through, she was probably never going to trust anyone that much.

It wasn't as if one of her former boyfriends had fallen for her either. Sure, those other guys might have been attracted to her looks, but like Spencer, they'd always had a problem with what she did for a living, whether it had been vice cop or female bodyguard.

But she wasn't about to admit that to Spencer. Hell, she wasn't even about to admit that she was pregnant. She snorted. "Luther must have been messing with you."

Spencer didn't reply; he just kept staring at her as if he was trying to see inside her.

And fear, nearly as intense as when Luther had held that gun on her, gripped her. She was afraid of what Spencer might see if he looked too hard.

The truth.

Spencer could see the truth on her face even as she uttered the lie: "Of course I'm not pregnant."

He shook his head.

"Why would you believe anything Luther Mills told you?" she asked.

"Because in this case—about this—I trust Luther more than I trust you," he admitted.

"Why would I lie about this?" she demanded.

"Because you don't want me to know."

"If I was pregnant," she said, her face flushing, "and I'm not saying that I am, it wouldn't be any business of yours."

"If I'm the father, and I probably am, it sure as hell would be my business!"

She snorted again, just as she had when he'd first shared what Luther had told him. Derisively. As if the idea was ridiculous. Hell, she'd even said as much. But he narrowed his eyes and glared at her.

She glowered back at him while her face flushed an even deeper shade of red. "What makes you think you would be the father? It could be any number of men."

He snorted now at her blatant bluff. "And when are you getting together with them?" he asked. "You've been my bodyguard around-the-clock for weeks now."

"I could be farther along than you think…"

"Then you damn well shouldn't be working as a bodyguard, putting your life in danger." Especially not for him, not after the way he'd treated her.

She held up a hand as if to hold him back even though he hadn't reached for her.

But he wanted to; he'd wanted to reach for her the minute he'd realized she was the one holding the gun on him. He'd wanted to close his arms around her and never let her go. But the fear he'd been feeling for her had frayed his temper and instead of being relieved, he'd been angry that she'd ever been in danger in the first place. Danger that she kept willingly putting herself in by insisting on going alone, without backup.

"You shouldn't be a bodyguard," he said again. "For anyone…"

"Stop," she said. "Just stop!"

"Keeli, you know—"

She silenced him—with her hand pressed over his lips. "Shh…"

His lips tingled from the contact with her skin. But she wasn't just shutting him up because she didn't want to listen to what he was saying. Instead she appeared to be listening to something else, her head cocked to the side.

Then he heard it, too. The sound of the front door creaking open. She'd been worried that Luther might come back. He should have listened to her. He should have gotten her the hell out of there.

They didn't have time now.

He drew his weapon as she lifted hers. But she had no bullets in her gun—no way of defending herself. That didn't stop her from stepping between him and the foyer—of trying to put herself between him and the threat.

As a bodyguard, that instinct was ingrained in her. But she needed to worry about herself now. About herself and the baby she might be carrying...

He reached for her, to move her aside. But she suddenly fell, dropping to the floor even though Spencer hadn't even heard a shot.

Did the intruder have a silencer on his gun? Had he shot Keeli before they'd even seen him?

Chapter 7

 As Keeli had turned toward the intruder, her head reeled with dizziness. Then her legs folded, and everything went black.

Who'd come into Spencer's house? Had Luther returned? If he'd come back, he'd probably brought more gunpower than just him and that guard.

So was she unconscious or dead?

And what about Spencer?

She fought against the darkness, but when she opened her eyes, she squinted against the light. With the day slipping into night, it had been pretty dark in Spencer's house, and neither of them had turned on so much as a lamp.

So where was she that it was so bright? Fluorescent bulbs flickered over her. And a machine beeped, and something squeezed her arm. She gasped and reached out, clawing at it.

"It's okay," a deep voice murmured. "It's okay. It's just a blood pressure cuff."

"Blood pressure?" She jerked fully awake, and as she sat up, that cuff pulled at her arm along with a line leading from a needle under her skin to an IV. She was on a gurney—behind a curtain in what was probably the emergency room of River City Memorial. That would have been the closest hospital to Spencer's house.

She turned toward the man sitting next to her gurney and studied him for any signs of injury. "What happened? Are you all right?"

Spencer released a ragged breath. "I am now."

She narrowed her eyes and visually scanned him from head to toe. "Really? Who came into your house?"

"It was me," another deep voice murmured.

Keeli turned toward the sound just as Parker pulled aside the thick vinyl curtain and stepped into the small space around her gurney.

"I had Nikki put a GPS tracker on Spencer's phone," he explained.

"And instead of knocking or ringing the bell, he walked right in," Spencer said.

"I didn't know the situation…" Parker looked from her to Spencer, as if he still wasn't sure of the situation. "And when I walked in, I found you lying on the floor."

She reached up and touched her head, remembering that wave of dizziness she'd felt. "I—I don't know what happened…"

"I thought you got shot," Spencer said.

Parker added, "And he nearly shot me."

"I was protecting her," Spencer replied.

And she was the one who was supposed to have been protecting him. But he had nearly been shot at the courthouse, and if that had been Luther sneaking into his house tonight, he could have been shot there as well. Maybe he was right. Maybe she shouldn't be a bodyguard anymore; she was losing her edge.

"I'm fine," she said. But she wasn't sure about that. She didn't remember anything that had happened after she'd turned toward the foyer.

"You're *not* fine," Spencer said, and his voice rumbled with frustration and something like concern. "You've been passed out for a while."

Maybe that was why they were monitoring her blood pressure and why she had that IV in her arm. "What did the doctor say?" she asked.

"She took some blood from you to run some tests." Spencer's face looked like all the blood had drained from it. He was so pale.

Was he that worried about her?

"I'm fine," she said again. And she did feel better now, less shaky than she had in those moments before everything had gone black.

The curtain moved as a dark-haired woman wearing green scrubs tugged it aside and stepped into the space. She looked at the men crowding the area around Keeli's gurney and then turned to her patient with her brows raised. "Do we need to talk privately?"

"No," Spencer answered for her.

And the doctor narrowed her eyes at him. "I didn't ask you," she said.

Keeli smiled. She liked the young woman already.

But she had a feeling that she might not like what she was about to tell her. She suspected that one of those tests the doctor had run was going to confirm what Keeli already knew. That she was pregnant.

Was the doctor wondering which of these men was the father?

But then she didn't seem to care. Her only concern was for Keeli. "It's up to you," the woman told her. "I can have security show them to the waiting room."

"I'll leave," Parker offered freely.

And the doctor smiled at him. "Can you take your *friend* with you?"

Spencer ignored the doctor and stared at Keeli. "I need to know the truth."

"And you're not going to believe what I tell you?" she asked him. She should have been used to that—used to not being believed when it mattered most. But back then, when she'd been a scared kid, she'd been telling the truth; this time, as an adult woman, she wasn't sure that she wanted to be honest.

He raised his brows at her now. He wouldn't trust what she told him, and that was her fault—because she'd already tried lying to him about what Luther had revealed. Why the hell had Luther told him?

To torture him?

To torture *her*?

What the hell was the killer up to?

Pure evil, no doubt.

And because of that, she should keep Spencer in sight. She was supposed to be protecting him—even though she'd done a piss-poor job of it that day.

She uttered a sigh of resignation and told the doctor, "He can stay."

Parker left then, probably rushing out to the waiting room to escape the tension between her and Spencer. When he'd passed out assignments, she'd told him that her protecting Dubridge was a bad idea. But she'd refused to give up the assignment because she hadn't wanted to let Spencer get to her.

Unfortunately he had.

"Are you sure?" the young doctor asked her again. "Is that really what you want or is he intimidating you?"

Spencer laughed. "Like anyone can intimidate Keeli Abbott..."

The doctor glared at him. "Why would anyone want to?"

Spencer's face flushed.

Keeli laughed now. "I like you," she told the doctor.

The woman smiled. "I hope you like what I'm going to tell you."

"I'm pregnant," Keeli said.

She nodded.

And Spencer sucked in a breath.

"Is that what made me pass out?" Keeli asked.

The doctor shook her head. "No. That looks like a combination of dehydration, low blood sugar and low blood pressure. Have you had a lot of morning sickness?"

Keeli nodded.

Spencer cursed and murmured, "I should have known it wasn't the flu..."

She'd worked hard to hide her nausea from him. Luther wasn't the only one to whom she'd wanted to betray no weakness. But clearly Spencer had been more aware than she'd realized.

"That'll get better once you're out of your first trimester," the doctor assured her.

"How far along is she?" Spencer asked.

The doctor ignored him, her total focus on Keeli. "How far along do you think?" she asked her.

"Probably eight weeks...almost nine."

Hearing that, Spencer dropped onto the chair that was wedged between the curtain and the gurney, as if his legs had folded beneath him. That night— that *incredible* night where they'd given in to their attraction—had happened eight, almost nine weeks ago. So he knew...

He was the father.

"We can confirm with an ultrasound," the doctor offered. And she reached for one of the machines wedged in on the other side of the bed. "If you pull up your gown, I will squirt some cool goo on your stomach and we'll take a look at your baby."

"What?" Keeli asked. "It's too small, isn't it?"

"We'll be able to see more than you think," the woman told her.

Keeli's hands trembled as she pulled up her gown. Then she gasped as the doctor squirted that goo on her skin. It was cool and weird feeling. But that was nothing compared to what she felt when she heard a weird throbbing noise and saw an image flicker on the screen of the machine.

"That's the baby's heartbeat you're hearing," the doctor explained. Then she pointed toward that peanut-like image on the screen. "And there's the baby. You can even see the heart beating."

Keeli gasped now.

"I would say you're right," the physician said. "Eight and a half weeks…"

"Is—is everything all right?" Spencer asked the question, his voice sounding hoarse and strained.

The doctor looked at Keeli, who nodded, before answering. "The baby looks fine. We need to get the mother rehydrated, so her blood sugar and pressure go up."

"She was kidnapped today," Spencer said. "At the courthouse…"

"That was *you*?" the doctor asked with a gasp of alarm. "I'm glad you escaped."

Keeli didn't bother telling the woman that her abductor had just let her go. She couldn't explain why he had. It had certainly had nothing to do with his better nature. Luther didn't have one.

"I'll get you a prescription for prenatal vitamins, and you should be good to go soon."

Spencer jumped up then. "Are you sure? Shouldn't she spend the night?"

"I'm fine," Keeli said.

"Yes, she is," the doctor agreed.

"But what about her work…?"

The woman's brow furrowed, then she nodded. "That's right. The news reports said you're a bodyguard."

Keeli appreciated that she didn't look at her skeptically as so many others did when she said what she did for a living. But it was more than a living to Keeli. It was her life. She loved being a bodyguard even more than she'd loved being a cop. As a bodyguard, she actually felt like she could protect people, and when she'd been on the police force, she hadn't been able to save as many as she'd wanted to. She'd seen so many lives lost—like Spencer's lost love—to drug overdoses or murder.

"She can't do that anymore," Spencer said. "It's too dangerous."

Keeli groaned in frustration. "You've been saying that even before you knew I was pregnant."

"Not just for you now," he said. And he touched his fingers to the screen of the machine, to the peanut on it. "For the baby, too."

"Until you're closer to your due date, you're physically able to keep working," the doctor assured her.

Spencer opened his mouth to argue but the woman shook her head. "I'm not going to debate the dangers of her work. Anybody can get hurt anywhere. As an ER doctor, I've seen it all."

Keeli could attest to that. She'd lost someone close to her not that long ago, someone who'd lived a dangerous life but hadn't died by gunfire or in a high-speed chase. She'd died because someone had been texting and missed a stop sign. And even the chief of police had been shot at the courthouse. She felt a surge of guilt that she hadn't asked about him yet. "Is he okay?"

"He?" Spencer stared harder at the screen. "Is it a boy?"

"The *chief*," Keeli clarified. "I'm asking about the chief. Luther said he shot him. Is he all right?"

Spencer nodded. "Just a shoulder wound. He's fine."

"And so are the baby and the baby's mother," the doctor assured him again. "I'll be right back with that prescription." She pulled the curtain aside and walked away.

Keeli wanted to call her back. She didn't want to be

alone with Spencer, who was certain to argue with her about her job and about the baby. But he said nothing at all; he just continued to stare in awe at the screen—at the miracle they'd made together. And something tightened around Keeli's heart, squeezing it.

She wasn't sure which of them she was falling for—him or the baby. But of course she couldn't really fall for Spencer... Even though, thanks to Luther, she now understood him a little better. She understood that he was actually being protective and why.

But that didn't change the fact that she didn't want him being protective of her. She could take care of herself.

And her baby.

He'd seen the look on the transport guard's face. He'd thought he was getting soft—letting Keeli Abbott live. So he'd put a bullet in the guy's brain.

Nobody better think Luther Mills was losing his edge.

He wasn't. But for some reason, instead of shooting her, he'd moved the barrel at the last moment and had directed the shot into the wall instead of into her small body. Maybe it had been the way she'd just stood there, not begging—not crying—that had impressed him.

But hell, Keeli Abbott had impressed him for a while. She hadn't gone after him like the others had. She'd worked the other vices in the vice unit. It wasn't until she'd been assigned to protect Spencer Dubridge that she'd gotten in his way.

And if she kept trying to act as Dubridge's bodyguard, she'd get in his way again. And she'd get dead for her efforts. He stepped over the guard lying on the kitchen floor of that house where he'd held Keeli.

He didn't need him anymore anyway. Or the house. Luther walked out of the door between the kitchen and the garage and got into the SUV that looked like one of the Payne's.

But he still needed someone else—his mole within the police department. He punched in the man's contact on his cell phone. "Do you have eyes on him?"

"The chief's at the police department."

"I'm not talking about the chief," he snapped. He was a little surprised and a hell of a lot disappointed that Woodrow Lynch hadn't been hurt so badly that he was unable to work, but with Luther on the loose, he probably hadn't had much choice. Lynch should have stayed with the FBI; it had probably been easier than his job here in River City.

Because River City belonged to Luther.

"Spencer Dubridge is at the hospital."

"What? Why?" Luther asked. Had someone else taken him out? He grinned. Had Keeli?

"I followed him to his house, but before I could get to him, Parker Payne showed up."

Luther cursed. Of course he had. Parker Payne had been a pain in Luther's ass for too damn long. He should have made damn certain he'd shot him in the courtroom.

"But Parker wasn't there that long before Spencer came out carrying that blond bodyguard."

Keeli…

"*Carrying* her?"

"Yeah, Parker drove them to the hospital," the guy informed him. "And I followed."

"Are they still there?"

"Yes."

Had Keeli lost her kid? Was that what had happened? Luther remembered how she'd put her hands over her stomach when he'd pulled the trigger. She'd thought to protect her baby before herself.

If only his mama had thought to protect him...

Then Luther wouldn't have had to do it for them both. He wouldn't have had to kill and turn to a life of crime to take care of them. But his mother hadn't been like Keeli Abbott. She wasn't strong and sassy.

Maybe that was why he'd moved the barrel so the bullet wouldn't hit her. He'd felt a twinge of something for her—something like respect. And Luther respected few people.

But he couldn't go soft now—not even for Keeli. "Stay there until they come out," he ordered. "And when they come out, kill them all."

The man gasped, but he didn't argue. He knew better. And he knew the consequences if he didn't follow the order. That he would die, too.

Luther might kill him anyways—even after the man had done his bidding. He was leaving River City, and he would probably never be able to return, so he wouldn't need his moles anymore.

All he needed was his money and his revenge. He couldn't leave until they were all dead.

Spencer didn't like this. Not one bit.

"You should stay here," he said.

Keeli glared up at him. Per hospital regulations, an orderly had rolled her to the lobby in a wheelchair. She had to stay in it until Parker brought the Payne Protection Agency SUV to the entrance. But she gripped the arms of the chair as if ready to vault out of it.

"You heard the doctor," she said. "I'm fine."

And so was the baby...

Their baby.

But would it stay fine if she insisted on resuming her dangerous profession? Or would she lose it before it became much more than that bean pod it had looked like on the machine monitor?

"You don't look so good, though," she said, and her lips curved into a slight smile.

He was probably in shock. And he wasn't sure from what—from the shoot-out at the courthouse where Luther had abducted her, from finding out she was pregnant, from her collapsing in his living room... Or from seeing that tiny image on the machine monitor.

And realizing he was going to be a father...

She'd all but confirmed it when she'd told the doctor when she must have become pregnant.

He shook his head, but he had to swallow before he could reply, "I'm fine..."

"Who's the liar now?" she murmured.

Remembering that she had lied to him pricked his temper. Why did she infuriate him so damn much? Was it because of how she made him feel? Ever since the first moment he'd met her, she'd had him tied up in knots of frustration and concern and lust. That was why he'd always worried so much about her—because he couldn't imagine a world without her in it.

Even now he wanted her. But he pushed the attraction aside to warn her, "Don't lie to me again."

Her face flushed with embarrassment, but she narrowed her eyes. "I wasn't lying that it's none of your business—"

"It's my baby!"

Keeli glanced around as if worried someone might have overheard his outburst. Then, keeping her voice low, she said, "And it's my body."

He sucked in a breath. It hadn't occurred to him that she might not want to continue the pregnancy. "You don't want the baby?"

Her hands clasped her stomach and she shook her head. "That's not what I'm saying. I'm going to carry this baby. But it's *my* body. I decide what's good for me." She pushed up from the chair then.

And he was too relieved that she was keeping the baby to argue with her about getting out of the wheelchair. Then he heard the beep of a horn and saw that Parker had pulled up to the doors.

Keeli headed toward the doors ahead of him, as if wanting to escape him. But as they stepped through them, she slowed down, shielding him like she had when they'd heard the door open at his house.

So she was right in front of him when the shooting started. Parker yelled and vaulted out of the SUV, but he was too late. Keeli had already fallen, but as she had, she'd managed to pull Spencer down with her.

They lay on the concrete side by side as bullets struck the hospital behind them, raining glass down onto them. Spencer couldn't tell if she'd just dropped to the ground to avoid getting shot.

Or if she'd fallen because she had already been hit.

Chapter 8

All the breath had left Keeli's lungs when she hit the concrete. And it wasn't because she'd fallen too hard. It was because of the fear. Sure, she'd been standing in front of Spencer, but he was so much taller than she was that he could have easily been hit and in his most vulnerable spot.

His head...

Hell, the shooter might have even been able to get his heart—although she'd once thought he didn't have one. She knew better now. She knew he'd lost it long ago when the love of his life had died.

She'd felt something whiz past her cheek, and her head had been in front of his chest. She lifted her hand to her face as she turned to look at him. She'd pulled him down with her as she'd dropped. Or so she'd thought.

"Spencer," she whispered.

The gunfire had stopped, leaving a silence so eerie that she was scared to break it.

He was staring at her, his dark eyes wide and shiny—almost as if they were glazed. Could he see her? Was he conscious?

"Spencer," she repeated urgently. "Are you all right?"

"Are *you*?" he asked, his voice even gruffer than her whisper. He reached out toward her, and his hand was shaking as he brushed his fingers along her cheek. And blood smeared his skin. "You've been hit."

She'd touched the cut, too. It was shallow. "Must have been glass…"

"It could have been a bullet," he growled. "You were in front of me again."

"That's how this whole bodyguard thing works," she reminded him.

He groaned. "You are not my bodyguard."

"The chief told you weeks ago that you can't fire me. If you want to stay on the job, you need to have me protecting you."

And she was well aware that it had been killing him the entire time. Not because he had a bodyguard but because he had a *female* bodyguard.

Footsteps pounded against the concrete, and Keeli's fingers twitched as she reached for a weapon that wasn't there. Spencer must not have brought it to the hospital for her. But he had his. He reached beneath his prone body and drew it from his holster. Then he rolled onto his back and pointed the barrel up—directly at Parker.

"Don't shoot!" she yelled at him.

"I won't."

"He's gone," Parker assured them. "Are you two all right?" He held out a hand to help them up.

But Spencer was already getting to his feet. And as he rose from the ground, he wrapped an arm around her waist and easily lifted her up.

Keeli's pulse quickened from his touch, but she couldn't let him distract her. Not now. Not when they'd nearly been killed again.

"He?" Keeli asked. "Luther? You saw him?"

Parker shook his head. "No. All I saw were taillights as the vehicle peeled away. I couldn't even get a look at the plate."

Spencer cursed.

"Was it an SUV?" she asked. "He was driving an SUV when he dropped me off at Spencer's house."

Parker shook his head. "It was a car. But I couldn't tell what kind."

She'd thought Luther had had plans for that SUV since it had looked like the ones Payne Protection used. He must have ditched it for another vehicle already. But she knew he hadn't ditched the city yet. He wouldn't leave until he'd taken the revenge he'd promised to exact on them all.

Spencer's arm tightened around her. "You need to go back inside and get checked out again."

Security guards swarmed the lobby now, as if finally daring to rise up from the ground. They pointed weapons at them through the broken glass.

"Stand down!" Parker said. "We're working for River City PD. Call Chief Lynch."

"I know you, Payne," one of the guards replied. But he didn't sound pleased about it. "Seems like the place gets shot up every time one of your family or bodyguards visit this hospital."

Parker's face reddened, but he didn't deny it. And Keeli remembered the stories of the shootings at the hospital. If her memory was right, several of those stories had indeed involved the Payne Protection Agency.

"Did you call it in?" Parker asked.

The guard nodded. "Of course. Anybody hurt?"

"She needs treatment," Spencer said, as he turned her toward those broken front doors.

"No. I don't," she insisted, and she wriggled free of his grasp.

"You were just shot at!" he said. "And you took a hard fall."

She pressed her hands to her belly. But it was still flat and for once it was settled. She didn't feel sick. But then morning had been a long time ago. And maybe that IV had restored all the fluids she'd lost, making her feel strong again. "I am fine."

"You're bleeding!" Spencer exclaimed, and he lifted his fingers that were smeared with her blood.

"You are," Parker agreed, his blue eyes filling with concern.

"It's just a scratch. I'm fine." Except that she was getting sick and tired of assuring everybody that she was fine. Because she was short and had a small bone structure, people tended to underestimate her strength. That was why she'd always worked so hard to prove them wrong, to prove that she could take care of herself. Keeli had always had to protect herself because nobody else ever had, not even when she was a child. She'd had nobody she could count on but herself. Nobody she could trust until she'd made friends with other members of the vice unit...except for Spencer.

He'd never been her friend. He'd never come to respect her like the others had.

Temper rising, she turned on him. "And thanks to me, you are fine, too. You're welcome. Although I'm questioning now if I should have bothered saving your miserable life."

"You shouldn't have," Spencer agreed. "You shouldn't have risked your life and the baby's life for mine." And he sounded appalled that she had.

"Baby..." Parker murmured, and all the color drained from his face now. Then he nodded with sudden understanding.

"Protecting you is my job," she reminded Spencer.

But it was more than her job to her. He was more than an assignment. That was how the hell she'd wound up carrying his baby. He was too damn much to her—too much temptation and aggravation and...

She could not be falling for him; it wasn't possible. Even now that she understood him a little better...

Now that she understood how helpless he'd felt being unable to save people he'd cared about...

And she'd never been in love, not like he'd been with the person he'd lost.

While she ignored Parker, Spencer turned toward him. "So fire her," he told him.

She gasped. But before any of them could say anything else, police cars with sirens wailing turned into the driveway to the hospital and pulled up next to them. Officers jumped out with their weapons drawn.

Luther, or whoever the gunman had been, hadn't shot them, but she wasn't so sure these officers wouldn't. Because of all the help Luther had had escaping from the courthouse, she didn't trust anyone not to be working for him.

Spencer released a shaky breath. "I'm glad you showed up when you did," he told his mentor, Detective Robertson. "I think those officers might have shot us first and then asked questions later."

Keeli, standing close beside him, nodded in agreement. "They didn't want to listen to us."

Instead they'd shouted at them to get down—with their hands in the air. And when Parker had reached for his ID, one of them had fired a shot. It hadn't struck him, but it had come too damn close.

Fortunately the detective had arrived then and yelled at them to stand down. Or the police might have started hitting them with their bullets.

And Spencer wasn't entirely sure it would have been a misunderstanding. The officer who'd fired might have been working for Luther.

Hell, they all might have been.

"I'm listening," Detective Robertson assured Keeli with a smile.

Frank Robertson had never had kids of his own. He'd never even been married. But he'd always had a fatherly way about him. Now that his hair had gone mostly gray and was thinning and his shoulders had begun to stoop slightly, he looked more like a grandfather than a dad now.

A dad…

That was what Spencer was going to be in seven months or so. The thought staggered him so much he worried that he might pass out like Keeli had earlier in his living room. But she'd had an excuse. She'd been abducted by a killer. Just remembering how close he'd come to losing her had him feeling like he might pass out now.

He was supposed to be the strong one. He *needed* to be the strong one—for her and for their unborn child. Like he should have been for Rebecca. He should have been able to help her, to save her...

"Are you okay?" Robertson asked him. "You look sick, Spence."

He swallowed hard and nodded.

But Robertson grabbed his shoulder and squeezed it. "Of course you're not okay. You just got shot at again. Was it Luther himself?"

Spencer shook his head now. "I didn't see anything." Because all he'd been able to think about was the baby Keeli was carrying. But she could have lost that baby. Hell, she could have lost her own life trying to save his.

Robertson turned toward her, but Keeli shook her head, too. "Just heard the gunfire ring out. I don't even know how many shooters there were."

Robertson uttered a ragged sigh. "That's a damn shame. What about Payne there...?"

Parker had gone into the lobby with some of the officers to make sure nobody had been hurt inside the hospital.

Before Keeli and Spencer could answer, Robertson said, "I better go in and take his statement." But he paused and stared intently at them. "Are you two sure you're both all right?"

"Yes," Keeli replied with a bit of an exasperated-sounding sigh.

Robertson arched an eyebrow, then chuckled. "Is old Spence here being a mother hen?"

"More like male chauvinist," she murmured.

And Robertson grinned. "In my day, they called that chivalry, Ms. Abbott."

She smiled. "I'm sure that's because *you* are chivalrous, Detective Robertson."

"Call me Frank," he told her. "You've known me too long to be so formal yet." He slapped Spencer's shoulder. "Not as long as I've known Spence here, though. I've known him since he was just a glimmer in his daddy's eye."

He'd probably caught Spencer looking at Keeli that same way—with so much desire that he couldn't stop thinking about that night, about what they'd done and now about what they'd made: a baby.

Keeli glanced back and forth between them. "You've known Dubridge that long? Are you related?"

"I grew up just down the street from Frank," Spencer explained.

She arched a brow. "Really? You're grown-up? Because I don't think you're all that mature yet."

Spencer chuckled, but he couldn't deny that he had often acted adolescent with Keeli. Something about her made him feel like an out-of-control teenager at the mercy of his raging hormones. He'd never been as attracted to anyone as he was to her, not even Rebecca. She reminded him of Rebecca, though, with her stubbornness and independence and recklessness.

Robertson cocked his head and studied them. "You must bring out something in him no one else has," he told Keeli. "Because Spence here was the most mature kid I've ever met. He's always had the drive to protect and serve—but mostly protect—everybody he's ever met."

Another look crossed Keeli's beautiful face, smoothing her brow and darkening her blue eyes. And Spencer felt a shiver of unease. It was as if she knew…

About his past.

Does she?

But how had she learned? She'd been surprised that Frank had known him so long, so they must not have talked about him before. And Frank, and only a few other people, knew about Rebecca.

Frank squeezed his shoulder again. "But he needs to be looking out for himself the most right now—with Luther Mills on the loose."

Spencer shrugged off his friend's concern. "I'm in no more danger than anyone else associated with Mills's trial."

"The hell you aren't!" Frank exclaimed. "You're the arresting officer, Spence. You've probably got a target on your back more than anyone else."

Maybe he did.

But Luther Mills wasn't the biggest threat to Spencer's life at the moment. Keeli was—because if anything happened to her and their baby while she was trying to protect him—it would kill him far more painfully and effectively than anything Luther Mills was capable of doing to him.

Soft hands closed around his neck and squeezed. They tightened before releasing. He exhaled a ragged sigh.

"Too hard?" a gentle voice asked, close to his ear, so close that the warmth of her breath heated his skin.

He shivered, though. How was it that he loved her so damn much?

Woodrow wouldn't have thought it was possible to love anyone as much as he loved Penny Payne-Lynch. "Perfect," he said, praising her neck massage. "Just like you…"

She reached over his shoulder and picked up the prescription bottle from his desk. "How many of these did you take?" she asked.

"I don't need drugs to make me realize you're perfect," he said.

She shook the bottle again. "Sounds like you didn't take any of these."

"I don't need them," he repeated.

"Woodrow," she said, and just his name was an admonishment. "You don't need to tough out the pain like this. Take something for it. I'm here. I'll drive you home."

He'd let her think that was why he'd wanted her close. His real reason hadn't been so that she could take care of him but so that he could take care of her.

Protect her…

Luther obviously wanted to hurt Woodrow. In the courtroom, Luther's crew had fired at the guards and even the judge. Luther was the one who'd turned his weapon on the chief—the one he'd shot. He definitely had it in for Woodrow.

"I'm waiting to get the report from the hospital," he told her.

She dropped the bottle back on his desk, then gripped his shoulders and turned his chair so he had to face her. "What report? The doctor said it was just your shoulder."

"It is," he assured her. "I'm fine. But there was a shooting at the hospital."

She gasped. "Who?"

"Spencer Dubridge and Keeli Abbott."

"She got away from Luther?" Penny asked.

Woodrow shrugged, then flinched at the pain going through his wounded shoulder. Penny quickly released him, even though she hadn't been touching anywhere close to his bandage. "I don't know all of the details yet," he said. "It just happened. So I'm waiting to find out what exactly happened."

"Are they okay?"

"I think so," he said. There had been no reports of casualties as far as he knew.

"Was anyone else involved?" She tensed as she asked the question so she must have already guessed that someone she knew had been involved as well.

Woodrow nodded. "Parker. But I'm sure he's fine, too."

She nibbled on her lower lip for a moment before nodding. "Yes, of course he's fine. I didn't have any feeling about him."

"Good," Woodrow said.

"Nothing like I had about you..." She shuddered. "I was so worried that I would get to the courthouse too late."

And he'd been so worried to see her—to know that if she'd been a few minutes earlier, Luther might have taken her instead of Keeli Abbott.

Nothing would hurt as much as losing her. That would kill Woodrow more effectively than any bullet.

Chapter 9

"Damn him…" Keeli murmured.

"Who?" Parker asked. "Spencer or me?"

She was furious with them both at the moment. After giving their report at the hospital, Parker had brought them back to the Payne Protection Agency. Then he'd called Keeli into his office for a private meeting.

"I'm madder at him for telling you I was pregnant," Keeli said. "And I'm mad at you for discriminating against me because I am. I agreed to come to work for you because I didn't think you were sexist."

Parker's face flushed with color. "I'm not."

She arched a brow. "Then why doesn't your sister work for you? Why does she work for your younger brother?" Nikki, along with several other bodyguards, was only on loan from Cooper Payne's franchise of the agency.

Parker's face turned a darker shade of red. "That's different. She's my baby sister."

"And she's a damn good bodyguard," Keeli said.

Parker nodded. "Yes, she is."

Pride coursing through her, she lifted her chin. "And so am I."

"Yes, you are," he agreed.

"And my being pregnant doesn't and will not change that," she said.

Parker shook his head. "Of course it does. How can you not realize that having a baby is going to change everything?"

She could not think that far ahead—to having a baby, to raising a child alone. Keeli wouldn't let her mind go there. That was more frightening to think about than Luther Mills on the loose. But her friend Hart Fisher was raising his daughter alone and had been a single father and a bodyguard for a while now.

She could do it, too—when the time came.

"Not now," she said. "Nothing's changing yet. I'm only a few weeks along."

Parker tilted his head and studied her as if he could figure out when she was due just by looking at her. But then with the way his wife and most of his family procreated, maybe he could.

She patted her flat stomach. "I'm not even showing yet." Because of the morning sickness she'd had, she was actually a little thinner than she usually was.

"I'm not taking you off this assignment because you're pregnant," Parker told her. "I'm taking you off it because you're in danger."

She snorted. "I'm a bodyguard. I'm in danger during every assignment."

"But you were kidnapped," he said—as if she needed the reminder.

"Yes," she said. "And if Luther was going to kill me, he would have when he'd had the chance."

He narrowed his eyes and studied her face. "Why didn't he?"

She shrugged. "I don't know."

"Did he know—did you tell him—that you were pregnant?" he asked.

She felt the heat crawl into her face. "Uh, he found the positive test in my purse."

"Well, I'll be damned," Parker murmured. "I wouldn't think that would make any difference to him. Maybe Luther has a heart after all."

Keeli had been in court during the eyewitness's tearful testimony about how Luther had shot her brother dead right in front of her. A man with a heart wouldn't have been capable of that kind of violence.

She shook her head. "No, he doesn't. And I doubt that's the reason why he didn't kill me. I think he was just messing with me." Or with Spencer.

"Which is why I don't want you working this case anymore," Parker reiterated. "Hell, I don't want you in River City anymore."

Keeli gasped with outrage. "You can fire me, but you can't banish me from the city."

But maybe he could; the Paynes were related to everyone who was anyone in River City either by blood or marriage or extremely close friendships. Keeli had once thought she was Parker's friend as well; that was why she'd come to work for him.

"I'm not firing you," he assured her. "I'm trying to save your life!"

"But my life isn't in danger!" she said.

"Mine is," a deep voice murmured.

Maybe her life was in danger, because she hadn't heard the office door open, and she should have been more aware, especially since Spencer was the one who'd stepped into the small office with her and was now listening to their conversation. Usually she was aware of everything but most especially of his presence.

In a delayed reaction, her skin heated and tingled now, and her heart raced even faster.

"And since you insist on protecting me," Spencer continued, "then your life is in danger, too."

She opened her mouth to argue, but he held up a hand and reminded her, "You were nearly shot at the hospital."

She uttered a low growl of frustration. "But I wasn't. And neither were you. I am a damn good bodyguard, and that's not going to change because I'm pregnant."

It would, eventually, but she had already decided not to think about that now. Not yet…

And especially not with Spencer present—because then she pictured him as part of that future. A frustrating part of that future. Would he try to wrap her and their baby in Bubble Wrap to keep them safe?

Nobody was putting Keeli in Bubble Wrap or protective custody. "And I'm not going anywhere," she told her boss. "So if you want me off this assignment, you're going to have to fire me."

Parker arched a dark brow. "Assignment?" He glanced back and forth between them. "Is that all this is?"

Obviously he'd realized who the father of her unborn baby was. Her face burned even more as embarrassment joined her anger. But pride surged through her again, lifting her chin. "I've done a good job. He's still alive."

That was mostly because she'd refrained from murdering him herself.

Parker nodded, then admitted, "I've been worried that you might kill him."

A smile tugged at her lips that her boss knew her so well. And since he did, why didn't he trust her to do her job?

Was it because she'd slipped that once—with Spencer—that he was worried she was too distracted to protect him and herself?

"I was tempted to kill him," she admitted. At least she hadn't given in to that temptation like she'd given in to their undeniable attraction. She cast him a sideways glance, and his good looks jolted her heart into overdrive. Then she added, "Because he kept trying to get me removed from his assignment."

She turned and glared at him.

"I don't want that now," he said.

"Really?" Parker asked, clearly as shocked as she was by the admission.

"Nope," Spencer said. "I want her to protect me— like Tyce Jackson is protecting the judge's daughter— somewhere far away from River City."

"You son of a bitch," she murmured—furious at his latest ploy to keep her out of harm's way. She probably should have given in to the temptation of killing him. Her life would be a lot easier now. But she remembered hearing the heartbeat of their baby and seeing that image on the screen, and she didn't regret what they'd done.

* * *

If looks could kill…

Spencer would already be dead.

She glanced away from the road just long enough to cast him another of those arctic glares across the console of the SUV as she drove.

Which made his fingers twitch with the need to grab the wheel. Not that she was a bad driver…

As a matter of fact, she was a damn good one. Some of those impressive skills she possessed were in driving as well as marksmanship and hand-to-hand combat. He'd worked with former Marines who weren't as skilled as she was. Maybe that was why he hadn't been able to sleep well since she'd been guarding him. He had been worried that she might murder him in his sleep.

But his tense and needy body called him on the lie he'd tried telling himself. He couldn't sleep because he needed her. So damn badly…

But not as his bodyguard.

He'd always been attracted to her. And maybe that was why he was such an ass to her. He didn't want her putting herself in danger over and over again. He didn't want anything happening to her like it had to Rebecca.

He flinched as pain jabbed his heart at the thought of losing Keeli. How empty and bleak his life would be without her arguing with him, glaring at him, driving him crazy with desire…

"What's wrong?" she asked. "Did you get hurt when I knocked you down at the hospital?"

"No," he replied gruffly. She had saved his life. Of course he hadn't shown her much appreciation for doing that; he'd been more concerned about her life. Hers and their unborn child's.

"So it's just your conscience attacking you now?" she asked.

He snorted. "Why would that be?"

"Because you're a sellout," she said. "Just like you accused every one of us of being for leaving River City PD to go to work at the Payne Protection Agency."

He flinched again. He had called them sellouts. And now seeing for himself how hard they worked and how many lives they'd saved, he knew how wrong he'd been to accuse any of his former coworkers of selling out. But he wasn't one either. "What the hell are you talking about? I'm not—"

"Yes, you are!" she interjected. "You're running away from your sworn duty to uphold the law."

"I'm not running away," he said.

"Yes, you are," she protested. "You made a promise to serve and protect, but you're going to leave here with a killer on the loose. You're going to let him rain terror on the city you're duty bound to defend." She shook her head as a grimace of disgust contorted her beautiful face.

Guilt gripped him. He did have a duty to protect the city; that was why he'd worked so hard all these years to bring Luther Mills and so many other criminals to justice. He hadn't been able to save Rebecca, but once he'd joined law enforcement he had saved other lives. However now, since learning of her pregnancy, he had a new duty—to his unborn child.

"Come on, Keeli," he began, trying to defend himself. "You know why—"

"I do," she agreed. "And that's what makes it

worse—because you're trying to get me to run with you. And I am damn well not going to run away."

He was already well aware of that. She'd told her boss she wasn't leaving River City. If Spencer really wanted to, he would finally get his wish for another bodyguard.

Then she added something under her breath, something he barely heard, but it sounded like she murmured, "Not this time…"

Had she run away before?

Was that why she'd left River City PD? Had she been running from something?

Or *someone*?

Spencer didn't want to leave the city either. He just didn't want her and their unborn child in River City with Luther Mills on the warpath. She was lucky the killer had let her go once. Spencer had no doubt that Luther wouldn't do that a second time.

He should not have let her go.

What the hell had he been thinking? Just because she was knocked up now didn't mean that she wasn't still going to be a pain in his ass like the rest of those Payne Protection bodyguards had proven to be.

Because, if she'd overheard any of the conversations he'd had while holding her in that house, she could prove more of a liability than any of the rest of them.

Especially if she shared that information with Spencer Dubridge.

He was the biggest pain in Luther's ass. The son of a bitch had taken way too damn much pleasure in slapping the cuffs on him. And Dubridge had made sure to do it right in front of Luther's crew, leading him from his home in one of those disrespectful perp walks. Like Luther was just a common criminal.

Luther should have had him killed right then.

Hell, he wanted him dead more than any of the rest of them. For how he'd treated Luther, for how he'd disrespected him, Spencer Dubridge deserved to die.

And he would have been dead—had Keeli not thwarted the last damn attempt at the hospital.

Even knocked up, she was too damn good a bodyguard. The only way she might be a worse one was when she was a dead one.

And that needed to be soon.

Chapter 10

A rumble of deep voices reached Keeli's ears, making her strain to listen. She couldn't make out the words, only that low murmur.

Who was talking?

Where the hell was she?

It was so black—she couldn't see anything. And she could hear...

Was that Luther?

Goose bumps lifted on the bare skin of her arms. Had he found her? Had he abducted her again?

What was he saying?

Something about a plane...

He was going to fly away—to escape justice. Keeli strained to hear what he was saying. He wasn't going to do it yet.

He had scores to settle. Several scores...

And he was going to do that...

When?

Keeli jerked awake from the dream that had been so damn real. Except it hadn't been a dream.

It was real.

Luther had abducted her from the courthouse. Had held her in some dark room. A room very like the one in which she was now lying on a bed, like she'd lain on that mattress. Where the hell was she?

A memory tugged at her, but it was just from the dream. Or *had* she been dreaming? Had she heard something while Luther had held her captive?

She heard something now: the creak of a floorboard. Someone was in the room with her, and she shuddered as she remembered how many times that had happened in the past. Not that anyone had believed her then...

Not that anyone had helped her. So she'd helped herself. She sat up and reached for the holster she'd left next to the bed. But before she could draw her weapon, a strong hand wrapped around her wrist and another pressed over her mouth.

Even though she recognized who the hell had grabbed her, she tensed—ready to fight. And not just for her life but for her heart as well...

She was going to struggle. Spencer felt it in how her body tensed beneath his hands. "Shh," he told her. "It's me..."

Even though he'd identified himself, she didn't relax.

"Someone's outside," Spencer whispered.

Ironically she relaxed now. Was she happier that

someone was trying to break in than that he'd broken into her bedroom? Of course it had only taken a paper clip to push open the lock so he could turn the knob and sneak in.

Did she think he'd come to her for another reason? For something else?

His body tightened with the thought of that something else. He wanted her—so damn badly. His skin tingled where it touched hers, which was smooth as silk and warm with sleep.

Spencer leaned closer and moved his hand from her mouth. He wanted to replace his hand with his mouth, but she tensed again and sucked in a breath.

She must have heard something, too.

Whispering like he was, she asked, "Was it a backup bodyguard?"

He shook his head. Then remembering how dark the room was, he voiced his reply, "I don't think so..."

Hell, he knew so, but he didn't want to admit to her that he hadn't given Parker the right address where to send backup bodyguards.

Luther knew too much and had too much help. And Spencer wasn't sure that it was just from inside the police department or the jail or the district attorney's office...

He was beginning to suspect that Luther had someone within the Payne Protection Agency who might be working with him. That was why Spencer had kept this location to himself. Not that Parker probably wouldn't have been able to figure it out, since it was the house where Spencer had grown up and where his parents still lived.

But they only spent half the year here now and half

at their home in South Carolina. They were at the other house now or he wouldn't have risked coming here.

Spencer hoped that by the time Parker figured out where they were, he would have been able to talk Keeli into going away with him—to somewhere a hell of a lot safer than River City right now. But when they'd arrived at his mom and dad's house, she hadn't wanted to talk. Or anything else...

She'd gone into the guest room he'd showed her and closed the door, locking him out. Just like she had since that night they'd made love.

Keeli had never let him back into her bed after that. Not that he'd tried. He hadn't been sure it had happened at all when she'd kept acting like nothing had transpired between them, and anytime he'd tried to bring it up, she'd shut him down. But it was too late. They'd already made a baby together.

And when the strange noises outside the house had awakened him, Spencer had worried that it was also too late to talk her into going away. If the house was surrounded, like Luther's crew had surrounded previous Payne Protection safe houses, they would get shot the minute they stepped outside. But if they didn't step outside, that crew was certain to storm inside and start firing.

He'd heard a tap on something. It could have been someone trying to break a window. But it had sounded like something striking metal more than glass. A gun against a pipe? He had no idea.

But before stepping outside to investigate, he'd wanted to check on Keeli. To make sure whoever was trying to get in hadn't already gotten to her.

She was fine. For now...

But she tugged away from him and reached for her weapon again. Her gun glinted in the darkness as she drew it from her holster. Before leaving Parker at the hospital, she'd gotten some ammunition from him, so that she was fully armed now. "I'll check it out," she said. "You stay here."

"Like hell I will," he growled.

He shouldn't have awakened her. He should have known that she would put herself in danger, just as she had so many times before, without any fear or hesitation.

But this wasn't like so many other times before. It wasn't just herself that she was putting in danger anymore. Didn't she care about the baby she carried?

"And you're not going out there either," he said.

"I need to find out who the hell is out there," she insisted as she scrambled out of the bed.

He heard the rustle of clothes, and he knew she must have been pulling on some. Had she been sleeping naked? She had that night she'd slept in his arms. But they'd both stayed naked that night and so damn hungry for each other.

How had she just forgotten about that night—about all the mind-blowing pleasure they'd given each other? He hadn't forgotten. He replayed it in his mind all the time.

Which was why he struggled to sleep. But it was good that thoughts of her had kept him awake or he might not have heard their potential intruder.

Her silky hair brushed his bare arm as she moved past him. But he caught her wrist again, like he'd caught her before she could draw her weapon on him when he'd first approached her bed to awaken her.

Maybe she had already been conscious, or maybe she was always that quick to react to danger.

But he'd been quicker. And whoever was creeping around the house might be as well.

"Let go of me," she said between gritted teeth.

"You're not going out there," he repeated. "You could get your head blown off."

She made a noise—that sounded suspiciously like a sniffle. Was she crying? No matter how harsh he'd been to her in the past he'd never made her cry before. He'd never even brought tears to her eyes.

But she was pregnant now. And he'd heard that the new rush of hormones made some women really emotional.

"Hey," he began, his heart aching with regret for upsetting her. Sure, he'd tried to piss her off in the past, but she'd always given as good as she'd gotten from him—sometimes better.

But she pressed a hand against his chest and shoved at him. "We both need to get out of here," she said with a new urgency in her voice.

At least she didn't want to go outside alone anymore to investigate.

"But then we'll both get our heads shot off," he said. If they stayed inside, they might be able to pick off the intruders as they broke into the house.

She shoved harder at him. "No," she insisted. "If we stay in here, we're going to get blown up."

Then he smelled it too—the gas.

And he realized that sound he'd heard must have been someone messing with the utility line outside his bedroom window. If that same someone struck a match...

His parents' house—the house where he'd grown up—could be blown up. And he and Keeli and their unborn baby would be blown up along with it.

"We need to get the hell out of here!" she said.

He agreed. But that didn't mean that the minute they stepped outside, someone wasn't waiting to shoot at them. They were trapped.

Damn it! Fury gripped Parker.

Spencer had lied to him. He'd given him the wrong address to send backup bodyguards. Not only hadn't the guys been protecting Spencer and Keeli but they'd nearly been arrested when the occupants of the house they'd been guarding had noticed them lurking in the shadows and had called the police.

Damn him!

What the hell had Dubridge been thinking?

Since the chief had hired the Payne Protection Agency, the detective had been insisting that he didn't need a bodyguard. But Parker had thought that insistence was only because Keeli had been assigned as his bodyguard.

And he'd thought Spencer was every bit the chauvinist that Keeli had always accused him of being…

But after finding out about her pregnancy, Parker had begun to think that Spencer had another reason why he hadn't wanted his bodyguard putting herself in danger. It wasn't because he didn't think she could handle it. It was because he cared about her and didn't want anything to happen to her.

Keeli had called Spencer's overprotectiveness chauvinism, and she hadn't appreciated it.

But something must have changed between them

because it sounded as if they were both going to become parents to the baby she carried.

And because of that, Spencer shouldn't have lied about where they were going. He should have wanted all the backup Parker could give him—if he really cared about keeping Keeli and their baby-to-be safe. So why the hell had he given Parker a phony address?

Then he remembered that the assistant district attorney had had doubts about Parker's agency—about his bodyguards. Jocelyn Gerber had once thought one of them might be working with Luther. She'd since realized how wrong she'd been, though.

But what if Spencer shared those doubts?

What if he didn't trust Parker or the guards who worked for him and his brothers? Dubridge had made it clear to all of them that he hadn't appreciated their leaving the River City Police Department for the private security business. He'd even gone so far as to call his former coworkers sellouts.

Did he think one of them had sold out to Luther Mills?

Parker's stomach knotted with the thought—not that one of his team or his brothers' teams could actually be working for Luther. He knew that wasn't true. But he hadn't liked it when ADA Jocelyn Gerber had been suspicious of them. And he hated even more that a detective, one with whom they'd worked, could think one of them would be unscrupulous enough to give up someone they'd been hired to protect.

Parker and his siblings didn't make their bodyguards swear to an oath like the police department. But they had a code of honor and integrity by which they and their entire teams lived. There was no way

Luther had gotten to anyone at the Payne Protection Agency.

And Parker would make damn sure that Spencer knew that—when he found him. The people at the house to which the detective had given the address hadn't even known who he was. He must have pulled the street number out of the air.

So where had they gone?

Not to the airport.

There was no way Spencer had convinced Keeli to leave River City. They were somewhere within the city.

Keeli hadn't heard the address Spencer had given him as she'd already slammed out of his office. But she'd known it was for a house, so he couldn't have brought her to a hotel or apartment. She would have known then that he'd lied to Parker, and she would have called to give him the right address for backup.

So Parker had had his sister, Nikki, run down a list of houses deeded to the last name Dubridge. And he'd found the house where Spencer's parents lived. He doubted, though, that the detective would have gone home and risked putting his parents in danger.

Especially after what had happened to the home of the parents of the crime scene tech who'd processed the evidence against Luther...

If Wendy Thompson's father hadn't had a safe room installed in his cellar...

They all would have died.

But Spencer was being careless with the family he was going to have in seven months with Keeli, so maybe he had been careless with the lives of his parents, too.

Parker glanced at the addresses of the houses on

the street where the detective had grown up. But he didn't need to read the numbers to know which house was Spencer's.

He knew the minute it blew up—flames and debris blasting into the night sky with such force that it rocked the SUV, which was still more than a block away, on its tires.

Parker froze with horror and dread. There was no way anyone could have survived the explosion. Luther had claimed his first victory in his quest for revenge.

Parker had lost a team member and a friend.

Chapter 11

Keeli lifted her face toward the water, blinking against the spray as it rushed over her. Bits of debris and ash circled the drain as it washed from her hair and her skin. She reached for more shampoo, lathering up again to get rid of the scent of the gas and the smoke.

They'd been a few houses away when the explosion happened, but it had knocked them to the grass and engulfed them in a billowing cloud of smoke and debris. For several moments they'd lain there, too stunned to move.

But then she'd remembered that someone had been outside. Fortunately whoever it was hadn't shot at them when they'd slipped out the window in the guest bedroom. But what if he'd seen them escaping…?

"We need to move," she'd whispered to Spencer.

He hadn't moved. But he probably hadn't been able

to hear her over the roar of the fire. So she'd shaken his arm. And finally he'd reacted.

Not only had he jumped up, but he'd lifted her from the ground before she could force herself up. And he'd nearly carried her as he ran from the fire. They didn't run far—just a few houses down the block.

"We can't stay here," she'd told him.

"We're not."

He reached inside the wheel well of a car parked in the driveway and pulled out a small metal container. Then he unlocked the car—a vintage Mustang—and tugged her inside with him.

She'd slid across the bench seat. "You're stealing a car?"

"Frank won't mind," he'd said. "We need to get the hell out of here."

She hadn't argued with him then. She'd acquiesced *until* he'd wanted to go to the emergency room. Then she'd gripped his arm and told him, "No."

"You should be checked out."

"I'm fine," she assured him.

"We were knocked down hard."

"I'm still fine," she insisted.

And finally he'd turned away from the hospital entrance, with its boarded-up windows, and had driven toward a hotel near the airport.

She knew he probably intended for them to leave on one of those planes. To get the hell out of River City. But she had no intention of running away.

Why hadn't Luther done that yet?

He had to be behind the explosion. But how the hell had he known where they were?

Of course he seemed to know everything about

Spencer. Far more than she'd ever known, and she had worked with the man for years and had protected him for a couple of months, spending 24/7 with him.

And now she carried his baby.

She slid her hand over her belly. Everything felt fine. No more nausea. No nothing.

But that was good. Right before releasing her, the ER doctor had told her that she only needed to be concerned if she was cramping or bleeding. She wasn't.

Just as she'd told Spencer, she was fine. And so was their baby. But would they stay that way if they remained in River City? Was he right to insist that they leave until Luther was brought to justice?

Would the criminal be brought to justice if they ran away? She felt like she was the one who could find him. Like she had a clue locked in her head...

In that dream...

Or had it been a memory? The rumble of those voices...

She turned off the faucet, and she heard that rumble again. But this voice sounded even deeper than the one she remembered.

And she immediately identified it as Spencer's. Who was he talking to?

He sounded upset or, at least, concerned.

Who the hell was in the hotel room with him?

She grabbed a towel from the rack and quickly wrapped it around herself. Her hands shook slightly as she reached for her holster on the sink and drew out her weapon.

She'd been doing a piss-poor job of protecting Spencer lately. He could have been killed at the courthouse or the hospital and at the house...

He was the one who'd awakened her. And he was the one who'd lifted her up from the ground and found the car for their escape. But she should have insisted on driving it.

Because someone must have followed them to the hotel.

She pushed open the bathroom door and rushed out, her gun drawn. But the only person in the sight of her barrel was Spencer, his cell phone pressed to his ear.

Still, when she saw the look on his face—the intensity of his desire as his gaze went up and down her barely clothed body—she didn't lower that barrel. She felt like she needed it to protect herself.

From the lust rushing through her, too.

The blast rocked Spencer all over again. And it felt nearly as powerful as when his childhood home had exploded, destroying all his mementos and so many of his family's possessions. That had stunned him. This feeling was a blast of desire that shot through him the minute he saw Keeli standing before him in nothing but a damp towel. Water glistened and dripped from her body.

He wanted to brush those droplets off with his fingers and his lips. He needed to touch and kiss every inch of her, like he had that night—that felt so long ago now.

"Spencer? Are you okay?" a voice called out.

It wasn't Keeli. Her lips hadn't moved although they were parted as if on a soft gasp. Or as if she was struggling as hard as he was just to breathe...

She'd knocked the breath from his lungs just like

the explosion had. He nearly had to pant for air as his head began to lighten and his knees shook a bit.

Maybe he was just in shock from the explosion. Perhaps that was all he was feeling—a delayed reaction to their near-death experience.

No. It was more than that. And he knew it. Hell, it was probably more than desire, but he wasn't ready to admit that. Not even to himself...because he wasn't sure he would survive if something happened to her and he'd fallen for her...

"Spencer!" the voice called again. "Are you there?"

And he remembered the cell phone pressed to his ear. "Yeah, yeah, I'm here."

"Where's here?" Frank asked. "I need to come there and take your report."

Spencer didn't want anyone there with him and Keeli. He wanted to be alone with her. Really alone...

"I just told you everything that happened," he said. "I can sign a statement later."

"I'll bring it to you," the detective offered.

Spencer chuckled. "I know what you really want..."

And he knew what *he* really wanted. Keeli.

Finally she lowered her weapon. Then she leaned against the bathroom jamb. She must have realized who he was talking to—and that it wasn't some intruder in their hotel room. It was just one room. One bed.

Fortunately only single rooms had been available. And since he hadn't wanted to use a credit card that could be traced, he'd only had enough cash on him for one. Or maybe *unfortunately* because if he had to share a bed with Keeli and couldn't touch her...

That would be torture.

"What—what do you think I want?" Frank asked.

"Your car."

"What?"

"I took your Mustang," Spencer said. "I thought you knew."

"I don't care about the car," Frank said.

It wasn't the only vintage automobile the older detective owned. But Spencer knew it was one of his favorites.

He snorted. "Like hell you don't."

"I care about you," Frank said. "I want to make sure you're all right."

"I am," Spencer said with a sigh. He'd already told him that a few times.

"And Ms. Abbott?"

"Fine," Spencer said. And he sucked in a breath all over again as he stared at her. She was more than fine. She was so damn gorgeous even with that scratch on her cheek from the glass that had struck her at the hospital shoot-out.

She was also strong and unflappable.

It didn't matter what happened; she handled it. She would make a great mom.

To his child...

Panic gripped him now. Would he be a good father? His father had been. And Frank had acted like a second father to him. So he had role models—very good role models—to help him be a dad.

He groaned as he thought of his mom and dad. He counted his lucky stars that they were at their winter place in South Carolina and hadn't been put in harm's way by the explosion. But now he had to tell them that

their home here was gone, along with all the possessions in it and so many memories.

"You don't sound okay," Frank persisted.

Spencer sighed. "I'm tired." Tired of arguing with
his old friend. But he hadn't slept either. He'd only
been lying in bed for an hour when he'd heard that
noise outside the house.

Thank God he had.

He shuddered to think of how close he'd come to
losing his life. But his wasn't the life that mattered
most to him. Not anymore...

"I'll talk to you later," Spencer told his friend before disconnecting the call.

"You called the police?" Keeli asked him.

Spencer smiled. "I am the police."

She sighed. "You know what I mean."

"I called Frank, so he wouldn't worry about his vehicle," he explained.

"Sounds like he was more worried about you," she
remarked.

Spencer felt a twinge of guilt that he'd been so short
with his old friend. Frank had sounded genuinely concerned. "He's a good guy."

"Did he see the explosion?" she asked. "Did he notice
anyone hanging around the house?"

Spencer shook his head. "He said he was asleep
until it happened. Then he was disoriented, trying to
figure out what went down. I should call my folks,
too, let them know..." But he dreaded the thought of
doing it, of devastating them.

"I'm sorry," Keeli said. "It was a nice house, and
all the pictures of you in it, it must have been a happy

home…" Her voice cracked a bit as she trailed off, as if she was wistful or envious.

He narrowed his eyes to study her beautiful face. "What? Didn't you have a happy home?"

She shrugged her bare shoulders as if it was no big deal, but somehow Spencer suspected it was. "Not everybody's as lucky as you are, as the Paynes are. I should call Parker," Keeli said. "He must be freaking out."

Spencer shook his head. "I don't think so…"

Keeli inhaled sharply. "How can you say that? You don't think he cares about us?"

"I don't think he knows about the explosion."

Her blond brows drew together in confusion. "How could he not?"

"Because I didn't tell him where we were really going," he admitted.

Keeli gasped. "What the hell were you thinking? No wonder somebody nearly killed us. We didn't have any backup. Hell, if I'd known that I wouldn't have gone to sleep."

She hadn't slept long. Dark circles marred the skin beneath her gorgeous blue eyes. She looked exhausted.

So exhausted that he felt a pang of guilt for how badly he wanted her. He needed a shower, too, and not just to wash off the debris and smoke. He needed a cold shower to cool his desire for her.

"That's why I didn't tell Parker," Spencer said. "I wanted to make sure we were safe."

Her forehead furrowed now as she narrowed her eyes to stare at him. "What the hell are you talking about? You don't trust Parker Payne?" She didn't give him a chance to explain his suspicions before she added in outrage, "He's the police chief's stepson—a former vice cop. He wants Luther Mills brought to justice as badly as we do."

Spencer snorted then. "I'm so sick of you all saying that. You left. I stayed," he said. "I'm the one who finally arrested him."

Color flushed her face. But then she lifted her chin with pride and defensiveness. "So why do you want to run away now when he's on the loose?"

When he'd picked the hotel near the airport, she'd informed him that she wasn't leaving River City. But she hadn't sounded as determined to stay as she had earlier in Parker's office.

"I want to make sure you're safe," he said.

"Then you should have told Parker where we were going, so he could send a backup team to protect us," she pointed out.

And now heat rushed to *his* face. "I told you... I wasn't sure we should trust him."

"Parker—"

"I know," he muttered. "But I don't know everybody who works for him and—"

"You know everyone who works for Parker," she said. "You've worked with all of us, too."

"And you all walked away two years ago without arresting Luther Mills."

"So you think one of us was working for him? On his payroll?" she asked, and she nearly bristled with outrage, so much so that her towel began to slip. But she grabbed at it before it could fall.

Unfortunately.

Spencer's body reacted, though. Desire surged

through him, making him so damn hard and needy for her.

"I don't know what to think," he admitted. Actually he couldn't think—not with her nearly naked standing in front of him. "That's why I didn't tell Parker where we were."

"Then that proves you can trust him," she said. "He had no idea where we'd gone."

"He could have had someone follow us. You could have been followed when you left the office," he pointed out.

She snorted derisively. "Nobody followed me."

"Then how the hell did someone know where we'd gone?"

"It was your parents' house," she said.

He'd never specifically told her that, and she hadn't asked. But the hallway leading to the guest room had been like a photo gallery depicting every special event in his life, so it had been easy for her to figure out how happy his home had been. But he'd never realized she might not have had the same. He flinched. Had it been like Rebecca's house? So dangerous she hadn't been able to stay?

"I'm sorry," Keeli said again; she must have misinterpreted his flinch being over the loss of his childhood home, not his childhood sweetheart.

"It was a nice home," she continued. "Clearly filled with a lot of love."

Her compassion struck him just as hard as her sexuality—maybe harder. She had so much strength and depth to her.

Spencer groaned. "I need to tell my parents...just

Treat Yourself
with 2 Free Books!

Suspense

Suspenseful Romance

GET UP TO 4 FREE BOOKS &
2 FREE GIFTS WORTH OVER $20

See Inside For Details

Claim Them While You Can →

Get ready to relax and indulge with your **FREE BOOKS** and more!

Claim up to FOUR NEW BOOKS & TWO MYSTERY GIFTS – absolutely FREE!

Dear Reader,

We both know life can be difficult at times. That's why it's important to treat yourself so you can relax and recharge once in a while.

And I'd like to help you do this by sending you this amazing offer of up to FOUR brand new full length FREE BOOKS that WE pay for.

This is everything I have ready to send to you right now:

Try **Harlequin® Romantic Suspense** books featuring heart-racing page-turners with unexpected plot twists and irresistible chemistry that will keep you guessing to the very end.

Try **Harlequin Intrigue® Larger-Print** books featuring action-packed stories that will keep you on the edge of your seat. Solve the crime and deliver justice at all costs.
Or **TRY BOTH!**

All we ask in return is that you answer 4 simple questions on the attached Treat Yourself survey. You'll get **Two Free Books** and **Two Mystery Gifts** from each series you try, *altogether worth over $20*! Who could pass up a deal like that?

Sincerely,

Pam Powers

Harlequin Reader Service

Treat Yourself to Free Books and Free Gifts.

Answer 4 fun questions and get rewarded.

We love to connect with our readers! Please tell us a little about you...

DETACH AND MAIL CARD TODAY!

	YES	NO
1. I LOVE reading a good book.		
2. I indulge and "treat" myself often.		
3. I love getting FREE things.		
4. Reading is one of my favorite activities.		

TREAT YOURSELF • Pick your 2 Free Books...

Yes! Please send me my Free Books from each series I select and Free Mystery Gifts. I understand that I am under no obligation to buy anything, as explained on the back of this card.

Which do you prefer?
- ❏ **Harlequin® Romantic Suspense** 240/340 HDL GRCZ
- ❏ **Harlequin Intrigue® Larger-Print** 199/399 HDL GRCZ
- ❏ **Try Both** 240/340 & 199/399 HDL GRDD

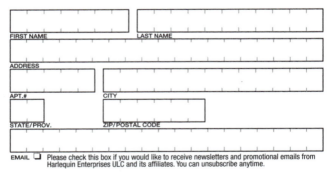

FIRST NAME   LAST NAME

ADDRESS

APT.#   CITY

STATE/PROV.   ZIP/POSTAL CODE

EMAIL ❏ Please check this box if you would like to receive newsletters and promotional emails from Harlequin Enterprises ULC and its affiliates. You can unsubscribe anytime.

Your Privacy – Your information is being collected by Harlequin Enterprises ULC, operating as Harlequin Reader Service. For a complete summary of the information we collect, how we use this information and to whom it is disclosed, please visit our privacy notice located at https://corporate.harlequin.com/privacy-notice. From time to time we may also exchange your personal information with reputable third parties. If you wish to opt out of this sharing of your personal information, please visit www.readerservice.com/consumerschoice or call 1-800-873-8635. **Notice to California Residents** – Under California law, you have specific rights to control and access your data. For more information on these rights and how to exercise them, visit https://corporate.harlequin.com/california-privacy.

HI/HRS-520-TY22

© 2022 HARLEQUIN ENTERPRISES ULC
™ and ® are trademarks owned by Harlequin Enterprises ULC. Printed in the U.S.A.

Accepting your 2 free books and 2 free gifts (gifts valued at approximately $10.00 retail) places you under no obligation to buy anything. You may keep the books and gifts and return the shipping statement marked "cancel." If you do not cancel, approximately one month later we'll send you more books from the series you have chosen, and bill you at our low, subscribers-only discount price. Harlequin® Romantic Suspense books consist of 4 books each month and cost just $4.99 each in the U.S. or $5.74 each in Canada, a savings of at least 13% off the cover price. Harlequin Intrigue® Larger-Print books consist of 6 books each month and cost just $5.99 each for the U.S. or $6.49 each in Canada, a savings of at least 14% off the cover price. It's quite a bargain! Shipping and handling is just 50¢ per book in the U.S. and $1.25 per book in Canada*. You may return any shipment at our expense and cancel at any time — or you may continue to receive monthly shipments at our low, subscribers-only discount price plus shipping and handling. *Terms and prices subject to change without notice. Prices do not include sales taxes which will be charged (if applicable) based on your state or country of residence. Canadian residents will be charged applicable taxes. Offer not valid in Quebec. Books received may not be as shown. All orders subject to approval. Credit or debit balances in a customer's account(s) may be offset by any other outstanding balance owed by or to the customer. Please allow 3 to 4 weeks for delivery. Offer available while quantities last. **Your Privacy** – Your information is being collected by Harlequin Enterprises ULC, operating as Harlequin Reader Service. For a complete summary of the information we collect, how we use this information and to whom it is disclosed, please visit our privacy notice located at https://corporate.harlequin.com/privacy-notice. From time to time we may also exchange your personal information with reputable third parties. If you wish to opt out of this sharing of your personal information, please visit www.readerservice.com/consumerschoice or call 1-800-873-8635. **Notice to California Residents** – Under California law, you have specific rights to control and access your data. For more information on these rights and how to exercise them, visit https://corporate.harlequin.com/california-privacy.

▲ If offer card is missing write to: Harlequin Reader Service, P.O. Box 1341, Buffalo, NY 14240-8531 or visit www.ReaderService.com ▲

BUSINESS REPLY MAIL
FIRST-CLASS MAIL   PERMIT NO. 717   BUFFALO, NY

POSTAGE WILL BE PAID BY ADDRESSEE

HARLEQUIN READER SERVICE
PO BOX 1341
BUFFALO NY 14240-8571

NO POSTAGE
NECESSARY
IF MAILED
IN THE
UNITED STATES

maybe not quite yet." He waited for her to call him a coward.

But instead she nodded as if understanding his reluctance. She did say, "Because you grew up there, it would be easy for someone to find that house."

It had been—too damn easy. But hopefully nobody would find them here. He'd even parked the Mustang a few lots away—in case Frank had filed a stolen vehicle report before he'd had the chance to reach him.

"I should call Parker," Keeli said. She stepped back into the bathroom.

And he felt a flash of regret that she was probably getting dressed. But then she came back out in just the towel, her cell phone clutched in her hand. "You can shower now," she said. "And I'll call Parker."

He wanted to protest. But he had no proof that his suspicions of the Payne Protection Agency were founded. And he needed that shower.

That *cold* shower…

Before he closed the bathroom door, he told her, "Don't tell him where we are."

"You're being ridiculous," she huffed.

"I'm being cautious," he said. "We're safe here because nobody knows where we are. Let's keep it that way."

She drew in a deep breath, as if bracing herself for an argument. But surprisingly she agreed, "Okay…"

Maybe she wanted a moment, too—a moment just for the two of them.

But after Spencer closed the bathroom door, he grimaced at himself in the mirror. He was an idiot if he thought Keeli wanted him the way he wanted her.

She only wanted to be safe.

And he hadn't done a very good job of protecting her and their unborn child. Spencer just hoped Keeli didn't tell Parker where they were. They were safer with nobody knowing.

"Do you know where they are?" Luther's informant asked the tech.

The young woman studied her computer screen. "His cell signal is pinging off a tower near the airport. Could he be leaving town?"

Not Spencer Dubridge. He was too damn stubborn and stupid. He hadn't realized yet that it was no use. There was no way to stay ahead of the criminals anymore—no way to bring them all to justice.

Hell, it felt most days like there was no way to bring any of them to justice. Certainly not Luther Mills.

He was too rich. Too powerful.

Too intimidating.

But Spencer was too stupid or naive to be intimidated. Naive and trusting...

And because of that, he should have been easy to kill. But his bodyguard was too damn good. Was she the one who'd heard him outside, breaking open that gas line? She must have been the one who'd gotten them out of the house before he'd had time to toss that lit flare toward that open pipe.

Maybe he'd been too cautious in getting as far away as he had. If he'd been closer, he might have been able to stop them—with a bullet in each of their brains. And then the explosion would have covered up his crimes for him.

Unlike all the years he'd had to cover them up himself. For himself and for Luther Mills.

That was why he needed to kill Spencer—because Luther had ordered the hit and had commanded him to carry it out.

"He's not at the airport," he told the tech.

"There are a lot of hotels out that way…"

Of course. Spencer had checked himself and his hot little bodyguard into some hotel. While Spencer was naive, he was smart enough to have probably used cash and skipped providing an ID.

It would take a little while to track him down. Hopefully not that long because Luther was antsy. He wanted Spencer dead more than he wanted any of the others gone. The drug lord should have thought about that before he'd released Keeli Abbott.

It would have been a hell of a lot easier to kill Spencer if Keeli wasn't protecting him. That was why he needed to take them out together.

He'd nearly succeeded tonight.

But nearly wasn't good enough.

Not for Luther Mills.

If he failed again, it wasn't just the money that Luther had promised him that he would lose. He had no doubt that Luther might take his life, too.

He had to find Spencer and Keeli as soon as he could.

And he had to make damn sure that this time neither of them survived.

Chapter 12

Keeli didn't call Parker. Not because Spencer had actually gotten to her with his suspicions.

It wasn't possible that someone at the Payne Protection Agency could be working for Luther Mills. At least not within Parker's franchise.

Keeli knew all her team members too well to believe any of them could be bought or intimidated. Sure, Tyce Jackson might be related to Luther, but he had even less use for the killer than the rest of them did.

Luther had had the woman Tyce loved abducted. He would have killed her—had Tyce not rescued her. Unfortunately he'd nearly died in the process.

No. Her colleague was not working for Luther, and neither was anyone else with whom Keeli worked. They were like her brothers. But Parker's brothers...

She didn't know everybody who worked for them.

And they'd been the bodyguards acting as backup at the safe houses. The safe houses that Luther's crews had stormed with guns blazing. She shivered as the suspicions she hadn't wanted to entertain suddenly washed over her.

Goose bumps rose on her bare skin, and she realized she wore only that towel. She'd left her clothes in the bathroom, but Spencer was in there now.

Naked.

The running water spraying his skin.

Her heart slammed against her ribs as it began to pound at a maddening pace. The goose bumps left as heat rushed through her instead. She wanted him.

And from the way he'd looked at her when she'd stepped out of the bathroom in only her towel, it was clear that he wanted her, too.

Maybe that was why she hadn't called Parker. She had to think. Not about Spencer's suspicions but about what she wanted. Spencer...

He was all she could think about—just a door separating her from his naked body. She doubted he'd locked it. But before she could reach for the knob, the water shut off. And she froze, uncertain what to do now.

She must have made some noise, something, because the door opened and just as Spencer had done moments ago, she stared down the barrel of a gun. His gun.

But unlike her, he quickly directed it away from her. "I'm sorry. I didn't know it was you. I just saw the shadow under the door."

And also unlike her, he'd grabbed his gun before he had a towel. Nothing covered him but droplets of water dripping from his wet black hair and running down his smooth skin over all his rippling muscles.

With her gaze, she followed the path the water took. But she wanted to follow it with her hands—with her mouth. She wanted to touch him like she had that night.

The night they'd made their baby.

His body reacted—maybe to her gaze and the molten hot desire that was probably burning in her eyes—and his erection jutted toward her. Spencer's mouth also curved into a faint grin. "Did you want something, Keeli?"

She wanted him. And he damn well knew it.

That was why she'd fought the attraction for so many weeks after giving in to that one exhilarating night. She'd already believed he didn't think she was as strong as he was, as smart, so she'd been too proud to even acknowledge what they'd done that night, how they'd made love and how much she'd wanted to do it again. He was so damn infuriating. So smug and…

Sexy as hell.

"Damn you," she murmured.

He chuckled.

"I don't want you."

"Liar," he said as he stepped forward. "Yes, you do."

She didn't move. Didn't back away. Instead, she lifted her palm and planted it against his chest. Damp hair covered his muscles, tickling her skin. She didn't push him back. His heart leaped beneath her palm—beating as fast and furiously as hers was beating. "I don't want to want you."

He chuckled again. "Now that's probably the truth."

It was. She *didn't* want to want him. But that was a

fight that even she couldn't win, especially now that she knew what she'd interpreted as chauvinism might have been the chivalry his friend and neighbor claimed it was. It also might have been because he hadn't been able to protect the woman he'd cared about the most that he tried so hard to protect everyone else. Even himself...

Keeli knew what that was like, trying to protect yourself from more pain, from disappointment, from disillusionment. She'd done that her whole life. And the truth was, she wasn't sure she'd ever be able to fully trust anyone. But even if she couldn't trust him, she couldn't deny any longer that she wanted Spencer Dubridge. She ran her hand over his chest to his shoulder and then the nape of his neck, and she tugged his head down so that she could kiss him.

She ran her lips over his, which were cool from the shower. He must have had the water on cold. And she smiled against his lips. "Cold shower?" she asked. "Guess you didn't want to want me either."

"I didn't want to make a pass and have you kick my ass," he said.

And she laughed.

This was why she couldn't hate him like she wanted to. As much as he infuriated her, he also charmed her into wanting him. He was so quick-witted and funny and smart. And with his black hair, dark eyes and chiseled features, he was so damn handsome.

He lowered his head and kissed her again. And his lips were warm now as they slid over hers. He nipped and nibbled at her mouth until she opened it, and he deepened the kiss.

Her breath escaped on a wistful sigh. He was such a

good kisser. She could have gone on and on just kissing him. But then he touched her. Or he touched the towel because it dropped away from her body.

But he replaced the terry cloth with his hands, running them over her body—over her breasts. Her nipples peaked, begging for his touch.

He obliged as he cupped her breasts and ran his thumbs over the tight points.

Sensations shot through Keeli. She was more sensitive to his touch now than she'd been before. Maybe it was the pregnancy and all those raging hormones. Her breasts were bigger now—fuller—than they'd been even though her stomach wasn't showing yet.

The baby inside her was just the size of a peanut now. But it would grow...

And she would grow.

Would Spencer still be attracted to her?

She didn't want to care, but she did. Keeli wanted him to want her as much as she wanted him. She hated this feeling—this vulnerability. That was another reason why she'd wanted to pretend that night had never happened. She didn't want to need anyone the way she needed him. She'd prefer to go off alone, to be independent, because she had been the only person she'd ever really been able to count on. Her parents had never had photos of her like his parents had lining the walls of his house. She hadn't been loved and celebrated like he'd been.

But he was celebrating her now.

"You are so sexy," he murmured, then almost reverently added, "And beautiful..."

He wanted her now. She felt his erection straining toward her. And she touched it.

He groaned as if she'd kicked him.

"Are you okay?" she asked.

"No," he said. "You're killing me... I want you so damn badly."

She swallowed down the lump of pride choking her and admitted, "I want you, too."

His breath shuddered out in a ragged sigh of relief. "Good!"

Maybe he wasn't quite who she thought he was. Maybe he was just old-fashioned. Or he wanted to protect every female like he hadn't been able to protect the one he'd loved and lost so long ago.

But he had to know by now that Keeli could protect herself. Or could she?

She had a feeling making love with him again would put her in even more jeopardy than being his bodyguard. Because she was in danger of falling for him...

He stroked his fingers over her breasts again, and the desire that rushed through her pushed aside her fears. She needed him too much to deny either of them now.

She touched him like he touched her, stroking her hand up and down the length of him.

A growl tore from his throat now, as his control snapped. He picked her up in his arms and carried her the short distance to the only bed in the room. She'd been there when the clerk had claimed there were only single rooms available; otherwise she might have suspected him of planning this.

But then he would have had to know the house would explode. And he'd clearly had no idea.

Sympathy rushed over her again. She was truly

sorry that he'd lost his childhood home and all the mementos and pictures of what had looked like an idyllic childhood. She'd never really had a home or a childhood, so she didn't fully understand how big a loss it probably was to him. But she offered him comfort— with her touch, with the kisses she pressed to his lips and then his cheek and his chin.

His breath shuddered out in another ragged sigh. "You are incredible," he rasped.

What was incredible was the potency of the passion that burned between them. She'd never wanted anyone the way she wanted him.

She trembled with the need as tension wound tightly inside her. He laid her on the bed, but he never let go of her, joining her on the soft mattress.

She wanted him to join their bodies. And she reached for him again. But he pulled back. And he focused on her instead. He moved his mouth over her body, kissing her everywhere. His lips closed around a nipple, and she arched off the bed. "Spencer!"

"Did I hurt you?"

She shook her head. But she was hurting—with the intensity of her need.

He groaned. And it was clear that desire was gripping him as well. He paused though, with his mouth on her stomach and looked up at her. "Is it…is it okay?"

She nodded. "Of course. We won't hurt the baby." The doctor had told her that—that having sex wouldn't harm the baby even in the last trimester. Had she seen the attraction between them then?

Keeli was glad now that she'd told her even though she'd said the information was irrelevant at the time.

She hadn't thought this would happen again—that she would give in to her desire.

But they'd both nearly died—so many times that day. She could have lost him—could have lost the chance to ever be this close to him again. But this wasn't close enough. She needed him inside her—needed him to be part of her and her part of him.

However, Spencer hesitated yet again. Maybe he'd changed his mind. Then he moved his lips, sliding them down her stomach to her mound. And he made love to her with his mouth.

She arched from the bed and called out his name as pleasure rushed through her. "Spencer!" Her heart pounded frantically. He'd given her a release, but it wasn't enough. She wanted more. She wanted all of him.

Keeli was already clutching his shoulders—but then it had been to hold him where he'd been. Now she dragged him up. Finally he eased inside her. He was so big but somehow he still fit her perfectly. And like she had the first time they'd made love, she felt a completeness she'd never known.

For so many long, lonely years she'd had a hollow ache inside her. But she wouldn't have thought Spencer, of all people, would be the one to finally fill that emptiness. But it wasn't just physically that he sated her. It was the rush of emotions that flooded her, that made her feel whole.

But she didn't recognize—or maybe she didn't want to recognize—anything but the desire. He'd just given her pleasure, but already that need for more was building inside her. She arched and shifted beneath him, meeting his thrusts—which were far too gentle.

He was holding back with her—as if he thought she might break. He should have known her better by now, like she was beginning to know him.

She knew what drove him wild. So she arched up and kissed his neck and she ran her short nails down his back. Muscles rippled beneath her fingers. And his pulse leaped in his throat and she felt his breath shudder out.

"Keeli…" He uttered her name between gritted teeth, as if desperately trying to hang on to control.

She wanted him to be as out of control as he had made her. So she moved beneath him, thrusting up faster and faster until his control finally snapped. And he met her frenzied rhythm.

And then the tension that had built inside her snapped with his control. She yelled as she came again. Then he joined her with a shout as his big body shuddered with the intensity of his release.

He dropped onto his side next to her, his body still shaking. He panted for breath, his gaze intense as he stared at her. "Are you all right?"

She was struggling to catch her breath, too. And her heart was still beating so fast. But it wasn't with pleasure now. It was with fear. Fear that now that she realized he was more overprotective than chauvinistic, that he was more caring than caustic, she was falling for him.

She'd told him she was fine, but Spencer didn't believe it. He'd seen the fear on her face. Maybe he could finally get through to her—get her to go away with him somewhere safe until Luther was apprehended.

He was the one who'd arrested the drug lord the last

time. Like she'd said, it felt like he was neglecting his duty as a detective if he ran away.

But he had a more important duty now. To Keeli and the child she carried. He was not going to let them down. There was a vulnerability to Keeli that she didn't want to show. She'd showed it when she'd mentioned his happy home; she'd revealed her longing and her envy. What had she been through?

He tightened his arm around her. She'd fallen asleep with her head on his shoulder, her soft breath whispering across his skin. Warming it even as goose bumps rose on it.

He wanted her again.

Still.

Always...

He'd never felt anything like what he felt with her. Not even with Rebecca.

Something about Keeli had always reminded him of his old friend; maybe that they were both small in stature and delicately boned, fragile looking. Rebecca had been so much more fragile than he'd realized.

Of course, he and Rebecca had only been kids. Their friendship had ended when Spencer had shared Rebecca's secret homelife with Frank. When child protective services had gotten involved, Rebecca had run away from foster care and from Spencer. Mixed in with his friendship for Rebecca was so much guilt and regret.

But even those bittersweet emotions were nothing compared to what he felt for Keeli. These emotions scared the hell out of him. If he lost her...

Not that he really had her. Even though they'd made love again, she'd made it clear that she didn't want to want him. She didn't even like him, which was his fault.

He'd always been such an ass to her. And it hadn't been fair of him to judge her just based on her resemblance to Rebecca; he should have given her the chance to prove herself. And when she had—over and over again—he should have given her his respect. But he'd been so afraid that she was going to get hurt.

Or worse.

If anything happened to her...

He couldn't contemplate it. He wouldn't *let* anything happen to her. He had to get her out of River City—before Luther found them again.

How *the hell* had he found them?

Not that it would have been that hard. Luther had threatened the evidence tech by threatening the lives of her parents and had discovered where they lived. Maybe he'd done the same with Spencer's parents.

He was even more relieved they weren't in Michigan now. Keeli shouldn't be either. Maybe he could convince her to stay with his parents in South Carolina.

No. Luther might track them down at their vacation home like he'd tracked Spencer down at their house in River City. And it was Spencer he was after.

He'd had the chance to kill Keeli and he hadn't taken it. If she'd died tonight, she would have just been collateral damage. Spencer was the one Luther wanted dead—because he'd arrested him, which was something nobody else had done. So maybe he needed to stay in River City just like Keeli had said. But she didn't have to stay.

She would be a hell of a lot safer the farther she was

from him. Nothing separated them now but skin. Their hearts even beat with the same fast rhythm.

But how was that possible when she was sleeping?

She shifted against him and murmured. And he realized it was her dream that had her heart racing again. No, it wasn't a dream. It was a nightmare.

"Shh..." he murmured soothingly. "I have you. You're safe."

She jerked awake—at first he'd thought it was because he'd spoken—but then she spoke. "I know where he is!"

"Who?" he asked.

"Luther," she replied. "I know where he took me."

"You said you couldn't see anything," he reminded her.

She nodded. "I couldn't. But I could feel each turn of that van, and I could hear. I know where we were."

"That doesn't mean Luther's still there," he said.

If he was smart, and Luther Mills was too damn smart, then he'd already left River City. But even as smart as Luther was, he was more arrogant and vengeful. He didn't think he could be caught—again. And he wanted to take down everyone who'd tried taking him down.

No. He hadn't left yet. But would he still be at the place where he'd held Keeli captive?

Spencer was afraid that they were about to find out—because Keeli would insist on going there whether he agreed to go along or not.

He could only hope that Luther was already gone—because if he was still there, there would be another treacherous encounter. And Spencer wasn't sure how many more of those he and Keeli could survive.

* * *

He'd screwed up and not just because he'd let Keeli Abbott live. It was because he'd left something behind. The nagging feeling in Luther's gut persisted. He knew he'd left something at that house—something that would give up his future plans.

His escape.

Not from jail but from River City.

He had to go back. It was risky, but only if she'd figured out where he'd been holding her.

And he had that nagging feeling twisting his stomach into knots that she had. She was so damn resourceful. That was the only way she kept surviving and saving Spencer Dubridge, too.

She was also smart. Too smart...

He had to go back. Had to make sure nothing was left behind. But he wasn't going back alone—just in case. He had to level the playing field because if she had in fact figured out where he'd kept her, she wouldn't be alone. She would have Spencer with her and probably a bunch of the Payne Protection bodyguards.

That knot in his stomach eased as he grinned. That wouldn't necessarily be a bad thing. Maybe he could get his revenge there—with all of them.

Chapter 13

"It's too dangerous," he said as Keeli stepped out of the bathroom, dressed again in her black pants and black sweater. "You can't go."

Keeli sucked in a breath. She was so sick of his thinking she couldn't handle herself. If she couldn't, she sure as hell wouldn't have made love with him again—because that was far more dangerous than going back to the house where she'd been held captive.

"If Luther wanted me dead, he would have killed me when he had the chance," she reminded him. She still couldn't believe that he'd fired that shot at the wall instead of her.

Even if the houses around that one were vacant, like he'd claimed, the sound of the gunshot would have carried farther than her screams. Someone might have heard it. Might have reported it, wouldn't they?

So Luther had probably not returned after he'd dropped her at Spencer's house. But she knew that there was something in that place that might lead them to where Luther had gone or was going.

She remembered some of those words she'd overheard now. Something about a plane...

What plane?

Had Luther written it down?

And a new identity. Passport. Birth certificate. All in a different name.

He was going to start over as someone new—once he'd killed everyone he thought had wronged him.

"You nearly died in that shooting and in that house explosion," Spencer reminded her. He had dressed as well in the suit pants he'd worn to court what seemed like so long ago. But he'd left the jacket and dress shirt at his parents' house and wore only a T-shirt, smeared with dirt, with the pants.

"But you were the target," she said. "So you're the one who should stay here. Not me."

He grimaced. "Not going to happen."

"So you do actually want to bring him to justice?" she asked. Then she continued, goading him like he'd goaded her and her team members so many times. "I thought you'd given up..."

He grimaced again. "That's not the case at all and you know it."

"I know that you want to run."

"I want you out of danger!" he shouted. And clearly, she'd snapped his control again but this time on his temper instead of his desire. "You have to stop risking your life!"

"It's my life to risk!" she shot back at him.

"It's my baby whose life you're risking along with yours!"

She was so mad that she arched a brow and asked, "Is it?"

Color rushed to his face but then he laughed and shook his head. "Nice try."

She arched her brows, feigning innocence. "What do you mean?"

"I have no doubts that baby's mine."

She'd all but admitted it already, so she just sighed. "The baby. Not me. I am not yours. You cannot tell me what to do."

He cursed and nodded.

But she didn't for a minute believe that he had accepted that and would stop trying to control her. That was why they could never be together. Someone had tried controlling Keeli before, and she'd run away. She'd run away from the abuse and from the disbelief when she'd reached out for help. Nobody had helped her then, so she'd helped herself.

She'd been a child then. She was an adult now. She wasn't running away from anything or anyone. Not anymore...

"If you're determined to do this," he said wearily, "then we need backup."

"We would have had backup all night if you'd told Parker where we were really going."

"Have you called him?" But he asked the question like he already knew the answer. Had he checked her cell when she'd been sleeping?

Heat rushed to her face. She was embarrassed that she kept falling asleep. And she was embarrassed that she hadn't called her boss to report in. Parker had to have found out about the explosion at Spencer's parents by now. He had to be wondering where they were—if they were even alive. It could take days for firefighters to sort through the debris for any traces of survivors.

That debris had once been Spencer's home. Was still his parents' home...

"Have you called your mom and dad?" she asked.

He flinched. "I haven't. The neighbors or the fire department probably have, though."

"I am going to call Parker now." She'd have to do it with his phone, though. While Luther had given hers back along with her empty gun, she hadn't had time to charge it. And the battery had been low before she'd made love with Spencer. She glanced at the screen, but it was completely black.

Spencer pulled his phone from the pocket of his jeans. "I should probably call my folks—"

"You don't have time to call them now," she told him. They had to get to that house. Luther might have gone back to it after setting that explosion at Spencer's childhood home. He might not know yet that they'd made it out alive.

They barely had.

She shuddered and reached for Spencer's phone. But he held it out of her reach. "Mine's dead. I need to use yours."

"I'm calling the police," he said.

And she jumped up and knocked the phone from his grasp. "You can't do that! You know there's a leak in the department." She retrieved the phone from the carpet.

Spencer closed his hand over hers before she could dial anyone.

"And you can't be sure you can trust Parker, or you would have already called him," he said.

"I trust Parker," she insisted.

He tilted his head and narrowed his dark eyes as he studied her face. "But you don't trust all the other bodyguards."

"I trust my team," she said. "I trust all of them with my life."

"And mine?" he asked.

She nodded. But then she had to admit, "I'm not sure about Parker's brothers' teams, though."

Spencer tensed. "I know Logan has a couple of ex-cons working for him."

Her head shot up. "Really?"

How could Logan, a former detective himself with the River City Police Department, trust an ex-con?

"They're his brothers-in-law," Spencer added.

And she nodded with sudden understanding. "Okay…"

"One of them is married to the district attorney."

"The Kozminskis." She'd met both Garek and Milek when they'd been working as backup to protect the other people associated with the trial. "Milek is the one who's married to Jocelyn Gerber's boss."

Could he also be working for Luther?

"I'll ask Parker to only use his own team," Keeli said.

Spencer shook his head. "That's not possible. Tyce is out of the country with the judge's daughter. Once the evidence tech testified, Hart took her back to where her parents and his daughter are hiding out from Luther. Clint did the same thing with the eyewitness—

whisked her away right after her testimony. That leaves Landon, and he's not about to leave Jocelyn's side."

Keeli knew he was right. Landon was so in love with the assistant district attorney that there was no way he would leave her unprotected. And he wouldn't bring her to the house where Luther might be hiding out either.

She cursed.

"We have to call the police," Spencer persisted.

But she shook her head. They'd found the leak in the district attorney's office. The man had nearly killed Jocelyn and Landon. But the only person in the police department who'd been caught, and killed, had been a rookie. He couldn't have been the one supplying Luther with all the information he'd had about the investigation. Sure, there'd been someone within the evidence lab who'd been working for him, too. But there had to be someone else...

She shook her head. "We can't."

"We can trust the chief."

She couldn't argue that; he was the one who'd hired the Payne Protection Agency. He trusted them. "I'm calling Parker," she reiterated. And she tugged free of his grasp and punched his number into Spencer's phone.

"Where the hell are you?" her boss bellowed.

He probably thought Spencer was calling him since she was using his cell. "That doesn't matter," she said.

"Keeli!" he exclaimed, and a ragged sigh rattled the phone. "You're alive."

"Of course," she said.

"I saw the house explode."

So he'd found it. He was good.

But his voice cracked with emotion when he added, "I thought I was too late. I thought you were dead."

"I'm alive," she assured him. "I'm fine. And I think I've figured out where Luther took me."

Another sigh rattled the phone, but then he chuckled. "Of course you did."

And she knew she'd done the right thing to call him. Although it was hard for her to trust anyone, she trusted Parker Payne. She wasn't sure she could trust herself, though.

Why had she slept with Spencer again?

It was only making her fall for him.

And that was the last thing she should do—even farther down the list than having a baby with him.

Spencer should have knocked the phone from her hand like she'd knocked it from his. But he didn't want her getting hurt—by anyone but most especially not him. When she disconnected her call with her boss, he scowled at her. "You shouldn't have done that."

"We can trust Parker," she said. "You know that."

"I would have called him myself if I felt that way," he pointed out.

"You know Parker."

He did. "It's not Parker either of us are really worried about," he reminded her. "It's all the other bodyguards. Luther could have gotten to one of the other ones."

She sighed and said, "He could have...but one of those bodyguards isn't going to try to take us out at the house with Parker and his brothers present."

"All the Paynes will be at the house?"

She nodded.

That tight knot of tension in his stomach eased slightly. "Okay, that's good." He did trust the Paynes. "As long as one of the other bodyguards doesn't tip off Luther..." Because they both knew the drug lord wouldn't just leave—he would set a trap for them before he left. Maybe he already had.

Keeli handed back his phone, then headed toward the hotel room door. But before she could turn the handle, Spencer caught her arm.

"Stay here," he implored her. "Please..."

She uttered an exasperated sigh. "We've been through this over and over again. This is my job, Spencer. It's what I do. Stop trying to stop me from doing it. From being who I am."

That tension in his gut wound tighter. This was who she was—the one who kept putting herself in danger. Over and over again...

And that wasn't something he thought he could handle—especially not when she was carrying his baby. That was why he'd fought his attraction to her for so long. But that was a fight he'd lost.

And he lost this one, too, as she pulled open the door and stepped out into the hall. Unless he physically overpowered her—and he wasn't convinced he could if she really fought him—and tied her up in the hotel room, he couldn't keep her from going back to that house.

All he could do was stick close to her and try to keep her from getting hurt. So he hurried after her, letting the hotel room door close behind them. He doubted they would be coming back here—even if they survived what would probably be another confrontation with Luther or his crew.

"Wait," he called after her.

She was shorter than he was, but she moved faster, almost running toward the stairwell at the end of the hall. Maybe she was worried that he would try to overpower her because she kept going. But like before, when she reached for the door handle, he caught her wrist.

Keeli tensed and through gritted teeth warned him, "You grab me again and I will drop you."

She hadn't seemed to mind earlier that evening—when he'd carried her to the bed. But he knew better than to point that out now. She would certainly drop him then—probably with a blow to his groin.

"I'm not trying to stop you," he said. "I'm just trying to slow you down now."

She tugged free and turned and glared at him. "So Parker and his brothers will beat us to the house?"

"Yes."

"They won't know which one it is," she said. "I need to get there first and figure it out."

That was his only hope. That she might be wrong about how many turns and the distance and that damn train whistle she remembered hearing before she'd felt the vibration of the train as it rumbled down tracks that must have been close to the house. That was what she'd shared with Parker on her call—which was more than she'd shared with Spencer.

"They'll figure it out," he said. "If you give them time."

She shook her head. "We don't have time." She opened the door to the stairwell. "We need to catch Luther—to get him back behind bars."

He couldn't argue with that; putting Luther in prison was the only way any of them would be safe. But he wasn't sure how safe that would actually be even after that happened. Luther had managed to wreak havoc and danger from behind bars when his bond had been denied and he'd been in jail awaiting his trial.

Keeli was so eager to get to that house that she ran down the three flights of stairs to the exit that opened to the outside. Spencer wanted to reach out again and grab her, but he didn't doubt that she'd meant what she'd said. So he backed off.

She opened the door, but she didn't rush out headlong into the parking lot. Instead she drew her weapon and looked around, then she beckoned him. "It looks clear."

Dawn had broken, but it was only a faint lightening of the darkness. He couldn't see that clearly yet. But he noticed no movement in the parking lot either.

All the other occupants of the hotel must have still been in bed. Like he wished he was—with Keeli snuggled against his chest, asleep in his arms. But even then she hadn't been resting; she'd been having a nightmare—a nightmare that wouldn't end until Luther was no longer a threat.

"I parked the Mustang two lots over," he reminded her. "It would be safer if I went to get it and came back to pick you up."

She held out her hand, palm up. "Give me the keys, and I'll do that."

He groaned. "Keeli—"

"I'm going to need to drive anyways," she said. "It's the only way I'll be able to remember exactly the number of turns and the distance in order to trace my way back to that house."

"So once I get the car and bring it back here, you can drive then," he agreed. He didn't want her trying on her own to cross all those open parking lots again. Of course they'd already done it safely once when they'd arrived earlier that evening.

But then nobody might have realized yet that they'd survived the explosion. Now people knew and were probably out looking for them again. He didn't want her risking her life and their baby's life for his.

"Just to be safe," he said, "let me get the car."

"You're the one who needs protecting," she said. "And I'm your bodyguard. Luther doesn't want me dead like he does you."

"He would—if he had any idea that you figured out where he'd been holding you." Luther had let her live, but he had probably regretted that since she kept thwarting the attempts made on Spencer's life. He ignored her outstretched hand and started across the lot.

She, of course, kept pace with him now, staying between him and whatever threat might lurk in that lingering darkness. Spencer doubted there was one. They hadn't been followed from the explosion, and she hadn't told Parker where they were staying. Had the call been long enough for someone to trace though?

It could have been—especially for Parker's tech-genius sister, Nikki Payne-Ecklund. Because of that thought, he was just reaching for his weapon when the first shots rang out.

Predictably, as she had before, Keeli knocked him to the ground. They sprawled on the pavement just a few yards from the Mustang—and from any other vehicles. They had no cover. And the shots continued to ring out.

Spencer knew it was only a matter of time before they were hit.

* * *

Had he hit them?

He'd fired so many damn shots. At least one of them had fired back at him, though, the bullets striking too close to where he'd taken cover at the edge of a building. He was too far away to see clearly—to see if they were bleeding.

And he didn't risk getting any closer just in case one of them was alive. He'd been lucky that none of the bullets had struck him. But if he stepped away from his cover, he was certain to get shot.

And even if he wasn't killed, his life would be over anyway and not just because Luther would probably send someone after him to put a bullet in his brain.

His life would be over—because everyone would know the truth about what he had done. About who he really was...

No. He had to believe that this attempt had been successful—that he'd killed them.

Chapter 14

Keeli's ears rang from all the shots—the ones they'd fired and the ones fired at them. She shook her head to clear it and droplets of blood flew from her face.

Spencer reached out a shaking hand and touched her cheek. "You're hurt."

"I probably just reopened the wound from where the shard of glass cut me at the hospital," she said, dismissing the wound. It wasn't deep. But it stung like hell, so she didn't really think it was from the previous injury.

"I think you got hit with a bullet this time," Spencer said, and now his deep voice was as shaky as his hand.

She touched the wound and grimaced. "It must have just grazed me. It's not in my face." Or she wouldn't have made it up from the asphalt.

Of course Spencer had helped her up—once they'd heard a car careen out of the lot. Hopefully that had been the shooter leaving—although it would have been better had he not been able to leave because one of them had hit him. But she doubted she had, since she hadn't really even been able to see where he'd been hiding.

But *he* had been hiding and waiting for them. How the hell had he found them?

"Did you see him?" Keeli asked. There had been just the one shooter. But she hadn't gotten so much as a glimpse of him.

Spencer was focused only on her, his gaze intent on her face as he continued to press his fingertips to her cheek. "We need to get you to the hospital."

She shook her head. "I'm fine. And we have no time. We need to get to that house."

"You don't think that was Luther shooting at us just now?" Spencer asked.

"If it was Luther, he wouldn't have come alone like that," she said. "He's never by himself."

"That's why we need to stay here," Spencer said. "We need to file a report and investigate to see if anyone saw who the hell was shooting at us."

She wanted to catch the son of a bitch who'd been shooting at them, too. But she wanted to catch Luther more. Whoever had been targeting them had only been carrying out Luther's orders anyways. Mills was the one they needed to stop.

She held out her hand like she had before the shooting started. "Give me the damn keys!"

Spencer knew better than to argue with Keeli anymore. She wasn't just determined now; she was also bristling with fury. He pulled the Mustang keys from his pants pocket and dropped them into her hand. As she'd unequivocally stated earlier, she needed to drive to be able to find the house again.

He would rather she didn't find it. She'd already been through too much recently. While she believed she and the baby were fine, he wasn't so sure. And if they found the house and Luther was still there, Spencer knew that none of them would be fine.

Since the car was too old to have power locks, he had to wait at the passenger door for her to reach across and pull up the lock. And she hesitated just long enough that he thought she might drive away without him. He held on to the handle tightly because he doubted she would keep driving if she was dragging him along with her.

But then he wasn't sure if she was mad at just the shooter or at him, too.

She was still his bodyguard, though, so she unlocked his door. Maybe she'd been worried that the shooter would return. "I would leave you here," she admitted, "for your protection…but we both know you're not safe anywhere."

"*We're* not safe anywhere," he corrected her. And he knew he spoke the truth. Keeping her safe wasn't going to be possible. "Unless we leave River City," he said. And he gestured at the signs leading to the airport. "Let's leave."

"And miss this chance to catch Luther?" She shook her head. "I can't do that."

He uttered a ragged sigh of resignation. Neither could he. Luther on the loose was even more dangerous than Luther behind bars had been, and with all the destruction he'd caused from jail, he had been very lethal there, too. Spencer didn't want anyone getting hurt because of the killer, but most especially not her.

"I understand that you need to find the house," he said. "But once we get there, you should stay in the car."

She snorted in derision.

"Damn it, Keeli, it's not that I'm telling you not to do your job," he said—although he had probably told her that, many times. He'd been so worried about her getting hurt even then, but despite his fears and her recklessness, she had survived. *Then.* "Just that you're not equipped to do it right now."

She gasped. "Because I'm pregnant."

"Because we're probably out of ammunition," he said. And because she was pregnant. But if he admitted that now, she would probably shoot him if she had any bullets left.

She was still bristling with fury and driving fast because of it. Even once she approached the courthouse and that back alley where Luther had whisked her into the van, she didn't slow down. And she said nothing to him, just murmured numbers beneath her breath, counting each turn she made. Maybe she was driving fast because the guard had, too. He would have been afraid that they were being followed.

Spencer had wanted to follow them. But Parker had been concerned Luther might carry out his threat to harm her. Keeli's boss had probably saved her life. But they couldn't hope that Luther would spare it again.

Especially if they cornered him.

A train whistle pealed out. And Spencer's pulse quickened. He knew they were getting close—even before he noticed the row of black Payne Protection

SUVs pulled alongside the street onto which she turned after crossing the railroad tracks.

"Is this it?" he asked.

"We're close," Keeli said, and her voice sounded a little strained.

He couldn't tell if she was afraid or in pain. The wound to her cheek wasn't much deeper than the one slightly below it where the shard of glass had nicked it. Thankfully, the bullet hadn't done much damage. But she was so damn beautiful it would be a shame if she was left with any scars from those close calls.

But scars were obviously the least of her concerns. How could such a stunning woman be so totally devoid of vanity?

Keeli had always been a mystery to him—why she'd chosen such a dangerous profession, why she willingly and what had seemed to him, *recklessly*, put herself in peril...

But he realized now that they weren't all that different. Both of them were determined to protect people. It was too bad that the person he wanted to protect most was her.

She drove up next to the SUV at the beginning of the row of them and rolled down her window. "Did you see anything?" she asked her boss.

At least Spencer thought it was Parker to whom she spoke. The man sitting next to him looked exactly like him with the same black hair and blue eyes. It could have been his twin, Logan, or one of his other brothers who looked eerily similar as well.

Parker paused for a long moment before he nodded. "We heard a lot of vehicles driving onto a street just one over from this one, and we saw the headlights through the side yards between the houses."

It was still too early for that much activity. Nobody was throwing a party at this hour of the morning.

Luther had called in reinforcements. He must have guessed she would figure out where he'd been holding her. And he'd set his trap. Hell, maybe he'd counted on her figuring it out so that he could set a trap for them.

"So they were here before us?" Spencer asked.

Parker nodded. "Why? Do you think you were followed?"

"We were just shot at," Spencer told him. And he'd probably let some of his suspicion creep into his voice because Parker narrowed his blue eyes.

Then her boss turned toward Keeli. "Is that true?" He gasped as he noticed her cheek. "You were hit again?"

She shrugged. "It's nothing."

The wound had stopped bleeding at least. But he wished she would have gone to the emergency room. She needed stitches. Maybe a tetanus shot as well.

Parker turned back toward Spencer. "We were here before you, too," he said, as if to point out that none of them could have been the shooter.

But the assailant had left before they had, too. Hell, the shooter could have been any of the Payne Protection bodyguards or anyone sitting in those vehicles idling one street over—waiting for them to turn onto it.

"This is too dangerous," Spencer said. For so many reasons. "We need to get the hell out of here!"

As if she hadn't heard him at all, Keeli didn't even glance at him. She was totally focused on her boss. "How are we going in?" she asked Parker.

Spencer knew it wouldn't matter what he said now, just like it hadn't back at the hotel parking lot where they could have been killed. She wasn't going to listen to him. Keeli didn't care what he thought. She probably didn't care about him at all except for carrying out her assignment to keep him alive.

"I got them this time," he said, his voice rising with his declaration. "Spencer Dubridge and Keeli Abbott are dead."

Luther held his cell phone to his ear with his shoulder while he held a pair of binoculars to his face. From his vantage point between two houses, he had a clear view of the Payne Protection SUVs lined up at the curb of the street one over from the house where he'd held Keeli Abbott—where he should have killed the bodyguard.

If only he could take back that moment when he'd directed the bullet into the wall instead of her heart…

But that bullet might not have annihilated her anyway. It appeared she wasn't an easy woman to kill.

Peering through the lenses, he asked, "So tell me, Frank, do you still have that little green vintage Mustang?"

A long silence followed his question, and Luther wondered if he'd accidentally muted his caller. But then the old detective finally replied—with a question of his own. "Why do you ask?"

"Because it just drove up with Keeli Abbott and Spencer Dubridge inside."

Detective Robinson cursed.

"Yeah, they're not dead." But the detective would be soon. Robinson had been good at getting the information Luther had needed; he was useless at carrying out orders. Of course not everyone had the skill and the guts for killing that Luther possessed.

And Robertson had only gotten the information Luther had needed because Spencer had seen him as a mentor and a confidant. Eventually Keeli or someone else at the Payne Protection Agency would figure out that Spencer was the leak at the police department.

Luther chuckled.

He just didn't know he was…

And he might never find out. None of them might if Luther had called in enough shooters to take out all the bodyguards that had showed up in the area.

He should have known that Keeli would figure out where he'd held her. She was too damn smart and resourceful.

But then she'd lived on the streets, and not just while she'd been working vice, so she knew them well—probably as well as Luther did.

He was going to hate leaving them.

But he had no choice for now.

Maybe he would eventually be able to come back. When the search for him died down…

When he changed his appearance enough…

Hell, he had enough money that he would hire some doctor to make himself even better looking than he was. Then he'd come back to River City and reclaim it as his.

When Keeli and Dubridge and all the Paynes left, they would never be able to return. Because there was no coming back from the dead…

Chapter 15

Keeli cursed. And not just because chaos suddenly erupted on the street. She might have been cursing the hardest because Spencer had been right.

Luther had set a trap for them. Parker had just handed Keeli some extra ammunition through the vehicle's open windows when the shooting began. She barely had time to duck before the windshield exploded, spraying shattered glass over her and Spencer.

He reached across her and pressed his foot onto the accelerator, sending the car speeding away from the row of SUVs as they came under fire.

But the shots continued to ring out, striking the car and the tires. His hands covered hers on the wheel but still the Mustang careened out of control, jumped a curb and crashed against a small tree.

"We have to get out of here," Spencer hissed.

She didn't want to run, but she couldn't argue with him since it was the smartest thing to do right now. The car was totally disabled, so they would have to make a break for it on foot.

More bullets struck the car, shattering the side and rear windows. It seemed as though the shooters were advancing on them now that the car had stopped moving. They needed to make a run for it or they were sitting ducks.

"Get out!" Spencer said. "I'll cover you."

"No!" she said. "I'll cover you." That was her job—to protect him.

But he'd already sat up and directed his barrel through those shattered windows and started firing. Keeli slammed the full magazine into her gun and did the same, raising her weapon to fire.

The shooters, also coming under fire from the bodyguards, began to retreat.

She pushed open her door and rolled out of the vehicle, keeping low as shots continued to fire into the night.

But Spencer didn't bother ducking down as he vaulted out of the car behind her and tried to cover her body with his. "Get off me!" she yelled at him.

She didn't want him to take a bullet for her. And she wanted to stop a few more of the shooters. But she couldn't see anything now with his big body blocking hers.

Then the gunfire stopped.

Keeli shoved at Spencer. She didn't know if he was still on top of her because he was protecting her or because he was hurt. "Are you all right?" she asked.

He lifted his head and peered around before he began to ease off her. "Are they gone?"

Footsteps pounded across the asphalt of the street, and Spencer covered her again.

"Are you guys okay?" Parker asked.

Keeli wasn't. She was so mad that she elbowed Spencer off her, making his breath rush out with a whoosh of air that stirred her hair.

"Stop trying to save me just because you couldn't save your ex!" she shouted. "I can take care of myself."

Spencer's breath escaped in another whoosh, as if she'd struck him again. And he stared at her through dark eyes wide with shock. "What? How do you—"

"Are you okay?" Parker repeated as he held out his hands to them both.

"Yes," she replied for them both. "How about everybody else?"

"Good, good," Parker replied, but quickly. Adrenaline must have been pumping through him like it was Keeli.

She rolled to her feet on her own, but Spencer lay sprawled on his back now that she'd shoved him off. At least she'd thought that was why he was just lying there. But now she noticed some blood on him, running down the side of his face from his thick black hair.

"Are you all right?" she asked him again, as concern and guilt replaced her anger. Momentarily. If he was fine, she would be even more pissed that he'd been hurt trying to do her job for her. She was the bodyguard—not him.

When was that going to get through his thick head? When he got it blown off trying to protect her? Of course then it would be too late.

Panic clutched her heart, squeezing it tightly. She crouched down next to him and touched his head, looking for bullets. But she flinched as she felt sharp edges of glass instead. Shards of it slipped through her hair as well. So much had rained in on them that it was no wonder he would have some cuts. Fortunately, that was all it appeared to be.

But she trembled as she considered how much worse it could have been. They all could have been killed.

"My head's still there," Spencer assured her.

And she realized her hands were still in his hair, gently brushing that glass out of the thick black strands. She jerked back and straightened up. "You're lucky," she said. "You could have been killed."

"You, too."

Too angry with him to speak, she just shook her head which sent another spray of glass raining from her hair. Then she stomped off to join the others as Parker leaned over to help Spencer to his feet.

Parker could keep him safe now.

"I think she meant that you're lucky she didn't kill you," Parker said as he helped Spencer to his feet.

Spencer had to grip the other man's arm and shoulder for a moment to steady himself as his legs threatened to fold beneath him. It wasn't just the glass that had hit him.

A piece of the metal from the car had jabbed his head when the vehicle had crashed into the tree. But the wound wasn't much deeper than those from the shards of glass. He had been lucky he hadn't gotten hit with a bullet.

He couldn't believe that nobody else had either. "Everybody is really okay?"

Parker nodded grimly. "Well, my brothers and the other bodyguards are…"

Then Spencer noticed some bodies lying on the ground and heard the distant wail of sirens. Fortunately, the police and ambulances were on their way.

Where the hell had Keeli gone?

He looked around the area for her but couldn't catch a glimpse of her blond hair. If she was anywhere close, he would have been able to see her, since the sun was up now and sunshine always shimmered in her golden hair.

"Where is she?" he asked.

He'd been right when he'd suspected that she knew about Rebecca. But how? Had she had him investigated?

But only a few people knew about his high school sweetheart, and he doubted that Keeli had spoken to any of them. So how did she find out?

More importantly, where the hell had she gone?

Parker was looking around, too, and since he was a little taller than Spencer, he could probably see around all the other bodyguards except for a few of the hulks that made up Parker's brother Cooper's team of former Marines. Those guys could have easily been blocking Keeli.

He hoped like hell that they were—because if anyone started shooting again, they would protect her. If they weren't working for Luther…

Spencer needed to be the one protecting her. He'd tried when he'd jumped out of the car after her and covered her body with his. But she hadn't appreciated his playing the hero for her.

She didn't understand that he didn't act that way because he was a jerk. He acted that way because he cared too much. But then she knew about Rebecca, so maybe she knew the truth. Hell, maybe she knew it better than he did.

He needed to talk to her. But first he had to find her and make sure she was safe.

Parker sucked in a breath and shook his head. "I don't see her either."

Spencer cursed. "She went to find that damn house." He knew it. She was determined to track down Luther or find some damn clue to where he was hiding. "Did you guys secure it?"

"We don't know which house it is," Parker admitted. "That's why we stopped on the street. And the shooters came from vehicles parked on the other street, but none of them came out of a house."

So what the hell was going on?

"Did you secure this area?" Spencer asked as he walked around the bodyguards. Some stood over the bodies on the ground or knelt beside them, giving aid.

Parker nodded. "Every one of Luther's shooters that was able to leave ran off," he said. "A few took off in vehicles. Others just fled on foot."

So they could be anywhere. They could have grabbed her the minute she'd walked away from the others.

God, what if she'd been taken hostage again?

Frank Robertson needed to pack up and get the hell out of River City. He'd heard it in Luther's voice—the finality. He was done.

Luther was done with him. He was of no use to him

anymore—especially since he hadn't even managed to kill Spencer and his damn little bodyguard.

How the hell did she keep saving him or maybe he was saving her? It didn't matter. Working together, were they both just that good?

Luther better hope not, or they would find him before he got the hell out of River City. Spencer would find him and arrest him just as he had before.

Would Spencer find Frank?

Had he figured it out yet that Robertson was the one working for Luther, feeding him the information he'd tricked Spencer into revealing to him?

The dumb kid had told him so much—because he trusted him. He was entirely too damn trusting, just like his parents. They were people who believed everyone was inherently good. They were the only ones who were, and he felt a little twinge of guilt that he'd fooled them all. They had no idea…

And neither did Frank; he didn't know how Spence had survived as long as he had in law enforcement. The job had made Frank tough and cynical years ago.

He'd known he was going to get nothing out of it—no sense of justice. So he'd settled for money from thugs like Luther Mills. It had bought all those vintage cars Frank liked to collect. But he couldn't take all those cars with him. He could only take one now.

He wished he hadn't left the Mustang in the driveway.

But he hadn't expected Spencer to survive that explosion and steal it from him.

He would have to take one of the others. One of them he hadn't sold yet. Once Luther had gotten arrested, Frank had started worrying that he might give up his leaks for some leniency with the assistant district attorney. Instead Luther had just leaned on his leaks.

Either way—Frank had known he might need to make a quick escape, so he'd liquidated some of his assets. Did he have enough?

How long would he be able to hide from Luther? Knowing Luther and his thirst for vengeance, he would probably have to disappear for the rest of his life.

His suitcase packed, he slammed it shut and grasped the handles. But as he stepped out the back door with it, shots rang out.

And he knew it was already too late. Luther had come after him before he'd even had the chance to run.

Bullets broke the glass in the door and splintered the wooden doorjamb. He ducked low and pulled the door closed. So much adrenaline coursed through him that he didn't know if he'd been hit.

Just like he hadn't known for sure if he'd hit Spencer and Keeli.

He shouldn't have told Luther that they were dead—not until he'd confirmed it. Because now Luther wasn't just done with him, he was pissed.

More shots rang out, shattering the glass in the windows, penetrating the wood of the structure. Pictures fell off the walls as bullets bored through the drywall. If he wasn't already hit, he was probably going to be soon.

Yeah, lying to Luther Mills had been a mistake. Because now it seemed like Luther was determined to make Frank pay for his lie…with his life.

Chapter 16

Keeli was lucky she didn't get shot by a homeowner whose windows she peeked into, looking for the house in which she'd been held. She glanced into each one on the street where Luther's crew had parked... Until she found it, at the end.

She recognized the green appliances, yellow countertop and old cabinets and the kitchen table made from some big wooden spool. It had probably been used once for utility wires. This was where Luther had brought her, and the guard who had helped him escape the jail lay dead on the floor, a hole in his forehead and a pool of dried blood beneath what was left of the back of his head.

She grimaced.

His body seemed like the only one in the house. But she listened intently at the window to hear if anyone was moving around inside. However, dead men couldn't move, so she heard nothing but the wail of sirens in the distance and the noises coming from the crime scene on the other street. Everyone's attention was focused there.

This house was her total focus. Even though Luther was gone, probably even before the shooting began, he might have left something behind—something besides that body. Some sort of clue that might lead to where he was now or where he was going.

Eventually he had to leave River City. Even he would have to accept that.

He didn't own the city anymore. But he owned too damn many people in it yet. Like the guard—who had paid for helping Luther with his life. How many others had lost theirs?

She'd seen the bodies of some of the shooters as she'd walked through what was now a crime scene to this street. Why would anyone work for Luther when they knew how it would probably end?

Like this...

She walked past that window where she could see the dead guard. The service door to the garage stood ajar, like someone had left in a hurry.

Her weapon was in her hand, held at her side, so that she didn't frighten any of those neighbors into whose homes she'd peeked. But it was ready, if she needed it.

The black SUV was gone—or hell, maybe it was parked a street over in that line with all the other Payne Protection Agency SUVs. That was probably why Luther had it. So he could move among them.

She found only the van inside the garage—the jail transport one taken from the courthouse. The side

was open, revealing the empty interior where Luther
had thrown her—where she'd ridden while keeping
mental track of all the turns and potential distances
between those turns. She had remembered; she had
figured it out.

But it was too late.

Luther was gone.

She stepped into the house then—through the door
from the attached garage that opened onto that kitchen
where the dead guard lay. Why had he done it? Why
had he helped Luther?

Money?

Threats?

Had Luther been holding someone he loved hostage
like he'd tried to hold the judge's daughter?

So much had happened before the trial to stop it
from ever starting. But once the trial had begun, they'd
thought it would all be over. No one had considered
that Luther might have planned an escape.

"Where are you going?" she murmured.

She holstered her weapon and leaned over the
guard. Despite how many dead bodies she'd seen in
her life, and not just as a cop, she grimaced. It never
got easier.

At least not for her.

She braced one hand on that spool table while she
rifled through the guard's pockets. They were empty.
He had taken no notes about Luther's plans. Or if he
had, Luther had taken them after he'd killed him. She
stood up and pulled her hand from the table, and a
splinter pierced her palm. The wood was scratched
up, and now so was her palm.

She cursed, but she knew how damn lucky she was

that all she'd gotten over the past few days were a couple of scratches and a sliver.

But maybe her luck had run out. A door creaked, and she noticed a shadow in the garage. Maybe she hadn't checked it thoroughly enough. Could someone have been hiding in the dark corners all along, waiting for the right opportunity to kill her?

Parker had known the police were coming; he'd heard the sirens in the distance. He'd thought first responders and patrol cars were coming to the scene. But the Special Response Unit rolled in as well in their big van and a long SUV followed behind it. The chief of police stepped out of the passenger's side of the SUV.

Woodrow looked tired. Maybe, like Parker, he hadn't slept at all the night before either. A lot of people probably would not be able to rest until Luther Mills was apprehended again.

"Everybody okay?" Woodrow asked as he approached Parker, his gaze intent as he visually checked him for injuries.

"Our people are," Parker replied. "Just some scratches. Luther's scraping the bottom of the barrel for backup. None of these guys were marksmen." Which had been damn lucky for them.

The chief shook his head. "How does he do it? How does he get so many people to keep helping him?"

When they knew they might wind up like the shooters lying on the ground? Dead or dying…

Parker shrugged. "I don't know. Maybe these kids don't feel like they have a choice. But what about the others—the leaks in the police department and the

DA's office and all the jail and courthouse guards that helped him?"

Woodrow cursed. "I thought Nick cleaned up most of the corruption in the police department before I took over as chief."

Nick was Parker's half brother and a former FBI agent who'd been assigned as interim chief of the River City PD a couple of years ago. He'd worked hard and had brought some of the bigger criminals in the city to justice. But Luther had always eluded the law and still continued to do so.

How was it possible?

"There are still some dirty cops," Parker said, and he pitched his voice to a low whisper. He wasn't concerned about the cops who'd just arrived overhearing him. He was worried about Dubridge. But when he looked around, he didn't see the black-haired detective in the area.

"I've been working hard to figure out who in the department could be on Luther's payroll," Woodrow assured him.

Parker knew that, but he wondered… "Have you looked at Spencer?"

The chief tensed. "Detective Dubridge? He's the arresting officer…"

"I know," Parker said. "And I wouldn't suspect him but…he took Keeli to the house where he grew up and they were nearly blown up. Then just before this happened—" he gestured at the crime scene that the officers were now cordoning off with yellow tape "—which he knew about, he and Keeli are nearly shot outside the hotel they were staying at after the explosion."

Woodrow's brows furrowed together. "But he was

nearly blown up and shot, too. It doesn't make sense that he would put himself in that much danger."

Parker uttered a ragged sigh. "Yeah, yeah, I know. If not for Keeli, I'm sure he would have died. And probably vice versa…" And there was no way Spencer would have knowingly put Keeli in danger. Even before she'd become pregnant, he'd been fiercely protective of her. "Maybe I'm just reacting to his suspicions about us."

"Us?"

"The Payne Protection Agency," Parker explained. "He acts like one of us is working for Luther."

The furrows left Woodrow's face as it went blank. Almost carefully blank…

And a knot tightened in Parker's gut. "No…you can't think that—"

"Ms. Gerber had concerns as well." Woodrow reminded him of the assistant district attorney's suspicions.

She'd thought one of Parker's team was working for Luther because they were all former vice cops. And when she'd learned that Tyce was probably Luther's half brother, she'd pinned all her suspicions on him. But she'd been wrong. Tyce, and the rest of Parker's team, wanted to bring Luther down more than anyone else did.

"Jocelyn was wrong," Parker bit out. "And you are, too, if that's what you believe."

"But how has Luther always found the safe houses and hotels…?"

And that knot tightened even more. "No…" He refused to believe that anyone with his agency could be working for Luther. "You know how well Logan, Cooper and I know our teams, how carefully we've chosen them. They're not employees to us. They're family." Some literally, some just of the heart.

Woodrow released the ragged sigh now. "I know..."

And because they were family to him, Parker had to make sure they all stayed safe. Where the hell had Keeli gone?

He needed to get someone to find her. He only hoped it wouldn't be too late.

Staring down the barrel of a gun, Spencer raised his arms. "Don't shoot," he told Keeli. "It's me."

But she didn't lower the barrel, just continued holding it out across the dead body over which she stood.

"What did he do to you?" he asked with a nod at the body.

"He helped Luther escape the courthouse. And Luther must have been the one who killed him."

It was obvious he'd been dead awhile. The blood beneath him had dried.

Spencer was sure—well, pretty sure—that she wouldn't fire her weapon, so he teased, "Don't shoot me. I promise I'll stop stepping in front of bullets for you."

Sighing, she finally lowered her weapon. "We both know the only way you'll do that is if I put a bullet in you myself."

He chuckled but he didn't argue. "I'm not going to apologize for that. Just like you putting yourself in danger is part of who you are—trying to protect people is part of who I am."

"Then maybe you should have left River City PD, too, to become a bodyguard," she said.

"Parker asked me," he admitted. "But I didn't want to leave until I put Luther Mills away."

"He thinks you blame him for her death."

He tensed with shock. "Luther is the one who told you about Rebecca?"

"That was her name?"

He nodded. "But I don't understand…how the hell does Luther know?"

"He made it sound like you accused him of killing her," Keeli said. "Like you blamed him for her death."

Spencer shook his head. "She ran away from home…" Keeli flinched like he'd struck her, and he wondered… "Did you?"

She shook her head. "We're talking about you… and Rebecca. Tell me about her."

"After she ran away from home, she lived on the streets, supporting herself with prostitution. She got hooked on drugs. Then eventually overdosed and died. That must be why Luther thinks I blame him. But I don't blame him."

Keeli stepped closer to him, and her fingers touched his face, skimming lightly along his jaw. He hadn't realized he was clenching it so hard until it began to ache. "You blame yourself," she murmured.

He nodded.

"Why?"

"I reported her parents for abusing her, for knocking her around, and when child protective services started investigating, she ran away," he said, his chest aching with his mistake.

"Spencer, this was your high school sweetheart, right? You were kids."

"I was a kid," he admitted. "I was naive, thinking I

was doing the right thing. I tried to help, but I couldn't protect her."

"She didn't run away because you couldn't protect her," Keeli said. "She ran away from that house—from the abuse." She released a quavering breath. "Rebecca didn't run away from you. She ran away because she didn't trust anyone."

He shivered—not because of the memories—but because of the way Keeli spoke, like she knew what she was talking about—like she'd gone through it herself. "Did you live through something like that? Did you...?"

"Run away from home?" she asked, then nodded. "Yeah, not that you could call it a home. And somehow Luther knows about that, too, knows how I grew up on the streets."

He flinched now, at what she must have endured. "How did you survive?"

"I didn't turn to drugs or prostitution. For the longest time I didn't want anyone..." Her voice cracked and she shook her head as if shaking off the memories. "I was a petty thief. I stole to support myself. Broke into cars, that kind of thing, and somehow Luther knew all about it, all about me."

Spencer's heart ached for what she'd endured. He wished he'd known because now her stubborn independence was beginning to make more sense to him. She hadn't been able to trust anyone. And he couldn't blame her. "I'm sorry—"

She shook her head. "No, don't pity me. I survived. I took care of myself. And that's what I'm doing now, trying to figure out how Luther keeps tracking us down."

"How the hell does he know so much about us?" Spencer grumbled. "I've never told anyone I work with about Rebecca…" He hadn't wanted to admit to how badly he'd failed his sweet friend. Rebecca had been such a gentle, loving person.

"I have no idea," Keeli replied. "I thought you told him."

"Admit any weakness to that sick son of a bitch? Not damn likely…" He would have used it against Spencer. And maybe he had. His head began to pound now, and it wasn't because of the wound from the car crash. Horrible thoughts—suspicions—had begun to creep into his mind.

"So who does know?" she asked. "Who have you told about her?"

He didn't want to admit it. Not yet. "What about you?" he asked. "Who knows you were a runaway?"

She hesitated, as if she didn't want to admit it either. "Parker. But that doesn't mean your suspicions about him or the other bodyguards at the agency are founded."

No. Spencer suspected they weren't. "He doesn't know about Rebecca."

"Luther might have just recognized me," she said. "From when I lived on the streets."

He looked at her now, and it was as if he saw her for the first time. And he finally understood her.

"I—I wasn't a prostitute," she insisted. "Or a drug user. I just did stupid stuff like breaking into cars and stealing wallets…until I got caught."

She was so strong. No wonder she was fearless. She had already been through and survived the worst life had ever thrown at her. And she'd just been a kid at the time. He could barely breathe through the pressure on his chest, through the pain of thinking of what she'd been through.

"But my path might have crossed Luther's from time to time," she added.

Like Rebecca's had. But he doubted that Rebecca would have ever mentioned her high school boyfriend to her drug dealer. Once she'd run away, she'd wanted nothing to do with Spencer anymore. All she'd wanted was drugs.

"What about you?" she asked. "How does he know about her?"

He sighed. "I don't know."

"I think you do," she said. Her blue eyes were narrowed as she studied his face. "I think you've figured it out."

He shook his head. "It doesn't make sense."

"Who would know about Rebecca and about your parents' house—because we weren't followed there. I drove, and there weren't any lights behind us. Somebody had to know about the house, about Rebecca, somebody who's known you for a long time..."

And he knew she'd figured it out, too.

"You called him when I was in the shower at the hotel," she reminded him. "I came out with the gun because I heard voices."

He cleared the knot of emotion from his throat before finally uttering the name. "Frank..."

"Detective Robertson."

"But I didn't tell him what hotel we were staying at," he assured her. Maybe even then he'd wondered... Since the house had exploded, the house just down the street from Frank's house. He had probably noticed the lights on and realized Spencer had brought her there.

"You know cell signals can be traced," she said.

And Frank had the resources to do it—all the police resources. He was such a revered detective that he was close to the chief, too. But he was closer to Spencer than anyone else.

His stomach knotted as he remembered all the things he'd told his friend. Of how he'd kept him apprised of everything related to Luther Mills's trial and the threats he'd made against everyone associated with it.

He groaned. "I can't believe what a fool I've been..."

She lifted her hand to his face again, running her fingers along his jaw. "Don't keep blaming yourself for everything and assuming responsibility for everyone."

He reached out then and closed his arms around her. Spencer wasn't protecting her now. He wanted her to protect him from the soul-crushing reality of what he'd done. Of how he was the one who'd put everybody in danger.

She wrapped her arms around his waist and hugged him, as if she'd instinctively known what he needed. It was like that when they made love, too. Like she knew deep down what pleased him.

He wanted to stay like that forever. But he had to face reality—the reality of what he'd done and the reality of his old friend's betrayal.

"We have to find Frank."

"He might know where Luther is," she said, and she pulled away from their embrace to head toward the door.

Before following her, Spencer looked down at the body lying on the floor. And he hoped that Luther didn't know where Frank was, or his old mentor might have already wound up like the guard.

Despite the betrayal, Spencer didn't want Frank dead. He just wanted the truth. And he hoped they could find him before it was too late for Frank to say anything anymore.

Chapter 17

Keeli's heart ached with the heaviness that emanated from Spencer. She glanced across the console of the Payne Protection Agency SUV and noted how his broad shoulders bowed with the weight of his guilt. It had to have been killing him that he'd, albeit inadvertently, put other people in danger. He was the one who always wanted to protect everyone else—even when they didn't need protecting.

"You didn't know," she reminded him.

"I knew there was a leak in the police department," he gritted out. "That's why the chief hired the bodyguard agency."

The chief *had* been there—at the scene—when they'd returned from the house. But they had been careful to avoid him and Parker while she'd bummed the keys for one of the SUVs off another bodyguard. She hadn't wanted to waste any time talking when they needed to track down Robertson before Luther got to him.

Spencer continued, "Lynch didn't trust his own force. And I shouldn't have trusted anyone either."

She didn't think he was talking just about Detective Robertson now. Reaching across the console, she touched his arm. "That's no way to live," she murmured softly.

He looked at her again. Even though she was focused on the road now, she could feel his gaze on her. It felt as intent as it had at the house when she'd admitted to being a runaway.

"Is that how you lived?"

She nodded. "I couldn't depend on anyone at home. My stepfather was a creep. He..." She shuddered. "And when I told my mom, she didn't believe me. She didn't trust me. So I learned fast to trust nobody either. It's how I had to live..." In order to survive on the streets, she hadn't been able to rely on anyone but herself. And she'd *had* to live on the streets because the house where she'd grown up had never been a home. The people who'd raised her had never been family, not like her Payne Protection Agency family.

"What changed?" he asked. "How did you get off the streets?"

Like Rebecca hadn't? She wondered if that was what he was thinking.

"A female vice cop reached out to me," she said. But man, she hadn't made it easy for Paula. "She got me into a safe foster home."

"That's why you became a cop."

She smiled and nodded. "Yeah..."

"Is she still on the force?"

She shook her head as tears rushed to her eyes and pain clutched her heart.

Spencer reached across the console and squeezed her arm. "Did she get killed in the line of duty?"

"Nope," she choked out. "She got killed in a traffic accident, driving her kids to soccer practice—years after she left the force to become a stay-at-home wife and mother." She turned to him then. "Because her husband thought being a cop was too dangerous."

He sucked in a breath as if she'd struck him. And she knew he'd gotten her point.

But just in case, she added, "I don't know how many more lives she could have saved—like mine—had she stayed on the job. One of those could have been her own."

"Or she could have died on the job," he said.

And she sighed—with frustration now—that he just didn't get it. Bad things happened all the time—to anyone—anywhere. Of course more bad things happened when people were associated with Luther Mills.

Like the dead guard...

"We might be too late," she warned him. "Luther looks to be tying up loose ends."

He sucked in another breath.

"You still care about Detective Robertson."

"Of course I do," he replied gruffly.

"But he betrayed you," she said. "He tried to kill you." He had to have been the one who'd rigged Spencer's parents' home to explode.

"We don't know that for sure," Spencer told her. "We don't have any proof of that. We could be wrong."

And it was clear that he hoped like hell that they were. But when they turned onto the street where his childhood home had exploded, she knew they weren't wrong. The tape, blocking off the area that had been evacuated since the explosion, was broken. The house from which they'd taken the Mustang was bullet ridden. The windows were broken, and there were holes in the walls.

It had been shot up.

She parked the SUV on the street and reached for her weapon. But before she could open her door, Spencer reached across and caught her arm.

"This was a bad idea," he said. "We should have brought along backup."

"Now you're worried about him?"

"I'm worried he's already dead," Spencer admitted. "And I'm worried that his killer might still be here."

Keeli shook off his hand and opened the door—to an eerie silence. No birds chirped. Nobody moved. Of course the area around the decimated house had been evacuated—maybe for a block or so—as a precaution in case the gas lines to the other homes caused explosions.

They could have told them that a faulty gas line hadn't caused the damage. Frank Robertson had—on Luther Mills's orders.

Spencer might have been holding out hope they were wrong about that. But Keeli was convinced of his guilt—even more so now that she had seen the detective's home. It was probably too late to save him. But maybe they could find a clue—something—to where Luther might be.

All she'd gotten from the other house had been the splinter in her hand. Some damn clue that had been...

She hoped Robertson, being a detective, had left more behind than his dead body.

Spencer rushed around the front of the SUV to join her in the street. She'd parked across from Robertson's house.

"You told me you were going to stop jumping in front of bullets for me," she reminded him.

But she'd known, even then, that he'd been lying. And now, knowing who might have been the one firing those bullets at them, she knew he'd hold himself even more responsible for keeping her and their unborn baby safe.

"Nobody's firing any," he said softly, his deep voice a low rumble of a whisper. He must have found the silence as eerie as she did.

There wasn't even a hint of sirens in the air. So maybe the shots had been fired through a silencer. Or someone would have reported the gunfire.

Unless no one had been close enough to hear.

But the detective.

He must have been inside his house. Was he still there?

Weapons drawn, Keeli and Spencer approached the house slowly—each trying to shield the other with his or her body. But Keeli wasn't as annoyed as she usually was with him. She understood more about him now.

She only wished she could shield him from what they would probably find inside the house.

Nothing.

They had found nothing inside. Nothing but shattered glass and broken pictures and shot-up walls...

Where the hell was Frank?

Keeli moved around the house, obviously looking for clues. She pointed out the massive TV and the sound system. "Expensive stuff…"

Just like all the pricy vintage cars he collected. Spencer should have known that something was going on—that Frank had been living beyond his means. But the confirmed bachelor had told Spencer he could afford all those cars and toys because he'd never married and had kids.

A family brings you down, kid. Don't ever get mixed up in all that love stuff…

Spencer had told him then that it was already too late, and he'd told Frank about Rebecca. He must have been the one who'd told Luther, like it was all some joke.

But no…

It couldn't be.

Spencer couldn't have been that wrong about his old friend. But he must have been. Who else had he been wrong about?

He looked at Keeli again—like he'd been looking at her since her revelation of being a former runaway. How had he not known that about her?

Because he'd been afraid to get to know her. He hadn't wanted to risk his heart on a woman who willingly put herself in danger. But it was too late for that.

She was carrying his baby.

"It's too late…" she murmured his words aloud.

And he tensed. "What?"

Had she found a body?

She was pointing but at the suitcases near the door. "He must have been on his way out when Luther and his crew showed up."

And that alone—those packed bags—confirmed all Spencer's worst fears. His old friend—his mentor—had betrayed him.

"How could he…?" he said, choking on the emotion overwhelming him.

Keeli slid her gun into her holster, then slid her arms around his waist. "I'm sorry…"

He was the one who owed her the apology—her and so many other people. "The things I told him…" He pulled away from her, unwilling to accept her comfort when he was the one who'd put her and the others in danger. His heart ached, and he felt physically sick over what he'd done. "I can't believe I didn't realize then that he was pumping me for information about the protection detail. I told him about the safe houses." He groaned at his stupidity.

But she said nothing.

"Here's your chance," he told her. "You can get back at me for all the asinine comments I've made to you over the years. You can tell me what a jackass I've been."

"You are a jackass," she said. "But that's for calling me Bodyguard Barbie."

A smile tugged at his mouth.

She continued, "Not for trusting a man you've known your entire life."

"He was like my second father," Spencer admitted. "I can't believe he's gone."

"He is," Keeli said, and her confirmation made him flinch with the twinge of pain striking his heart. "But I don't think he's dead."

Spencer gestured at the windows and the walls. "Look at this place."

"Exactly," she said. "There's no blood. There was no shoot-out inside here. And if there had been—if Robertson was dead—why would Luther have bothered moving his body? He left the guard where he shot him."

Spencer stiffened. "You're right…"

Frank wasn't dead. And he knew why. He remembered the detective's plan in case any paroled convict ever came after him looking for revenge. But before he could check the detective's hiding place, the older man stepped from it—from the secret reinforced compartment in the back of his closet—and pointed his gun. But not at Spencer, at Keeli.

"Don't move or I'll kill her…"

This was even worse than realizing Frank had betrayed him—because now that he knew how immoral his old friend was, he knew the guy would make good on his threat. He would have no compulsion against taking the life of the woman Spencer loved.

The old detective was wily. Luther had known that. The guy had been on his payroll for years without anyone ever catching on…

The FBI agent who'd been brought in years ago to clean up River City PD had arrested all the dirty cops he'd been able to find evidence against, and the ones he hadn't had enough proof to prosecute he'd forced into retirement. But good old Frank had survived unscathed.

Not even Dubridge had caught on…

But he must have figured it out now. Or maybe Keeli had. The former runaway was the one with all the street smarts. And even back when she'd been just a kid, she'd been tough. Despite her small size, nobody had intimidated or hurt her.

Well, someone must have had to or she wouldn't have run away. Maybe that was why Luther had spared her life back at the house. His home life hadn't been an easy one either—not like the one his half brother Tyce had had, growing up with his doting grandparents.

His grandparents had not been Luther's, though, so he'd been forced to raise himself. And he'd done good—damn good—for himself. He wasn't going to lose it all now.

And he wasn't going to succumb to sentiment with Keeli Abbott. This time he would kill her—along with Dubridge and Frank. The old man had been hiding in the house.

Luther could see all of them through the lenses of his binoculars he'd pointed at the broken windows. He'd been watching for a while, watching for Robertson to come out. And waiting for his reinforcements to arrive in case he didn't.

He was going in—but he wasn't going in alone. He was glad now that he'd waited for the others. Or he would have been outgunned.

Or maybe not...

He could just wait for the old detective to either blow away Keeli and Spencer or for one of them to blow him away. It was bound to happen.

But not fast enough for Luther.

He knew the Payne Protection Agency stuck together. Parker would be here soon enough, looking for Keeli and Spencer, to make sure they were safe.

He would find only their dead bodies.

Luther turned to the guys who had survived the

shooting with the bodyguards. They looked scared and tired.

But he couldn't blame them.

He felt a little uneasy as well. That was why he decided not to go any closer to that house himself. He just ordered them, "Go! Storm the house. And make sure all three of them die."

Spencer and Keeli couldn't keep getting away.

Luther had to make sure they perished, but he didn't follow the shooters as they slipped out of the yard where he stood. He only raised the binoculars to his face again to watch it all unfold. But his boys barely made it into the house before it exploded—the blast so strong that even almost a block away it knocked Luther back on his ass.

It was probably good that he was lying down—because nobody noticed him as the line of Payne Protection SUVs rolled onto the street. Too bad Parker and his bodyguards hadn't been a little earlier—then they all could have blown up together.

Chapter 18

The explosion turned the sky so black that the automatic headlights in the SUV came on, illuminating the street ahead of them. The vehicle rocked on its tires, and both Woodrow and Parker, who were inside the SUV, flinched. "Damn it," Parker cursed. "Not again..."

Parker stopped the SUV, and all the vehicles behind them halted, too, as debris rained down around them. It wasn't just parts of the house that Woodrow noticed. He shuddered as drops of blood spattered the window.

People had been inside when it exploded. And there was no way they had survived. Woodrow cursed now, too.

"What the hell happened?" Parker yelled, and there was so much frustration in his voice. "Why do we keep figuring out stuff when it's too damn late?"

They had just figured out who the mole in the police department was. Detective Frank Robertson—Spencer's former neighbor and current mentor. Between Woodrow and Parker, they'd realized that only the older detective knew Dubridge well enough to know where his parents' house was and at which hotel he and Keeli had been staying after that explosion.

Spencer and Keeli must have figured it out, too.

Parker pointed to the Payne Protection Agency SUV parked across the street from what was left of Robertson's house. "They beat us here." His voice cracked with emotion. "They must have been inside…"

He closed his eyes and laid his head on the steering wheel. And Woodrow reached across the console and squeezed his shoulder.

"I want to believe that they survived again, like they did last time," Parker said. "I want to believe that. But…"

It didn't look good; it didn't look like anyone could have survived this explosion.

"She's pregnant. She was…pregnant," Parker murmured, his voice gruff.

"Keeli…" Woodrow said quietly. "She would have been an amazing mother."

What a waste. What a damn waste of life…

So many lives had been lost because of Luther Mills. It had to stop. Luther had to be stopped.

Keeli was getting damn sick of having gun barrels pressed against her head. Luther had done it at the courthouse, and Robertson had done it at his house, using her to manipulate Spencer into following his orders.

But that might not have been such a bad thing…

The television in the corner of the small cabin glowed with the fire still burning from the explosion, which had spread to Robertson's garage and a neighbor's house. Fortunately the whole area had been under evacuation after the explosion at Spencer's parents' home, so there had been nobody in the other houses.

He cursed as he stared at the screen. "Lost my Chevelle in that garage."

"You didn't have to," Keeli reminded him. "You were the one who rigged the explosion." Just like he had at Spencer's parents' house.

"Yeah, to save our damn lives," he said. "You know Luther was watching it. We needed the diversion to escape."

But not everyone had escaped. The television news reported that there had been casualties. Luther? She doubted that—probably shooters that he'd sent into the house after her and Spencer.

"Are you expecting me to thank you?" she asked.

He snorted. "No, Ms. Abbott, I know that would kill you just like the explosion could have…"

And clearly he was regretting not leaving them in the house to blow up. But if he'd shot her like he'd threatened, Spencer would have gone after him— would have struggled with him until the trap he'd set for the house to explode had been sprung with all of them still inside.

No. He had done her no favor by letting her live. And she didn't expect him to let them live much longer. She strained against the zip tie binding her wrists together. It was too tight for her to wriggle her hands free of…and there was one around her ankles as well.

Spencer had put the zip ties around her wrists and ankles, but Robertson had pulled them tighter. He hadn't bothered putting any on Spencer—instead he'd struck him in the head.

Her heart pounded with fear as she stared down at him, looking so still on the old rug on the floor of the cabin. The color had drained from his face, so that trickle of blood looked even starker against his pale skin.

Had Robertson cracked his skull or just reopened one of the cuts from earlier?

She could see Spencer's muscular chest moving with breaths, could even see the flutter of his pulse in his throat. So he was not one of the casualties. Yet.

But she had no idea how much longer Robertson would leave them alive. She was certain that it was only as long as he had some use for them.

So she had to make sure he was aware they were useful to him yet. "So what's your plan?" she asked him. But she didn't give him a chance to reply before continuing, "Are you going to use us to negotiate with Luther or with the chief?"

His gray brows furrowed together as he stared at her. "What the hell are you talking about?"

"The chief has figured it out now," she said. "He has to know you're the leak." And if Woodrow Lynch hadn't figured it out, Parker would when he found his company SUV across the street from what was left of Robertson's house.

"So what if he has?" Robertson sneered as he swung his gun barrel toward the TV set. "He's not going after a dead man."

"He'll figure out soon enough that those aren't your remains in the house." At least she hoped he would. "Then everybody will be looking for you. Not just Luther."

He snorted again. "A dead man can't come after me either."

She laughed. "That's funny. You think Luther walked into that house as it exploded? You think he's dumb enough to fall for your stupid little trap? Then you don't know Luther Mills at all."

But it was clear that he did because all the color drained from his face—leaving him looking pale and old.

"He sent his guys in first because he knew it was probably a trap," she continued. "And now he knows that you tried to kill him." She grimaced and shook her head. "You better hope the chief finds you before Luther does. I can't imagine what he's going to do to you now."

But, actually, she could. Back when she'd lived on the streets both as a runaway and as an undercover vice cop, she had seen some of the bodies of the people who'd tried double-crossing Luther Mills. She shuddered as those images flashed through her mind. Then she glanced down at the floor, and she noticed that Spencer's body was tense now. He was conscious, but he was even more still than he'd been when he was unconscious.

He obviously didn't want Robertson to know that he was awake. But now she was more afraid for him than when he'd been unconscious. He was going to do something stupid—something heroic—to try to save her and their baby.

Damn it…

She opened her mouth, tempted to alert Robertson, but she worried that the detective might just shoot him this time—instead of knocking him out.

"Luther already tried to kill me," Robertson reminded her. "You saw my house—it looked like it had exploded before it even exploded!"

She nodded in agreement. "Yeah, you should have known better than to trust Luther Mills."

Just as Spencer seemed about to move from the floor, Robertson swung the barrel of his gun back toward Keeli's face. "That was your fault!" he shouted. "You kept saving Spencer's life. If you'd just let me kill him…"

"You think that's why Luther wants you dead?" she asked and emitted a pitying sigh. "He killed the jail transport guard that got him out of the courthouse. He doesn't care if you did what you were supposed to do or not. He wants you out of the picture."

"Then how the hell are you of any use to me?" he asked disparagingly. But he was curious, too, or he wouldn't have uttered the question at all.

"He wants Spencer dead more," she explained.

Now he swung his gun toward him. If Spencer saw it, he didn't so much as flinch.

"Then maybe I should just kill him now."

"No!" she exclaimed. "If you want to stay alive, you need to keep Spencer alive."

Robertson chuckled. "Don't try to play me like some stupid perp," he warned her as he swung the gun back toward her. "I was a cop a hell of a lot longer than you were."

"I'm not playing you," she lied.

But it was clear he didn't believe her—because he moved even closer—until that cold barrel pressed against her forehead.

Yes. She was getting really sick of having guns pointed at her head.

* * *

As he studied the scene through his lashes, with his eyes open barely a thin slit, Spencer forced himself to remain still. If he moved so much as a finger, he was afraid that Frank would instinctively move his and squeeze that trigger.

Then Keeli would die just like the guard had back at the house where she'd been held. Because Frank was right—she was playing him. She was biding her time.

She was as smart as she was strong and beautiful.

And she was fearless, too, because she ignored the gun pressed to her forehead and continued, "Think about it. Of everyone associated with his trial, he wants Spencer dead the most."

Frank made some noise—maybe another snort. Maybe a chuckle. "More than the witness?"

"He had a crush on Rosie Mendez. He only wanted to kill her so she wouldn't testify against him. It's too late for that now. Same with the evidence tech and the judge's daughter—they're of no consequence to him anymore. It's not like he intends to go back to trial."

"Then why does he want Spencer dead so badly?" Robertson asked.

She'd hooked him. Or maybe he'd already believed that Spencer was the one Luther wanted dead more than anyone else. Whatever his reason, he was listening now. And he'd eased the gun slightly away from her forehead.

"Honor," she said. "Pride. Spencer perp walked him in front of his crew, in front of the whole neighborhood he knows and owns. Luther counts that as disrespect. And just like he wouldn't tolerate Rosie Mendez's brother becoming a police informant against him, because that was a sign of disrespect, he won't tolerate Spencer arresting him."

Robertson leaned his head to the side. "So what the hell does any of that have to do with me?"

"You have Spencer," she said. "And you tell Luther you will make sure Spencer stays alive unless Luther helps you get out of River City the same way he plans on getting out."

Robertson let out a laugh and kept on laughing while he lowered the gun. But before Spencer could jump up from the floor, he swung it toward him. But Spencer had stilled again and closed his eyes. "I see why you fell for her, Spence. She's as brilliant as she is beautiful."

Robertson kicked him—hard in the thigh. "You can stop playing possum now, son. I know you're awake."

Spencer wanted to shout at him not to call him *son*— to never call him that again. He'd once thought of this man as a second father, but he was nothing like Spencer's dad, who was a good and honest man. The kind of man Spencer had always aspired to be, never more so than now that he was going to be a father himself.

If he and Keeli survived.

"I don't think I can even look at you," Spencer muttered, his disgust thick in his throat. But he opened his eyes. He looked at Keeli instead to make sure she was okay. Her blue eyes were flashing at him, as if she was trying to send him some kind of message.

Probably not to play a hero. But she didn't understand. He didn't want to protect her because he was trying to make up for not protecting Rebecca. He wanted to protect her because he loved her, even more so now that he knew what she'd overcome, how strong she'd always had to be.

Robertson kicked him again. "You sanctimonious

son of a bitch." He turned back toward Keeli, swinging the gun toward her again. "I really don't understand why you fell for him…"

She hadn't. But she didn't correct Frank. He just tried to figure out how to overpower him without that gun going off and a bullet hitting Keeli.

"Dubridge is a dick," she said. "He's a chauvinistic jerk ninety percent of the time."

"Is that all?" Spencer remarked.

Robertson chuckled. "I remember this banter when you both worked vice. Everybody around the department was always saying you should just get a room."

Banter? That wasn't what it had been at all.

Or *had* it?

And if Spencer had had his way, they would have gotten a room. He'd wanted Keeli long before the night they'd finally made love.

"Oh, it's true," Keeli said. "Spencer gets under your skin and makes you hate him."

Robertson had to realize how wrong he'd been now about her falling for him. Clearly she still couldn't stand him even after they'd made love, even after they'd made a baby.

"That's why Luther isn't leaving River City until he's damn sure Spencer Dubridge is dead," she continued. "And you know it. *Spence* here is your leverage."

Robertson nodded. "You're right. I need to turn Spence here over to Luther. But he needs to be dead when I do that." And he swung his gun toward Spencer again.

The last thing he heard was Keeli's scream.

Chapter 19

She awoke to darkness. At least she thought she was awake. The last thing she remembered was Detective Robertson hitting her with the butt of his gun. Hard. Hard enough that everything had gone black.

Maybe she was dead.

Luther would love that.

He had to be as pissed at her as Robertson was that she'd continually interfered with their attempts at killing Spencer. But she hadn't been able to save him this time. If she was dead, he certainly was, too.

But a groan rumbled in the silence. And it wasn't hers.

"Spencer?" she whispered, her heart lightening with hope and something else—something she wouldn't let herself identify.

"Keeli?" he answered her. "You're okay?"

"I don't know," she admitted honestly. "I can't see anything." Had the blow blinded her? Her hearing was fine, though. She could hear the creak of floorboards, a crash as something glass must have fallen, and then, finally, she could detect light emanating from the bulb in the fan hanging over the rug on which Keeli now lay.

"How long have I been out?" she wondered aloud. If it was so dark that she'd been able to see nothing without the light, then quite a lot of time had passed. But then she looked at the couple of windows that faced the small lake. They were dark, but it wasn't because it was night out.

Boards on the outside covered the glass. And when Spencer walked over to the door and tried to pull it open, it only rattled in the frame.

"He boarded us in," she murmured.

That was not a good sign. And probably neither was the fact that he hadn't restrained Spencer with zip ties. Either he'd thought he'd killed him with the blow he'd delivered before striking Keeli, or he had other plans to make sure they didn't survive.

She sniffed the air for the telltale odor of gas. But she smelled nothing.

"The cabin has no gas," Spencer assured her. "Only electricity, and I'm actually surprised he didn't already shut off that for the winter." He walked to the galley kitchen and opened a drawer. He pulled out a knife and headed back toward her. With the sharp blade he snapped the zip ties from her wrists and ankles.

She grimaced as feeling rushed back to her hands and feet. Before she could reach for them, Spencer rubbed her feet. Then he held her hands, moving his thumb over her palms and fingers until all sensation returned.

Too much sensation. She was still tingling but it wasn't from lack of circulation. It was from attraction. How could she want him so much—even now?

Maybe that was just the adrenaline. But she knew it was more than that. She glanced down at the knife he'd dropped on the rug and remembered how he'd walked right to the light switch. He'd also known about the utilities. "How do you know this place so well?"

"I've been coming up here since I was a kid. Frank would bring me fishing at his little lake house." He looked around as if seeing the place for the first time. Like he had seen his old friend. "How did I miss it?"

"Everybody missed it with my stepfather," Keeli said. "Nobody saw what he was really like, that all that niceness was just an act. Even my mother bought it. Maybe most especially my mother..." She shuddered as she remembered how alone she'd felt. "And he was a bad man."

Spencer pulled her into his arms and held her close, as if he wanted to protect her like he hadn't been able to protect Rebecca. He must have loved the girl so much.

Instead of taking comfort, Keeli offered it. "I protected myself," she told him. "And I got out of there. I'm fine."

He pulled back and stared into her eyes. He lifted his hand toward her face, and his fingers trembled as he stroked her jaw just below her twin scratches. "You're incredible..."

A smile tugged at her lips. "He must have hit you really hard."

He moved his hand from her face to his head and winced as he touched it. "Pretty hard..."

"Hard enough that you're being sweet to me," she murmured.

"I'm sorry," he said, "that I've been a jerk so much of the time."

"Ninety percent," she reminded him.

"You're being generous," he told her. "I thought it was more like ninety-nine."

Keeli smiled. "I was rounding down."

"Thank you."

She shrugged. "Not a big deal."

"I'm thanking you for all the times you've saved my life. And you tried really hard to get through to Frank," he said. "To save my life again. Thank you."

She released a shaky sigh. "I just bought us some time. We both know he's not going to let either of us live." She scrambled up from the floor. "We need to get the hell out of here before he comes back from wherever he's gone."

"Maybe he won't come back," Spencer said. "But either way, you're right. We do have to get the hell out of here."

Keeli picked up the knife from the floor.

He held up his hands. "So I guess this means you don't accept my apology for being a jerk?"

She chuckled at his sorry attempt at humor. "No, that son of a bitch took our guns." Her holster hung limply against her side. She missed the weight of her Glock. "But I'll be ready for him."

"Remember—you can't bring a knife to a gunfight."

"We have no choice now."

He didn't argue, just reiterated, "We have to get out of here."

The cabin was small—just one room with the couch that probably folded out to a bed, that ugly rug and a small round table near the kitchenette. Besides the outside door, there were two more. One stood open to the tiny bathroom. The other was closed until Spencer pulled it open. He looked inside, then cursed. "He took his toolbox."

"He probably needed it to nail all the boards on the outside," she pointed out.

Spencer headed back toward the kitchenette and pulled open more drawers and cabinets. He also took one of the chairs from around the table. Then he turned it so the legs pointed toward the window and smashed it through the glass. While the glass shattered and fell to the floor, the boards outside the glass didn't budge at all. He cursed again. But he didn't stop. He kept hammering the chair against the boards until its legs snapped off.

When he reached for another, Keeli grabbed it from him. "Let me try."

"You're not strong enough," he said.

"You're right," she said. "Ninety-nine percent…"

He chuckled. But his arms were shaking and sweat beaded on his brow and dampened his shirt. There was more blood oozing down his face from the wound on his head, too.

"And you've overdone it," she told him.

"We have to get out of here," he said.

"We will," she assured him. She had a feeling that Robertson wasn't coming back. He'd boarded them up so they couldn't get out, either to keep them captive for Luther or to give him time to get the hell out of the country.

Maybe he actually had a soft spot for Spencer after all. But she doubted it; he'd tried to kill him too many times to really care about him.

Spencer reached for the chair, but Keeli held tightly to it. "You need a break."

He didn't let go of the chair, just used it to pull her closer. "The chair isn't what I need…"

Her breath caught at the look on his face, the desire burning in his dark eyes. He needed her.

She needed him, too.

And it wasn't like anyone—even Luther—would be able to quickly get inside the cabin to get them— not with it as boarded up as it was now. So they were probably the safest they'd actually been in a while.

She let the chair slip through her fingers. But then Spencer let it drop, too, and he reached for her instead, pulling her up against his hard, hot body.

He lowered his head and kissed her deeply, passionately. His mouth made love to hers, his lips sliding across hers before he teased her with his tongue, too.

She gasped as desire overwhelmed her. He excited her as no one else ever had. Made her want him so damn much…

She grabbed his shirt in her hands like she had the chair. Fisting the material in her fingers, she yanked it up. The fabric pulled them apart but for just a moment. Then they were kissing again until he dragged her sweater up and over her head. The rest of their clothes were quickly pushed down and off as they moved their hands and mouths greedily over each other. Keeli needed more—as the tension wound inside her.

She needed release.

The powerful release only he had ever given her.

She wrapped her fingers around his erection and slid her hand up and down.

He groaned and slid his hands under her buttocks, lifting her. And he must have been as desperate as she was because he lifted her higher and slid inside her.

She cried out at the exquisite pleasure. But it wasn't enough. She needed more...

He kept moving inside, thrusting deeper and deeper. She wrapped her legs and arms around him, clinging to him. And he moved one hand from her butt and eased it between their sweat-slick bodies.

He touched her breasts, caressing them before moving his thumb over the nipple of one. She cried out at the sensations racing through her. Then he moved his hand lower, to her most sensitive place.

And she came, the orgasm raging through her like a flash fire burning her alive with passion and pleasure.

His whole body shuddered as he joined her in release. He was shaking, like he'd been from his exertion trying to escape, so he dropped onto the couch with her on his lap.

And she gasped as he drove even deeper inside her.

His hands grasped her hips and he tensed. "Are you okay?"

"Are you okay?" Spencer asked again, alarmed at the look on her face. If he'd hurt her or the baby...

He would never forgive himself. Hell, he wasn't going to forgive himself anyway. Not for how he'd treated her all these years. What he'd thought was reck-lessness was just her justifiable difficulty in trusting anyone, especially when she hadn't been able to trust the people who should have protected her most but from whom she'd most needed protecting. He'd been so stupid not to realize why she'd reminded him of Rebecca, and he'd been so stupid about Frank.

He should have caught on earlier that his mentor was the leak. Looking back, it all made sense now.

As much sense as a lawman going bad would ever make to him...

But he didn't give a damn about Robertson right now. All his concern was for Keeli whose beautiful blue eyes had gone wide with shock.

"Did I hurt you?" he asked. Or the baby?

Had he driven too deep inside her?

But she moved and moved again, and a moan slipped through her lips.

He was spent. He should have been spent—from trying to escape—from the sex. But her desire revived his, and he wanted her all over again. They made love quickly again—just as greedy as they'd been moments ago.

She came again, screaming his name. He loved the sound of it on her lips. He loved her. But he couldn't tell her that now—not when their future was so uncertain. He had to get them the hell out of the cabin.

He orgasmed again, too, but he felt no real release. Tension gripped him so tightly. When she dressed and headed to the bathroom, he threw on his clothes and headed back toward the window. The boards had to start coming loose.

But before he could lift the chair to swing it, he

heard a noise. The sound of a car approaching. All the other cabins had probably been closed up for the season already. The car had to be heading toward this one.

Was it Robertson returning? Or had he taken Keeli's advice and worked an exchange with Luther—their lives lost to save Frank's?

Parker paced his office, waiting for word from the chief. But it wasn't his stepfather who leaned against the jamb of his open doorway. His mother, Penny, watched him, her warm brown eyes soft with concern.

"Are you okay?" she asked.

He shook his head. "No. No, I'm not." A ragged sigh slipped through his lips before he admitted, "I think I lost her..."

"Keeli Abbott?"

He nodded. "Did you feel it?" he asked. She was legendary for getting this feeling when something bad was about to happen.

She shook her head, then asked, "Did you?"

He'd been getting premonitions, too, ever since opening his own branch of the Payne Protection Agency. He'd always known when something bad was about to happen to one of his team. But he hadn't sensed this—hadn't felt anything about Keeli—until he'd seen that house explode.

And even now he didn't have the certainty that she'd been inside. He was just worried that she had been— that she was one of the casualties. But the bodies had been too badly damaged to identify.

DNA had to be tested. So he'd retrieved her hairbrush from her apartment and had brought it to the police lab. Maybe he should have stayed there and waited for the results. But he'd thought…what if she was okay…?

What if she came to the office?

And so he'd come back here to wait for her—to hope that she would come to him.

"She's like another sister to me," he told his mother, his voice cracking with the emotions overwhelming him. "But I didn't treat her like one. I didn't take care of her like Logan and I always tried taking care of Nikki."

"That's why Nikki works for Cooper," Penny gently reminded him. "And that's why Keeli works for you. You respect her. You know she can take care of herself."

He released a shaky breath, relieved that his mother spoke of his friend in the present tense. Keeli had to be alive yet. Right?

She was Keeli. She was tough and resourceful. She had survived one house explosion. Certainly she could have survived another.

But after all the shootings, maybe her luck had just run out.

"Why are you here, Mom?" he thought to ask. Was she having a bad feeling now?

Her brow was furrowed, as if she was worried. But maybe she was just worried about him.

"We're having Sunday dinner," she reminded him.

"Mom, we're so busy—with Luther Mills on the loose—"

She stepped forward and pressed her hand over his mouth. "That's why we need to do this," she said. "We need to be there for each other. We need to take a little time to eat and rest and recharge."

He shook his head.

"It'll just be an hour," she promised. "You can see your wife and children."

He'd barely talked to Sharon since Luther's escape. She was at his mom's—all the wives and children were—just in case Luther came after their families, too. And there were bodyguards and even some FBI agents guarding his mother's house. They were safe there.

And maybe she was right.

Maybe he needed that hour to be with his family. But he wanted his whole family to be there—not just his blood relatives but his team that were all family to him, too. His team couldn't all be together until it was safe for all of them to return to River City.

And it wouldn't be safe until Luther Mills was apprehended. But even then, would his whole team be reunited?

Or was it too late?

Was Keeli already gone?

Chapter 20

The sound of the car engine raised goose bumps along Keeli's forearms. She'd dressed, but she wasn't completely recovered from what she'd done—with Spencer—from what she'd felt for the man.

She splashed some more cold water on her face, but her skin didn't cool off. And her pulse didn't slow either. In fact it raced even more.

She knew that the car was coming to this cabin. How much time did they have?

How long would it take someone to pull those boards loose? Or had Robertson gone for some cans of gasoline and he intended to burn down the cabin? That sounded more like him—like how he'd blown up the houses.

There was no gas hooked to this structure, so he would have had to go buy some. They needed to get out—before he took them out. Spencer must have thought the same thing because he was hammering at the boards across the window again. Hammering so hard that the legs snapped off this chair, too.

But she heard another noise—from the back of the cabin, and a section of the paneling slid aside to reveal a hidden door. As the knob rattled, Keeli grabbed up the knife and rushed toward the door. But just before it opened, Spencer lunged forward and threw himself in front of her—shielding her body with his—from whatever threat was coming at them.

Infuriated, she cursed at him. This wasn't chivalry. This was stupidity.

He had no weapon. She was the one with the knife—the one armed to defend them.

Would he ever trust her to do her job?

But he might never get the chance. Because now, with him trying to play hero again, he might die for his efforts. She didn't need his protection.

She just needed him.

Spencer tensed waiting for bullets to strike him from the front and for Keeli to stab him in the back. She was furious with him; he'd heard it in her curses. But he knew she would restrain herself.

He wasn't sure who the hell was coming through that door. He'd known about the hiding space in Frank's house. How had he never known about that sliding panel? Some mechanism from outside must have activated it.

But then he'd never known everything about Frank.

Had the guy sold them out to Luther? Was it his crew coming through the door with guns blazing?

He braced himself, waiting for a barrage of bullets. But the barrel of only one gun pointed at him. The man holding that gun was a stranger to him. But the face was familiar because he'd seen it almost every day of his life.

Now he knew that face was just a mask, and he'd never really seen the man beneath it. Frank had only shown Spencer what he'd wanted him to see—the superficial surface, not his dark interior.

Just because it was Frank who'd come through the door and not Luther or his crew, Spencer didn't relax. His body tense, he kept it in front of Keeli, shielding her. And miraculously, she didn't fight to get around him.

"You never showed me that door," Spencer remarked—because the terrible silence all around unnerved him. "But then you never told me about a lot of things."

The older detective's mouth slid into a smirk. "What happened to your hero worship of me, Spence? You used to claim I taught you everything you know."

He flinched. It was true. He had always accredited Frank with making him want to become a cop and then with making him a good cop.

But how was that possible when Frank had never been a good cop himself?

What the hell did that make Spencer?

Stupid.

Frank stepped farther into the room. While Spencer would have backed up, Keeli tugged on the back of his shirt—turning him. And he understood…she was trying to get them closer to the door.

Frank gestured at the broken window and the

chairs Spencer had smashed trying to break through the boards across that window. "I didn't nail those boards on, kid, I screwed them in place with very long screws." He shook his head and chuckled. "You weren't going to be able to pound them loose. But I applaud your efforts at trying to get out."

If only they had...

Because Spencer had no idea what the crooked detective had planned for them now...

But his nose wrinkled as he caught the scent of gas. And he groaned. "You're going to set the cabin on fire?"

Robertson nodded.

"That's a mistake." Keeli finally spoke from behind Spencer's back. "You're missing an opportunity to negotiate with Luther."

"You know the time for negotiations has passed," the older man told her. "If I agreed to meet with him— he'd kill me."

"He wants Spencer dead more than he wants you dead," she insisted.

And it was probably true—everything she'd said about Luther thinking Spencer had disrespected him with the perp walk. He had no respect for a drug-dealing killer. No respect at all...

And now he had no respect for his idol.

Frank shook his head. "You're not setting me up to get killed, Keeli Abbott. I know what you're trying to do."

"What are *you* going to do?" Keeli asked.

But Spencer suspected she already knew.

"I was just going to toss a match and burn the place down," Robertson admitted.

He had probably already doused it in gasoline. That was why he smelled like it.

"But then I started looking at the place and remembered bringing you up as a kid..." Frank remarked.

Maybe there was some sentiment in him after all.

Or at least some nostalgia.

But if there was, he shrugged it off now. "Then I figured it's probably more humane to just put a bullet in each of your brains." And he raised his weapon and pointed it at Spencer's head.

Keeli screamed. "No! Don't kill us!" she pleaded, her voice shrill with the sound of tears. "I'm going to have a baby. I'm pregnant."

Frank snorted. "And you think I care? You think that makes a difference to me?"

"Luther cared," she admitted. "That's why he didn't kill me when he was holding me captive."

Frank snorted. "Yeah, right, that's why he told me to kill you when I killed Spencer."

"But he couldn't do it himself," she said, and she sounded as if she was nearing hysteria.

Spencer had never heard such fear in her voice, and his heart broke with the need to protect her and their baby.

Was that why Luther hadn't killed her? Because she was pregnant?

But clearly it didn't make a difference to Frank. He didn't lower his weapon at all.

But suddenly Spencer dropped as Keeli kicked her foot against the back of his knee and made his leg fold beneath him. And as he fell, she lunged—toward Robertson—with the knife she clenched.

Spencer couldn't see if she'd connected or not. All he heard was the shot as Robertson fired his gun.

Woodrow loved the yellow farmhouse on the rural outskirts of River City, Michigan. He knew Penny had lived here with her first husband, and that could have intimidated him into wanting them to find their own home that they lived in together. But that part of her life was what made Penny the woman he loved so much. Not only had she lived here with her husband, but after his death, she'd raised her kids here.

Because it meant so much to her, it meant so much to Woodrow as well. So he was happy every time he came home to it and her. But he had to wait at the end of the driveway for security to let him go to his home and his wife. The FBI agent nodded when he recognized him, though, and stepped aside to let him continue up the drive to the house.

He had to get past a couple more guards standing on the wraparound porch before he was allowed to step through the door. The minute he did, the outside world receded to this realm of sunny warmth and brightness and mouthwatering scents emanating from the kitchen.

He couldn't remember the last time he'd eaten, but his stomach growled, attesting that it had been too long. But he'd had to wait for the results before coming home because he knew Parker was waiting.

His stepson greeted him in the foyer. "What did you find out? Were they in the explosion?"

"Let him sit down," Penny protested as she shoved aside her much taller son and closed her arms around Woodrow.

He hugged her close—she was like the house, so

warm and bright. And as he buried his face in her soft auburn curls, he breathed in delicious smells from her hair.

Keeping his arm around her, he turned back to Parker. He understood his stepson's concern. "It'll take longer to determine DNA matchups to the remains," he said.

Parker cursed.

"But the preliminary DNA markers on the remains indicate that all the victims were male."

Parker's breath shuddered out in a sigh of relief.

Woodrow expected he'd been holding that breath since the explosion. He reached out his other hand and squeezed Parker's broad shoulder. "She wasn't in the house."

"Then where the hell is she?" Parker murmured.

"Alive," Penny said hopefully.

There was no way even she could know that for certain. Just because Keeli's body hadn't been at the scene didn't mean she wasn't dead.

Parker must have realized that, too, because he said, "I have to find her." And he headed toward the door.

But Woodrow, with his hand on his shoulder again, stopped him. "Take a breath," he advised. "Eat the wonderful dinner your mother worked hard to prepare."

"Your wife cooked, too," Penny added. "And Sharon needs to see you—to make sure you're okay."

From the look on his face, Woodrow could see that Parker knew better than to argue with his mother. And it was obvious how much his stepson loved his wife, so it didn't surprise Woodrow when Parker turned and headed back into the house.

Penny didn't follow, though. She didn't rush off to the kitchen like she usually did when she was working on the family dinner. Instead she leaned against him, her body tense at his side.

And he knew...

She had had or was having one of those damn premonitions. Something bad was about to happen.

"What is it?" he asked. "Keeli? Spencer?"

Spencer could have still been one of the victims in the explosion. But Woodrow doubted it. He'd gotten to know Keeli Abbott well enough to know how seriously she took her job as bodyguard. She would have made sure that Spencer stayed safe—like he had at the courthouse—even if she'd been abducted again herself.

And she must have been, or she would have touched base with her boss. But then she hadn't before she and Spencer had taken off to find Robertson on their own either.

Woodrow could understand that Spencer probably hadn't been able to believe that his mentor could be working for Luther Mills. Woodrow struggled with the betrayal, too. He'd liked the veteran detective. He'd trusted him, too, more than he should have.

All the information Robertson had probably sold Luther hadn't come just from Spencer. Woodrow had divulged things he shouldn't have as well. Once Parker had suggested the leak could be Spencer, it hadn't taken Woodrow long to follow that leak to Robertson instead.

And when he'd checked his financials and his involvement in the past in crimes that Luther Mills had been suspected of committing, it was easy to see Robertson's complicity. There was a warrant out for his arrest now.

But was he already gone? Was he one of the bodies recovered from the house?

Woodrow suspected not—his gut told him that the detective had Keeli and probably Spencer as well. But where? And were they still alive?

He studied his wife's beautiful face. Her skin was pale, and there were lines in her brow and around her mouth—lines that usually weren't noticeable. She was worried. No. She was *terrified*.

And Woodrow realized she wasn't worried about just Keeli and Spencer right now. She was worried about all of them. That was why she looked so scared.

Woodrow didn't know if he'd suddenly developed that sixth sense himself—like her sons had after opening their own branches of the Payne Protection Agency—or if he'd just picked up on her feelings.

But he knew that Keeli and Spencer weren't the only ones in danger. They all were.

Chapter 21

There was so much blood. Had an artery been hit? Was that why blood pooled on the floor?

Keeli turned to Spencer, who lay on the rug beside her. "Are you okay?"

She had kicked him in order to knock him down and out of her way. But the problem was that Robertson's gun had still been pointing at him, and when she'd lunged with her knife, the gun had gone off. It lay now on the floor near the fallen detective.

Frank's fingers twitched, and he began to reach for the gun. His artery must not have been hit when she'd plunged the knife into his arm. And the blade was so short that she doubted it could have caused a mortal wound.

She grabbed up the gun before he could and turned the barrel on him. "Don't move!"

"You bitch," he growled at her as he rolled to his side on the rug. "I should have known you were up to something—cowering behind Spence and crying is not your style at all."

No. It wasn't. She would have taken him out the minute he'd come through the door if not for Spencer jumping in her way again.

She glanced over at him lying on the floor still. "Are you okay?" she asked again. "Spencer?"

He rolled over and groaned.

And panic struck her heart. "Were you hit?" She'd thought she'd knocked him out of the way—that she'd protected him.

He reached out and grasped his knee. "What the hell did you do?" he asked.

"Did you get shot?"

"No," he said. "But you kicked my knee. The same knee that I blew out playing football in high school." He groaned again as he gripped it.

Keeli felt a twinge of regret but just a very tiny twinge. She hadn't known about his old injury, and even if she had, she probably still would have kicked him—because she'd needed to get him out of her way so she could do her job.

"Yeah, and she saved your ass again," Robertson grumbled. "Bitch…"

"Hey!" Spencer yelled as he vaulted up and turned on his old mentor—as if ready to beat him up. Then he must have noticed that the man was already bleeding from the knife wound in his shoulder.

"You're welcome," Keeli told him.

Spencer glanced at her, but his dark eyes were narrowed in a glare. He didn't look very appreciative.

* * *

Spencer was fuming. Not because Keeli had stabbed Frank. He would have understood if she'd killed the man since it would have been self-defense. Robertson had had every intention of killing them. Spencer wasn't even mad that she'd kicked him.

But he was pissed as hell that she could have been shot when she'd brought her knife to the gunfight with a detective who'd been decorated for his marksmanship. She was damn lucky Frank hadn't turned his gun on her and killed her and their unborn baby.

How in the world was this kid going to make it to term if she didn't stop risking her life every other hour of the day?

He couldn't even look at her again. Instead he reached for Frank. He unhooked the man's handcuffs from his belt and then pulled his arms behind his back and snapped the cuffs around his wrists.

Frank yelped in pain. "Hey, she stabbed me! Take it easy!"

"I would have killed you," Keeli said. "But you're going to suffer a lot more behind bars than you would have in the ground."

"You are a bitch," Frank snapped.

And Spencer jerked his arms farther behind his back, making him cry out again. Even though Spencer was furious with her, he would not abide anyone insulting Keeli—not anymore. Not even himself...

Mortification swept through him as he thought of all the things he'd called her in the past—all the ways he'd goaded her, trying to get her to quit the River City PD and more recently her assignment as his bodyguard.

But if she had quit her assignment, he would probably be dead now because he didn't know if he would have ever figured out that Frank was the leak… Until it was too late.

Now, because of her, the leak had been stopped. "I'm placing you under arrest," he told his mentor. And then he proceeded to read him his rights.

"C'mon, Spence," Frank wheedled now. "You know if you put me in jail I'm a dead man. I put too many of those inmates in there, and they're going to want to get to me."

"You should have thought of that before you started working for Luther," Keeli reminded him.

"And Luther," Frank said, "he can get to me anywhere."

That was damn true—the man was trying to appeal to Spencer's overdeveloped need to protect people. But Spencer ignored him as he guided him toward that hidden door. As he pushed him through it, he coughed and sputtered at the overpowering smell of gasoline. Frank had soaked the cedar siding of the outside of the cabin. It would have gone up quickly—with no chance for Spencer and Keeli to escape if he'd lit the match.

"You have to get me a deal," Frank pleaded. "I'll give you Luther Mills. But I can't do any prison time."

"You know where he is?" Keeli asked, but she sounded skeptical.

Spencer was, too. He doubted anything the man would tell him now. If only he'd doubted him before…

"I'll testify against him for his other crimes," Frank offered. "I'll tell you everything he's responsible for."

She snorted. "It doesn't matter. He's going down for so many things."

"But you don't know where to find him," Frank said.

Keeli stopped walking now and turned back to study the older detective. And Spencer tensed, his grip tightening around Frank's arms. He felt like whirling him around to face him, but he knew that no matter how hard he looked, he wouldn't be able to see beneath the man's mask to the truth.

Keeli arched a brow. "And you do?" she scoffed.

"I—I have a pretty good idea," Frank said.

"Yeah, right…" She whirled away and started toward the car Frank had left idling in the driveway, probably so he would have been able to make a quick getaway after he'd set the cabin on fire.

"You're wrong!" Frank shouted after her. "Spence isn't the one Luther hates the most."

Spencer sighed. Should he be relieved that the drug dealer actually wanted someone else dead more than he wanted him dead? He didn't feel relieved; he felt concern.

But Frank couldn't be talking about Keeli. If that were the case, Luther would have killed her when he'd had the chance. Instead he'd let her go.

She kept walking toward the car and jerked open the driver's door. Of course she expected to drive.

But since there was no partition separating the back from the front, that might have been a good thing— because Spencer would have to sit in the back to make sure that Frank didn't try anything stupid. Like trying to get away…

And he was so desperate that he would probably make an attempt to escape.

"Don't you want to know?" Frank asked, but he twisted around to try to face Spencer now. He must have realized that he wasn't getting through to Keeli. And he already knew how damn gullible Spencer had been.

Spencer pulled open the passenger's door and leaned down to fold the seat forward, so he could shove Frank into the back. The car was just a two-door. One of his vintage vehicles again, so there weren't even any seat belts. Nothing that he could use to make sure Frank stayed in the back.

"C'mon, Spence," his old mentor implored him. "You have to wanna know. It's not like you to not want to try to protect everyone…"

While he hadn't known Frank at all, the man knew him too well. And finally Spencer forced himself to look at him. But like he'd suspected, he saw nothing different than any of the millions of other times he'd looked at the man. It wasn't as if Frank had suddenly grown horns or that honesty now burned in his brown eyes. He looked just the same as he always had.

But he would never be the same to Spencer.

Even so, his betrayal wasn't going to make Spencer change who he was. He was always going to try to protect people—even when, like Keeli, they didn't want protection. So he sighed and caved, "Who? Who does Luther want dead more than me?"

Frank hesitated for a moment. Maybe he hadn't thought Spencer would actually listen, so he hadn't had a name ready for him. And now he was trying to come up with one.

Spencer shook his head, disgusted with himself for even giving the guy the chance to talk when he knew he'd hear nothing but lies from him now.

"Get in the damn car," he said. But when he reached

for Frank's shoulder to shove him in the back, the guy cried out.

And Spencer's hand came away covered in blood. He'd momentarily forgotten that Keeli had stabbed him. If she hadn't, Spencer probably would have had a bullet in his head right now. His old friend had had no qualms about hurting him.

So he steeled himself and shoved again, forcing the guy into the back seat. "We'll take you to the hospital for some stitches," Spencer relented. "But you're going to jail right after that."

"Parker Payne!" the guy blurted out. "That's who Luther hates more than you. Parker messed up all his plans to get the charges against him thrown out."

Keeli snorted. "Parker was only doing his job. The chief hired him."

"He hates the chief, too," Frank said. "He hates both of them even more than he hates you, Spence. He could be going after either of them right now."

Keeli snorted again, as if she wasn't buying his story. But then her hands gripped the wheel tightly.

"Are you okay?" Spencer asked her as all the color drained from her face.

She turned toward him with wide eyes. "I know where Luther could take out both of them at the same time as well as a ton of other bodyguards and Paynes..."

"The Payne Sunday dinner," Frank confirmed as he leaned back against the rear seat.

"What time is it?" Keeli asked. Then she glanced at the clock on the dash. "Is that time right?"

Frank said nothing.

She turned toward him and shouted, "Is that the right time?"

He nodded at her.

She cursed. "If he's right—if Luther wants to take out the Payne family and the chief—he could have already done it."

And for the first time since he'd known her, Spencer saw fear on her beautiful face—but it wasn't for herself. It was for her boss and her friends.

Luther had brought in more gunmen for this job. But he still worried that he might not have enough. The yellow farmhouse was heavily guarded—outside and probably even more inside—because they were all inside. Through his binoculars, he'd watched as every member of the Payne family arrived.

The men all looked alike, so much so that he wouldn't have known which one was Parker if his shoulders hadn't been bowed as if he carried a big burden and his face tight with worry. He probably believed that he'd lost Keeli and Spencer.

Luther hoped that was true, but he had his doubts. Keeli Abbott was like a cat with nine lives; she just seemed to keep landing on her feet while carrying Dubridge along with her. No, Luther figured the casualties the news reported had been all on his side. But if Keeli and Spencer weren't dead, they would have been here with everyone else.

A grin tugged at his lips. Maybe old Robertson had come through in the end—maybe he'd finally, successfully, taken them out. Eventually Keeli had to use up all those lives of hers.

And the Paynes had to have used up all theirs by now as well. But damn, they had a way of surviving no matter what was thrown at them.

Had Luther brought in enough gunpower?

But even if they didn't take out all the Paynes, taking out any would cause a big enough distraction for him to slip away from River City—if he slipped away from this scene now.

That was why he'd ordered that SUV that looked so much like the ones they all used—so he could come and go around them without immediately arousing suspicion.

He wanted to stay—wanted to put more bullets in the chief like he had at the courthouse. And he especially wanted to put a bullet in Parker Payne. But if he stayed, he might never leave River City.

He might get planted in the ground.

No.

Even though he wouldn't get quite the satisfaction he deserved, he would be safer to take off now. And he would just make sure his men took out as many Paynes as they could. Before he gave the order, he offered them a little more incentive—a little more money per head.

No. Per dead…

He chuckled at his pun. Then he put down his binoculars and walked toward the SUV waiting for him. He was chuckling now, but he figured he'd be laughing later—when he was settled into his chair on the beach with a drink in his hand…

Chapter 22

Woodrow Lynch was a practical, pragmatic man. So Penny wouldn't have been surprised if he'd been unable to accept that she had a sixth sense that warned her when bad things were about to happen. But because he loved her so much, he loved and accepted everything about her—like her family.

They were all his family, too, now—even the ones who weren't related to her by DNA. He loved them just as she did, like they were her own.

So when he'd seen how worried she was, he'd alerted the guards outside to be extra vigilant. And he'd herded all the children to the basement, where no stray bullets could strike them within the concrete walls. Logan's wife, Stacy; Cooper's wife, Tanya; Nick's wife, Annalise; and Parker's wife, Sharon, all kissed their husbands and headed down the stairs to watch the kids. Nikki's sister-in-law, Emilia, went down with her baby, too.

But Nikki, of course, insisted on staying upstairs with her brothers and the other bodyguards. But knowing now how good she was at her job, Penny had no more qualms about her safety than anyone else's.

Unfortunately she had a lot of other qualms. That bad feeling had never been so intense before—so intense that she trembled with it. Woodrow hugged her close, but then his big hands gripped her shoulders and he steered her toward the stairs, too.

"You need to be down there—with the children," he told her. "You need to keep everyone calm."

But she was afraid that, with so much fear gripping her, she would only upset them more. She could hear Emilia's beautiful voice drifting up the stairs as she sang some cartoon movie tune to the kids. And tears stung her eyes.

All of these people—all of her family—had already been through so much, and they were finally happy. That could not all end now and not because of such a horrible man.

"Come downstairs with me," she implored Woodrow.

He was already hurt, his shoulder already wounded. He wouldn't be much help to the others. But he could help her. He could keep her calm and safe.

He leaned down and pressed his lips to her forehead. He held them there for a long moment while he breathed in the scent of her hair. "I love you," he said. "And I love the life we have. I love our family. I won't let anything happen to them."

And she believed him. She pulled back and opened

the door to the basement and walked down to join the others. But even over the beautiful sound of Emilia's voice, she heard the gunfire ring out.

She felt no satisfaction in knowing that her premonition had been right. Something bad was not just about to happen. It was happening *now*.

She wanted to believe her husband. Unlike the first man she'd married, every promise Woodrow had made to her he had kept. But she wondered if this time—if this promise—was beyond his control to keep.

Fear coursed through Keeli, fear like she had never experienced before. What if they were too late? What if they were all already gone?

Sunday dinners for the Paynes were legendary and open-ended. She had gone a few times. She knew what they were like—that the house was full of family and friends and food and children. Little kids were usually playing out in the yard and on the porch.

Tears stung her eyes, but she blinked to clear her vision. The road to the farmhouse wound around little lakes and fields in the rural outskirts of River City. She had to be careful so she didn't go off the road or sideswipe another vehicle like the black SUV she passed that was also taking the curve a little too fast. It was probably a bodyguard leaving the house. And if they were leaving, nothing must have happened yet. But she was still so certain it would that she forced herself to concentrate on the road and getting to the farmhouse before it was too late.

"Get his phone!" she yelled over the sound of the loud engine in the old car. Robertson had made them drop their cell phones in his house just before it had exploded. "We need to call and warn the others."

Keeli hadn't taken the time to drop off Robertson at the hospital or the police department. She couldn't have stabbed him that deeply because the blade of the knife hadn't been very long. And while he'd bled a lot, she hadn't hit an artery.

He would be fine.

It was the Paynes she was worried about.

"My phone fell out of my pocket when you attacked me," Robertson grumbled as if her attack had been unprovoked, as if he hadn't been trying to kill them.

She wished that blade had been a little longer now. He was such a bad man.

"We could stop," Spencer suggested, "and use someone's phone."

She knew what he was up to—that he didn't want her at the scene of a possible shoot-out. Keeli sighed. She would have blamed the fact that she was carrying his baby on his overprotectiveness, but he had always acted this way with her—as if she couldn't handle danger.

Frustration gnawed at her. "How many times am I going to have to save your sorry ass before you realize that I'm good at my job?"

"I'm not telling you not to go," he said. "I really want to warn the others."

Keeli did, too. But the cabin hadn't been that far from the Payne farmhouse. She was going to reach the house before they would have reached a town where they could use a public phone. And stopping along the way to talk someone into letting them use their private phone…

It could have been possible had Spencer had his badge to show them. But Robertson had made him drop it inside his house with his phone. He'd wanted everyone to believe they'd all died in the explosion, so he'd left his shield there, too.

She careened around another corner to find the road ahead blocked with vehicles. Only one looked like an official vehicle; the others looked like the ones that had been parked near the house where Luther had held her captive. Either rentals or beat-up personal vehicles.

Luther's crew was already here. She slammed her foot on the brake and threw the car into Park. Then she reached for the door.

"Wait!" Spencer said.

But she didn't listen, and when he tried to grab her arm, she jerked away. When she opened the door, she flinched at the gunfire blasting. They were too late.

Too damn late…

But she drew her weapon and headed toward the driveway anyway.

"No!" Spencer yelled even as he stepped out the passenger's door. "We're going to get shot."

And just as he said it, a bullet whizzed past her head. She ducked down. The next one struck the car, glancing off the metal. Another broke the windshield. Over and over someone fired at the car. And as each shot connected, Frank shouted a protest at the damage to his beloved car.

"Get back inside," Spencer shouted at Keeli from where he hunkered down near the passenger's side. "We need to get the hell out of here."

But Keeli wasn't going to run away. Not anymore…

Instead, armed with the gun she'd taken from Robertson, she ran to danger.

* * *

Spencer had never felt so helpless and it wasn't just because he was unarmed. It was because he couldn't stop her—as she ran right into the middle of the gun battle. Sure, she had a gun, but it only had so many bullets in it.

She seemed to make them count, though. Not that there were many shooters left. At least not Luther's shooters. FBI agents in their dark suits and Payne Protection Agency bodyguards outnumbered and overpowered them.

And finally the shooting stopped, leaving a long eerie silence. Then voices rumbled—people greeting each other, checking on each other.

"Are you okay?" a man who looked like Parker asked. Then he slapped Spencer's shoulder. "Well, hell, you're better than we all thought you were. We thought you blew up in that house explosion."

He shook his head. "No. I'm fine."

But he wasn't. He had a sick feeling in his stomach and a rushing sound in his head. He watched Keeli moving around the area, talking to FBI agents and bodyguards. Her face and body showed no reaction to what she'd just done. To how badly she'd risked her life…

Spencer was shaking. He couldn't believe that she'd run into the middle of a gun battle.

"Are you really okay?" Parker's brother asked.

He nodded. It was all he could do with the fury rising up in his throat, choking him. In his mind, he kept seeing a different outcome—he kept seeing Keeli lying on the ground like some of Luther's gunmen were. He saw her bleeding out, losing her life and their baby.

Spencer shuddered and forced himself to focus on the here and now. He recognized this Payne as the half brother, the former FBI agent who'd been running River City PD before Woodrow Lynch had taken over. Spencer had once worked for him. Had once respected and trusted him. But he didn't know if he could trust anyone again.

But Nicholas Rus had recently become an official Payne. More importantly than the name, though, he had always possessed the code of honor and integrity the rest of the family had.

"I arrested this man," he said, gesturing toward the back seat of the car against which he found himself leaning. His legs were shaking—not with fear now but with anger. "He needs medical attention."

Nick nodded. "Robertson." And he nodded again.

Maybe, when he'd been acting chief, he'd had his suspicions then.

Why hadn't Spencer?

"Is everyone all right here?" Spencer asked, worried that they might have been too late, that lives might have been lost. "Anybody need to be checked out?"

"We were ready," Nick replied.

"You were warned?" So Keeli had been right to not stop to find a phone. But he was too ticked with her to admit that as more than a fleeting thought.

Nick smiled. "Yes, my…mother…" His voice cracked with emotion. "She knew…"

"That's great," Keeli said as she joined them. "I've heard about Penny Payne's sixth sense about bad things." She looked around them and finally she shuddered in reaction. "It could have been so much worse."

It could have been—if Keeli had gotten shot.

Spencer's ears were buzzing again—as that image flitted through his mind of her lying on the ground, bleeding.

If he'd lost her... That loss would destroy him. He'd always mourned for Rebecca, had always felt guilty that he hadn't helped his friend. That he hadn't protected and saved her. But Keeli...

Keeli was truly the love of his life. He'd never been as impressed or as infuriated or as in love with another woman. He couldn't even fathom losing her.

But he didn't have her. And he probably never would. She would always run off without thinking, without caring about her own safety. Even now, she was concerned only with Luther.

"Did you see him?" she asked Nick. "I've asked everyone else and nobody has."

Nick shook his head as well.

So she moved closer, but only to push Spencer aside and lean in through the car window to address Robertson. The man was pale and shaking. He needed medical attention ASAP.

Nick had already motioned for an FBI agent to come over. But as the guy started to help Robertson out the other side of the car, Keeli interrogated him.

"Do you know where Luther is?" she demanded.

Frank must have been too weak to play any more games. He just shook his head. "I thought he'd be here..."

"He was," Nick said. "One of the shooters said Luther changed his mind at the last minute and left."

"What was he driving?" Keeli asked, and the color drained from her face.

"An SUV that looks a lot like the ones we use," Nick said. "Woodrow already put out an APB on it."

"We must have passed him!" she exclaimed. "We must have driven right past him!"

Parker walked up then—with the chief following close behind. Her boss gave her a quick hug. "I thought you were dead."

Before she could reply, Spencer's temper snapped. "She could have been!" he yelled. "Time after time she kept putting herself in danger! Robertson had a gun and she jumped him anyway. And then she ran straight into this gun battle by herself. She's suicidal!"

Keeli sucked in a breath and turned toward him. "What are you talking about? I've just been doing my job and doing it damn well."

He shook his head. "No. You take unnecessary risks. It's like you have a damn death wish, like you want to die!"

"That's ridiculous," she said.

"You'd be a hell of a lot more careful if you cared about your life and…" *The baby's.* But he didn't want to bring up her pregnancy in front of Parker again or the chief.

She flinched as if he'd said it, though. "I am careful," she said. "Despite all the attempts on our lives the past couple of days, you are fine. And I only have a couple scratches and a sliver." She lifted her palm to show off a red, swollen bump.

"That could have easily been a bullet in your hand or in your head," he said. His stomach lurched as he remembered how Robertson had held his gun to her head when they'd first come upon him hiding in his house.

If the gun had gone off...

Or if she'd been struck when she'd left Robertson's car...

"It was crazy running into the middle of a gun battle," he said.

"Dubridge," Parker said, and the way he uttered Spencer's surname was like it was a warning.

He didn't care. All he could think of was how many times he'd nearly lost her over just the past couple of days... And how he couldn't imagine a world without her in it.

"She acts so impulsively that she's a danger to herself and others," Spencer persisted.

Losing Rebecca had hurt, but that pain was just a dull ache compared to the gut-wrenching horror he'd felt at the possibility of Keeli being harmed. He ached even now for her and she was just a few feet away.

But then he noticed the look on her face, like he'd struck her, and he felt that distance grow. He felt her pull away from him. And he realized that his anger over the possibility of anything happening to her was what had actually hurt her.

He had hurt her.

But she'd hurt him, too. She made him think that she didn't care about the baby she was carrying—his baby. Despite what she'd said, maybe she didn't want it... Just like she didn't want him.

Hell, she didn't even like him. Protecting him was just an assignment to her, and that assignment kept making her risk her life for his. The only reason she'd nearly been killed was because of him—because Luther wanted him dead. If she wasn't protecting him anymore...

Then she would be safe. Spencer would make any sacrifice for her safety and the safety of their unborn baby.

"I don't want her as my bodyguard anymore!" he said.

He expected her to yell back at him—like she usually did. But she said nothing. She just shook her head and walked away. Maybe she was too angry to speak at all.

Or she didn't want to fight because she didn't want to be his bodyguard anymore either. Finally, after all these weeks of his trying to get her to quit, she'd given up?

Or had he gone too far? He was just so petrified thinking of what could have happened to her—of what nearly had.

Parker nodded and replied, "Agreed. I'll assign you someone else."

Spencer shook his head. "I don't even need a bodyguard." He gestured at the scene. "I'm sure this was Luther's last attempt at revenge before leaving River City. He's probably long gone by now."

"We don't know that," the chief said. "Until we catch him, I want everyone to have security." Woodrow focused on Parker now. "I want all the bodyguards to have bodyguards."

Spencer hadn't thought about that—hadn't considered that Keeli would still be in danger even if she was no longer protecting him. Sure, Luther had let her live before, but since then he'd ordered Robertson to kill her because she'd kept getting in the way of his plans to kill Spencer.

But even if she wasn't with Spencer, he knew she

wasn't about to give up on apprehending Luther Mills. And Luther had to be so desperate to not return to jail that he would kill anyone who came after him.

When Spencer saw a Payne Protection SUV pull away from the house and drive off, he knew it was Keeli and that she was going after Luther.

Alone.

How the hell could he find her? How could he save her?

Chapter 23

The splinter had made her think of something she hadn't realized earlier. Keeli had no idea how she'd missed it. Not the little sliver of wood—she hadn't had time to even try to dig that out.

The splinter had reminded her that when Luther had brought her into the kitchen from the garage, she'd noticed the table had a smooth top then that had been highly polished. But when she'd returned and found the guard lying on the floor beneath it, the surface had become so rough that the sliver had gone into her palm. So something must have been carved into the wood.

Maybe Luther had just been sharpening something and cut the wood. Or maybe he'd used it like a message board. She hoped the latter. But it was probably just the former, so she hadn't bothered sharing her thought with anyone else.

And truly, after the way Spencer had acted at Penny Payne-Lynch's house, she'd needed time alone. Thinking of how angry he'd been—and the things he'd said—had tears stinging her eyes. She blinked furiously. Had to be the pregnancy hormones making her so emotional.

After all, he'd said far worse to her before and it had never bothered her. Or at least it hadn't bothered her much. But since they'd made love and made a baby together, she'd begun to have feelings for him. But apparently her feelings were one-sided because the only feeling he seemed to have for her was disgust.

Now she knew that he would never accept her for who she was—for what she was. She was a bodyguard; it was her job to protect other people and sometimes doing that put her in danger as well.

But every time that she had been in jeopardy, she hadn't acted impulsively; she'd known what she was doing and how to minimize the risk. When she'd left the car, she'd kept low to the ground and had found cover. She hadn't just rushed off like he'd accused her of doing.

Keeli felt a twinge now, though, that she had rushed off before telling anyone where she was going. But it wasn't as if she was in any danger here. The house where Luther had held her was a crime scene because of the murder. Uniformed officers stood outside while evidence technicians inventoried it. She probably could have called and asked about the scratches.

But Detective Robertson might not have been the only dirty cop still on Luther's payroll. He could have more uniformed officers like the rookie he'd sent after the eyewitness. Or he could have had another crime scene tech doing his bidding, like the guy who'd tried to get the evidence from Wendy Thompson before the trial started.

So maybe coming here wasn't that safe—even with the officers on duty. She recognized one of the young men at the door. "Can I quickly check inside a moment?" she asked with a bright smile.

"You're not a cop anymore, Keeli," the man reminded her, but he smiled back.

She nodded. "I know, but this is where Luther brought me after the courthouse and I think I might have lost a necklace here…"

"You can't have forgotten that it'll have to go to the evidence room first anyway," he said.

"Can I just check anyway?" she asked. "I want to make sure it's here, or I need to keep looking. It's a family heirloom my mother gave me when I graduated the police academy." She was lying, of course, because her mother hadn't given her anything but disappointment. But she made her voice crack with emotion, which wasn't hard to fake. Her heart ached over how Spencer had treated her, over his thinking that she didn't care about the baby she carried. About *his* baby…

Realization dawned. That was why he'd been so angry. He must have thought she didn't really want his child. She did. But the baby wasn't all she wanted. She wanted him, too, but only if he could accept her the way she was.

If he could love her the way she was…

But nobody had ever loved and accepted Keeli like that.

She blinked against the threat of tears, and the officer groaned. "All right, you can go inside." And he opened the door for her.

She slipped through the garage to the kitchen door. The table was still there and dusted with the powder used to check for fingerprints.

Keeli leaned down and blew the dust from the gouges in the wood. It wasn't a doodle or a name. The gouges formed numbers. Numbers for what?

Not enough for a phone. Maybe an address? Or a flight number. She remembered Luther talking about a plane.

She didn't know if anyone else had noticed it and didn't dare point it out—not to people she could not trust. But who *could* she trust?

Parker must have sided with Spencer about her carelessness or why else would he have taken her off the assignment? Or maybe he'd just had enough of their constant bickering...

Keeli would miss that, and she would miss Spencer, too. But eventually she'd have to see him again—when their child was born. She pressed her palm to her stomach, wishing she could feel the baby move—wishing she could hear that heartbeat again and know that her baby was really all right.

But she knew nothing would really be okay until Luther was apprehended. Even if he left River City, he would find a way to still control his drug business and settle his old scores. Nobody would be safe with him free. Not Spencer—even with a new bodyguard—and not she and her child either.

They had to find him. She had to figure out what that number was. And she had some idea of where to look...

* * *

Spencer didn't know where to look. Keeli could have gone anywhere—to all Luther's old haunts. He owned so many businesses in River City and ran his business pretty much on every street corner and college campus, too.

"You don't know that she's trying to find Luther," Parker told him. He was in the driver's seat; as Spencer's new bodyguard, he had insisted on driving.

Spencer hated this—hated this feeling of helplessness he'd had since Luther had first made his threats from jail to take out everyone associated with his trial. He wanted to go back to driving himself—to worry about just the usual perps wanting revenge—not someone like Luther, who seemed to have unlimited financial and manpower resources.

With as much money as the drug lord had, he could be anywhere.

"You know that she is," Spencer said. "You know Keeli—she's not giving up on putting Luther away."

"That's exactly what you claimed she and the rest of my team did when they left the vice unit," Parker reminded him.

Spencer had talked a lot of smack over the past several weeks. Keeli wasn't the only one he'd given a hard time. "I'm sorry," he said, and admitted, "I shouldn't have said that." Since working with the Payne Protection Agency, he'd seen that they were every bit as dedicated to maintaining law and order as they'd been in the vice unit.

"You've said a lot of stuff you shouldn't have," Parker reprimanded him. "And I'm not the one you need to apologize to."

"I know," he said, and a tightness in his chest made it hard to breathe. He'd been such a damn idiot. "That's why we need to find her."

Before she found Luther...

"That's probably why she left," Parker said. "She wanted to get away from you."

"I've been a bigger ass to her than that, and she didn't quit," Spencer reminded him. "She didn't run away." Not even when she should have, but maybe, because she'd run once, she had vowed to never run away again.

Parker shook his head. "You're a damn fool, Dubridge. You can't see what's right in front of your face."

Heat rushed to his face right now along with his humiliation. "You're talking about Robertson."

"No," Parker said. "He fooled many of us. I'm talking about Keeli. You can't see how badly you're hurting her."

"I'm trying to stop her from getting hurt!" Spencer gritted out. "That's why I didn't want her to protect me anymore. I don't want her getting hurt because of me."

"That hurts them more."

"What?"

"Women like Keeli—like my sister, Nikki," he said. "They're strong, independent women. They deserve our respect."

"I respect the hell out of her," Spencer retorted, especially now that he knew just how much she'd survived—growing up on the streets.

Parker shook his head. "It doesn't sound like it—not when you're constantly doubting her abilities. She was a damn good cop and she's an even better bodyguard."

"She was a very good cop," Spencer said. That was

why he knew that she'd found Luther or at least a lead to where he was—even before Parker's cell phone rang.

Parker hit the Bluetooth connection and Keeli's voice filled the interior of the SUV. "It's an airfield."

"What?" her boss asked.

"I found an address scratched into a table at the house where Luther held me, and I remembered hearing him talking to someone—just a one-sided conversation. He must have written down the number then."

"How do you know what it's for?" Spencer asked the question.

She uttered a ragged sigh that rattled her cell phone and the Bluetooth speakers in the SUV. She didn't sound happy to hear his voice, but she answered him anyway, "Because I know...and I found an airfield that has the same street address."

"What is it?" Parker asked.

She read off the number and street for them. The airstrip had to be far out of town. "It's mostly just for crop dusters and small private planes," she said.

Spencer knew it. He'd suspected for years that Luther ran drugs through that airport. But he had never been able to trace it back to him because Luther had had his middlemen do all the work moving the drugs. That meant that Luther might not have had the address until he spoke to one of them and wrote it down.

It all made sense.

And Parker must have thought so too because he said, "I'll call the chief to get the FBI out there."

"I'm already on my way," Keeli said.

Spencer cursed.

And Parker echoed it. "Don't go near there!" he ordered. "He might see you."

There was no *might* about it. He would. Keeli was impossible not to notice.

"And he won't be alone out there," Spencer warned her. "You'll be outnumbered."

And then it wouldn't matter how damn good she was, she would still wind up dead. And losing her and their child would kill Spencer, too. He loved her too much to survive without her.

He wanted to tell her that, but he knew he'd said too much already, and she probably wasn't willing to listen to him say anything more. She confirmed that fear when she disconnected the call.

Parker looked across the console at Spencer and shook his head. "Hell, maybe you're right about her. Maybe she does have a death wish. She needs to wait until we get there."

But they both knew that if it looked like Luther might get away, she wouldn't wait. She would go in alone no matter how outnumbered she was.

He was going to get away with murder—with a lot of murders—just as he'd planned. It was all working out now. Sure, he had to leave River City. But he would make some physical changes, and he'd be back some day. Just not for a while...

And before he came back, he would make sure every damn Payne was dead, including the bodyguards who worked for them and the chief of police. Hopefully some of them had died today.

He hadn't stuck around to find out, though. He'd had things to do before he left, like picking up a briefcase of cash from the bank manager he'd been work-ing with for years. For a cut, the guy had been happy to help hide money and move it to accounts Luther could access wherever he wound up.

To start, he was going someplace warm—a nice area in Central America from which he'd received a lot of shipments. He'd always wanted to visit that part of the world. This was all going to work out for him. He could be semiretired from the business, running it from afar for a while.

Hell, maybe they'd all done him a favor—making him cut back and take life a little easier. He grinned as he waited for the pilot to finish inspecting the small plane. The trip was a long one; they would have to stop a couple of times to refuel. He wasn't as worried about that as he was to just get the hell out of River City.

He probably should have headed here straight from jail. But he'd been so pissed then that he'd wanted to settle those scores before he left. Now he knew he didn't have to be here to get his revenge.

He could get it even from thousands of miles away—where he would be very soon.

The pilot was taking a damn long time, though. Too damn long…

A chill chased down Luther's spine, leaving him as cold as he'd felt in jail. He could not go back there. But his gaze went beyond the plane and he stared at the airfield. There were just a few hangars along the strip. No commercial airport or security. The only ac-tual security was the crew he'd brought in to watch this hangar and the shipments that came in and out of it.

But that crew was thin right now. Most of his men were back at the Payne house, carrying out the attack there. He hadn't wanted any of them to come from there to here—in case they were followed.

Feeling that chill again, he lifted his binoculars to his eyes and peered around the area. It was nearly hidden on the other side of the fence around the airfield, parked behind some brush and scrubby trees. But he turned the binoculars and brought it into sharper focus. A black SUV.

And he cursed.

Sure, there were a lot of them on the road—including the one he'd driven here. But he just knew this one belonged to the Payne Protection Agency. He knew because he could see the blond hair of the woman behind the steering wheel.

Just like he'd thought, Keeli Abbott had a hell of a lot of lives. She had somehow survived Robertson's last attempt to take out her and Dubridge. Luther turned his attention to the passenger's seat of the SUV, but it was empty.

Where the hell was Dubridge?

Maybe he hadn't been as lucky as she was. Or maybe he just wasn't as smart. Instead of the detective tracking Luther down, Keeli had.

Luther knew now what he should have known when he'd nearly put that bullet in her head. He wasn't going to get away—until he took her out.

Chapter 24

He is going to get away. The plane was out of the hangar with the pilot inspecting it. They would take off soon. Keeli just knew it.

But she didn't know how to stop it. Alone…

Where the hell was everyone else?

Parker had ordered her to wait. So she'd parked outside the fence, behind some scrubby trees. Through the brush and the windshield, she studied the airfield. It was hidden on the rural outskirts of River City—not far from the Payne family home. If Luther had gone right here from the house, he probably would have already been gone.

He must have stopped somewhere—to get something. Probably money.

He would need a lot of it to disappear so that nobody could find him. And if he got on that plane, Keeli knew that was just what would happen—nobody would find him.

She had to stop him.

And she couldn't wait for reinforcements, not with time running out. She thought about calling Parker again. When she'd left the house where Luther had held her, she'd bummed a cell phone off the police officer who'd let her into the crime scene. But she knew that if she called again, he would tell her not to do what she was about to do, what she *had t*o do…

But how the hell was she going to stop Luther?

There was a fence all around the airfield—with just one gate in it. And of course Luther had armed guards stationed at that gate. They weren't going to just open it up and let her onto the airfield.

She could drive the SUV through the gates and maybe take out the guards in the process. But then the guards at the hangar would see her and start shooting.

Her best bet was to try to remain undetected until she had Luther. Where in the world was he now? She'd seen him moving around inside the hangar earlier. Or at least she'd thought it was him. It was hard for her to see clearly from this distance. Usually there was a pair of binoculars in the Payne Protection SUVs, but she hadn't found one in this vehicle.

Fortunately she'd found extra ammunition for the weapon she'd taken from Detective Robertson. Many of the bodyguards with the agency still used the same kind of gun that they'd had when working for the River City PD: a Glock. Keeli had a feeling that she would need all that extra ammunition—if she tried going after Luther alone.

But was she good enough to take out what was

left of his crew on her own? Or was she being reckless like Spencer had accused her of being? Was she knowingly putting herself in too much danger? When she'd first joined the police force, she'd been so determined to prove that her small size didn't affect her ability to do the job, that she could take care of herself. So she had refused backup when she probably should have had it...

She had taken chances she probably shouldn't have taken, but she'd also struggled to trust anyone else to back her up—then. For so long she'd struggled to trust anyone at all. But now, seeing things from Spencer's perspective, she finally understood why he had had a problem with how she'd done her job, with how she'd put herself in danger.

And it wasn't just herself she was putting in peril anymore. She pressed her palm over her belly. She couldn't feel anything. When would she?

She should have asked the doctor that. And the million other questions that flitted suddenly through her mind. But the sound of that heartbeat and sight of that little peanut on the screen had struck her dumb. She hadn't been able to think at all then—just react—as love had flooded her.

That love hadn't been just for her baby. It had been for the baby's father as well. Even as pissed off as he made her, she still loved the idiot. She didn't know how they could ever be together, though.

But if she did something stupid here and lost her life, they wouldn't have the chance to figure out how to coexist. And maybe even worse than that, she would have proven that Spencer was right about her. That she was too reckless.

Her lips curved into a smile as she thought of him. Stupid, chauvinistic bastard...

Damn, she loved him. And she loved their baby, too.

Too much to risk her life or the child's—even to stop Luther from getting away. She reached for the borrowed cell phone, needing to call Parker and see where they were.

Because they had to be close...

They had to stop him.

But before she could punch in Parker's number, the driver's door jerked open and strong hands dragged her from the SUV. She tried pulling her weapon from her holster, but when she reached for it, it was gone. Somebody had pulled it before she'd managed to grab it.

Then those strong hands whirled her around so that she stared down the barrel of that gun—into the cold eyes of Luther Mills.

Just like at the courthouse, he'd caught her unaware. But this time she knew that he wouldn't let her go like he had the last time.

This time she knew he was going to kill her.

He is going to kill her.

The minute Spencer saw the open driver's door of the SUV, that was what he thought. Not about himself killing her...

Because no matter how angry she made him, he could never hurt her. Physically. But Parker might have been right that he'd hurt her emotionally.

He hated how much of an ass he'd been to her and wanted to make up for his bad behavior. But that open door warned that he might not have the chance.

Because if Luther caught her again, he was going to kill her. If he hadn't already...

"We don't know what this means," Parker said, his jaw rigid as he slowed his SUV next to the one Keeli had driven there. "We don't know that she's inside the fence."

"We know she's inside," he said. They'd driven around the perimeter looking for her until they'd found the SUV. She hadn't been anywhere else outside the fence.

"But we don't know if she climbed over the fence and went willingly or not..."

Parker wasn't making him feel any better. "I almost hope she did."

Because then she might still have a chance...

If Luther had her...

Panic and dread clutched his heart.

Parker had stopped his SUV to step out and investigate. Spencer didn't care how she had left her vehicle— just that she was gone. And he had to find her before it was too late. So he climbed over the console into the driver's seat. He shifted and pressed on the accelerator.

Parker called out to him, but he couldn't hear what he said—over the roar of the engine as he barreled toward the gate. Maybe he'd wanted him to wait for the others.

But Keeli hadn't waited. And neither could he...

Not with her life on the line.

In his rearview mirror, he could see other vehicles, some with lights flashing, barreling down the road toward the airstrip. That just meant that Luther would take off faster in his plane—maybe taking Keeli with him.

Spencer drew the weapon Parker had given him

from his holster and pointed it at the guys guarding the gate. But they were too busy trying to avoid the metal and the bumper of the SUV as he crashed through the fence.

He headed straight to the plane. And as he did, he finally saw Keeli—being dragged from the hangar toward that plane. If she boarded it, he would never see her again.

So he pressed harder on the accelerator, racing across the airstrip before Luther could reach it with his hostage. And the SUV clipped one of the wings, tipping the plane forward. There was no way in hell it could take off now.

But he felt no satisfaction. Only fear…

More shots rang out, striking the SUV. He ducked, but he couldn't hunker down inside and wait for the others. Not with Keeli in Luther's clutches. He pushed open the door and, despite hearing her screaming, *"Don't,"* he stepped onto the tarmac.

"You should've known he wasn't going to listen," Luther said as he tightened his grip on Keeli. He had one arm locked tightly around her waist while his other arm was raised, with the barrel of his gun pressed to her head.

How the hell was Spencer going to hit Luther without Luther squeezing that trigger, even if just in reflex, and killing her? He didn't know, and his heart ached with his dilemma—the same one he'd faced at the courthouse when Luther had dragged her away from him.

Spencer couldn't lose her. He couldn't lose her and their baby. He had to figure it out this time. But did he have time?

The others were closing in; he could hear gunfire erupting all around him. And once Luther knew he had no hope, he would act. Once he knew he was going down, he would try to take down as many other people as he could with him.

And he would start with Keeli...

Unless Spencer could make him mad enough to turn that gun on him instead...

"How like you, Luther, to hide behind a woman," Spencer goaded him.

But Luther just laughed—as if he recognized Spencer's ploy. And then he turned the tables to remark, "How like you to suggest that women are somehow weaker than men."

Keeli stiffened and strained in Luther's embrace, trying to escape or to get to Spencer. She added her sentiment to Luther's remark, "He's a chauvinist ninety-nine percent of the time."

"Maybe I should let her loose," Luther told Spencer. "She'd probably take you out for me. She must not be your bodyguard anymore, or she wouldn't have showed up here without you. So it's no longer her job to protect you."

Spencer nodded. "It's true. I told Parker I didn't want her anymore." Not as his bodyguard. He wanted her as much more than that—as his soul mate, his wife...

"So then I'll take her," Luther said. "I'll take her and that Payne Protection SUV." He took a step toward the vehicle, pushing Keeli ahead of him.

Spencer glanced back at him and shrugged. "I don't know, man, I hit your plane pretty hard. Not sure it's drivable anymore."

The plane certainly was not.

"I'll find out," Luther said, and he moved Keeli a little closer.

"Don't let him get away!" Keeli shouted at Spencer.

He had no intention of doing that—no intention of letting Luther take her away from him again either. So he squeezed the trigger of the gun.

Air hissed out of the tire his bullet struck.

And Luther cursed.

But he didn't pull that gun away from Keeli's head like Spencer had hoped. He didn't point it at him instead. That was what he needed to do.

Even if he took a bullet, it would give someone else time to take a shot at Luther—time to take him down before he could put that barrel back against Keeli's head.

"Trying to piss me off?" Luther asked.

"He doesn't have to try," Keeli said. "He just does..." She knew what he was doing, too, and she stared at him intently, as if imploring him to stop.

Did she have a better plan?

Because Spencer couldn't see one...

He could see nothing but that barrel pressed against her head. He could see nothing at all in his life, in his future, if he lost her. He had to do something—because even if Luther shot her instead of him, Spencer's life was over without Keeli. He wanted to tell her that he loved her, that he needed her. But that would only give Luther more ammunition than he already knew he had.

How the hell many bullets did he have left in his gun? Would he be able to shoot Spencer and Keeli before someone stopped him?

Spencer wanted to look around—wanted to see if

Parker or any other bodyguards were close. But he didn't dare take his attention from Luther and Keeli.

If only he hadn't taken his attention from her before, if only he hadn't had Parker remove her as his bodyguard...then she wouldn't have been alone. Luther wouldn't have been able to get to her like he had.

In trying to protect her, Spencer had failed her—just like he'd failed Rebecca. And he was worried that he was going to lose her, too.

Luther savored the fear on Dubridge's face. The detective wasn't worried about dying, though. He was worried about losing Keeli. So maybe Luther should just pull the trigger now—with the barrel pressed right against her temple. Then he'd get the chance to savor Dubridge's horror and grief. But he had no doubt he wouldn't have much time to enjoy himself—before he died, too.

Dubridge would kill him, or the other bodyguards flooding the airfield would. Damn. His crew had failed dismally at the Payne house.

They must have been more heavily guarded than he'd realized. More prepared...or maybe even prewarned. Maybe he had a damn leak on his crew like the River City PD had had a leak.

"You know, Dubridge, I thought about recruiting you," he admitted. "Hell, I thought about recruiting you all. That's why I had Robertson find out as much as he could about everyone. He told me from the get-go that there was no corrupting you. That you had this white knight complex that made you want to be the hero you couldn't be to your old girlfriend."

Keeli flinched. He felt her face move against the

barrel. Was he pressing it too tightly? He didn't care. Where he had that barrel pressed, with his finger on the trigger, was the only thing keeping him alive.

Dubridge was afraid to fire at anything other than a tire right now. He knew that if he tried to hit Luther, Luther would take Keeli out with him.

Keeli as well as her and Dubridge's unborn baby…

"If you want to play the white knight now," Luther continued, "you need to help me get out of here. And then I'll let her live." Dubridge helping him escape the airfield was Luther's only chance of living. He knew it.

So did Keeli. Despite the barrel pressed to her temple, she tried to shake her head. And she murmured, "No… don't let him get away."

"Don't you want to live?" Luther asked her. "Don't you want to have that baby you're carrying? This is your only chance at surviving."

She tried shaking her head again. "It's your only chance," she said. "You won't let me live."

"I did the last time," he reminded her. But he'd regretted it ever since…

And she must have known it because now she snorted derisively. "That's a mistake you won't make twice."

No. It wasn't. Yet somehow he couldn't bring himself to squeeze that trigger. What the hell was it about Keeli that got to him?

He'd been willing to kill Rosie Mendez, so she wouldn't testify against him. And he'd had a thing for Rosie since they were kids in school together.

Hell, he'd even been willing to kill his brother Tyce—for getting between him and his leverage with the judge—namely the judge's daughter Bella Holmes.

But he wouldn't have been the one pulling the trigger for either of those murders. He'd ordered someone else to do it. Was that the problem?

Had he gotten soft all those long weeks he'd spent in jail—since Dubridge had arrested him? Had he lost the killer instinct he'd had since he was eight years old and put a bullet in his old man?

"You don't want to shoot her," Dubridge said, his dark eyes narrowed as if he was somehow reading Luther's mind.

He snorted. "You don't know me, Spence..." He mocked him with the nickname the old detective had used for him. "You didn't grow up like Keeli and I did."

Maybe that was it—the reason he couldn't just squeeze that damn trigger. Or maybe it was because he knew what would happen once he did: he would die.

He could see the shadows on the tarmac from other people rushing up. They were close but not close enough to have a clean shot. He stood between the plane and the SUV—protected—until he killed Keeli.

Once she dropped, he would, too.

So he had to try one last time. "Get me out of here," he told Dubridge. "And I will let her live."

The detective tilted his head. He was considering it; Luther could tell. The guy was obviously head over heels in love and would do anything to protect this woman and their unborn child.

Even help Luther escape?

But Keeli was just as determined to stop him. She didn't shake her head this time. She just murmured, "Don't..."

"Shut up!" Luther yelled at her. And with his arm around her, he shook her a little. Just a little…

But he'd moved her just enough that the barrel slipped away from her head. And she went limp, slumping low against him. Had she passed out?

No. She'd given Spencer a clear shot.

At least he wouldn't have to worry about going back to jail or to trial.

He flinched in anticipation of the bullet. And he squeezed the trigger—hoping like hell that he hit her, just as the bullet hit him… Right between the eyes.

Chapter 25

Keeli fell—hitting the asphalt hard. The breath whooshed from her lungs, leaving her stunned and immobile. But even while she lay still, everyone around her moved. She heard footsteps running across the tarmac, heard voices shouting and sirens wailing in the distance.

Spencer reached her first, dropping to his knees beside her. "Are you hurt?" he asked, his deep voice gruff with emotion. "Did he hit you?"

She turned her face to stare up at him. He looked so pale—so shaken. "Are you okay?" she croaked out.

She wasn't sure where Luther's gun had been pointing when he'd fired it. She felt no wounds. She'd barely scraped her hands when she hit the ground. But a bullet could have hit Spencer. She studied his face, which looked pinched with pain. He was hurting.

She just wasn't sure if it was physically.

Not that he was probably too upset about hitting Luther. He had hit him—hadn't he? She doubted the killer would have let her go if he hadn't been wounded.

Or worse.

She struggled to sit up. And she saw his body lying just a few feet away from where she'd fallen.

Luther wasn't going to escape now. He was clearly gone, blood pooling beneath his head. His eyes stared up at them, and she couldn't be certain but it looked like defeat in his gaze. He must have known that Spencer wouldn't help him escape—no matter how hard he'd tried to negotiate.

"What the hell were you thinking?"

She stiffened at the question, but it wasn't Spencer who hurled it at her. Parker shouted it as he joined them.

"I told you to wait!" He continued his rant while Spencer remained curiously silent.

His hands shook as he helped her up from the ground. And she looked at him again—trying to see if he was hurt. He looked fine. She could see no blood on him—nothing to indicate that he'd been shot.

But she remembered how Tyce had been wounded without anyone noticing when he'd rescued the judge's daughter. Before she could reach out to check him, though, he stepped back. Or maybe Parker had pushed him aside.

"Why did you disobey a direct order?" Parker asked.

"I didn't," she defended herself. "I was sitting outside the fence. I didn't think he'd notice me there…" But Luther must have had the binoculars she'd wished she'd had. If she'd been able to see where he was, he wouldn't have sneaked up on her like he had, which was embarrassing to admit. "I didn't see him coming until he pulled me out of the SUV."

"You got too close," her boss said.

She groaned as she realized that he was right. And maybe Spencer had been, too. Maybe she took unnecessary chances in order to prove herself just as good as her male counterparts. She nodded in agreement. "I know—I know... I'm sorry."

Parker uttered a weary sigh. "I'm sorry, too," he murmured. "You just scared the crap out of me. I couldn't get a clean shot off. Nobody could..." He turned toward Spencer and grabbed his shoulder. "But you—you did damn good."

Spencer shrugged off Parker's hand and his praise. Shaking his head, he said, "I only got the shot because Keeli set it up. She got the barrel away from her head..." He shuddered now.

And as she realized exactly how close she had come to dying, her knees began to shake and she nearly fell again. But Spencer reached out, his hand closing around her shoulder, and he steadied her.

Steadied and unsettled her at the same time. He looked so intense, his dark gaze so piercing as he stared down at her. "Are you okay?" he asked again.

He was probably worried about the baby, worried that either her recklessness or Luther's rough handling of her had endangered her pregnancy. She had no pain in her stomach, though.

The only pain was in her heart. She wished he was worried about her for her sake—that he loved her like he already seemed to love their baby.

She sucked in a breath and nodded. "Yeah, I'm fine." Then she curved her lips into a smile and added, "You can yell at me now, too."

That was probably the only reason he'd refrained from shouting at her like Parker had—because he hadn't known if she was all right.

He shook his head. "I don't want to yell at you," he said.

That was hard to believe—considering that she'd been in more danger with Luther than she'd been with Detective Robertson or during the shoot-out at the Payne-Lynch farmhouse.

But maybe he'd just given up on her quitting her dangerous job. Maybe he'd just given up on her.

But then, to her surprise, he said, "What I want to do is marry you."

His statement nearly had her knees giving out. The shock of his proposal almost had her tumbling to the tarmac again.

But she knew why he'd proposed and it had nothing to do with love for her. She'd promised herself years ago—when she'd run away from home—that she would never live with someone again who didn't love her. Because she knew how much it hurt…

Like she was hurting now, her heart aching.

She just shook her head and walked away from him.

Spencer's face burned with humiliation as everybody stared at him. Nobody could believe he'd proposed. Hell, *he* couldn't believe it. But he'd known in that moment when he'd nearly lost her that he didn't want to be apart from her ever again.

But when she walked off, he wasn't allowed to follow her. Too many people fired questions at him, taking his weapon—taking his statement. He was sure that somewhere on the airfield she was doing the same, giving her report, telling what had happened and how Luther had died.

Spencer was glad the killer was dead and no longer the threat he'd been to so many people. But he took no satisfaction in having taken a life—even a life as reprehensible as the one Luther Mills had lived.

So he ignored the accolades, even from the chief.

"Good work, Dubridge," Lynch said as he literally patted his back. "You'll certainly get a promotion for this."

He didn't want a promotion. He wasn't even sure he still wanted to work for River City PD. He was beginning to think that, like Keeli, he might make a better bodyguard than a cop. But he wasn't going to ask Parker for a job until he got an answer—a real answer—to the question he'd asked her.

But she was gone.

He'd been so intent on saving her from Luther that he hadn't realized he'd already lost her. No. He'd never really had her. That was the problem.

All the years he'd treated her like crap had ruined whatever chance he might have had with her. Sure, they'd made love. No. He had made love. He loved her.

She must have just been attracted to him. That was all. But Keeli was so intent on doing her job and doing it well that he was surprised she would have even given in to just attraction. It had to be more than that.

His feelings couldn't be this intense if they were one-sided. Because what he felt for her was so much more than he'd ever felt in his life.

"Go to her apartment," Parker said.

He hadn't realized the man had been watching him so intently that he'd pretty much read his mind. But maybe they were both reading the situation wrong. Spencer really knew very little about Keeli. He had no idea how she really felt about him. Maybe she still hated his guts like she always had. "I don't know where she lives…"

Parker gave him the address. Then he encouraged him, "Ask her again."

Spencer hesitated.

"What's the worst she can do?" Parker asked. "Say no again?"

"Shoot me," Spencer corrected him.

Parker sighed. "Well, that too…"

So a short while later, when he knocked at her door, he braced himself when she opened it. But she didn't hold a gun on him—just a hard stare.

"What do you want?" she asked, and her voice was as hard and cold as her blue eyes.

"I told you at the airfield," he said. "*You*. I want you."

But she just shook her head again. She stepped back and allowed him inside her place, but maybe that was just because she didn't want any of her neighbors to overhear their conversation. Her apartment was small and tidy but she'd spent very little time there since becoming his bodyguard.

When he saw it, he understood why she hadn't brought him there. With soft pink walls and flowered furniture, it was dainty and girlie—all the things he'd always teased her about being.

"No," she said. "You don't want me. You want the

baby. You want to be able to keep it safe. You don't trust me to do it."

He hadn't gotten hit, but his head began to pound—maybe it was from where the metal had struck him. Had that been earlier today or days ago? He couldn't remember when... So much had happened.

Or maybe that pounding was the sound of his racing pulse. He was almost as scared as he'd been when Luther had held that gun to her head.

"What are you talking about?" he asked her.

"Same thing Luther was talking about," she said. "Your white knight complex. You want to try to protect this baby like you weren't able to protect Rebecca."

He shook his head now. "That's not it."

She snorted derisively. "You can't tell me that you would want to marry me if I wasn't pregnant with your baby. That's what this is about..." She pressed her palm to her stomach. "That's the only reason you're proposing."

She believed that; he could see the certainty on her beautiful face. That wasn't all he saw either. He saw the longing. And he hoped he was reading it right—that she wasn't saying no because she didn't have feelings for him. She was just afraid that he didn't have genuine feelings for her.

He stepped forward and wrapped his arms around her. Then he lowered his head and he kissed her with all the passion burning inside him for her. But he didn't just give her the desire, he gave her the love that overwhelmed him.

When he pulled back, he was panting for breath and so was she. Her face was flushed with desire while her eyes were wide, as if she was dazed. Or stunned.

And he hadn't even said it yet.

So he said it now, "I love you. That's why I want to marry you—that's the *only* reason why. Because I love you!"

All the color drained from her face, leaving her eyes wide. Her voice trembled as she replied, "Don't lie to me. Please, don't lie to me…"

She had called him a lot of things over the years—things that he admittedly deserved to be called. But not this one. "I'm not lying," he insisted.

But she shook her head, refusing to believe him.

And then he realized, it wasn't that she didn't believe him. It was that she didn't believe she could be loved after how badly her family had let her down all those years ago when she'd been forced to run away from home.

He reached for her again, pulling her close, and his heart ached with the pain she must have suffered. He wanted to make sure that she never felt that way again—that she was never hurt again.

"I love you," he told her. "I love you."

Keeli wanted to believe him—so badly. But it was too convenient. She pulled back and stared up at him again. "If you love me, you have a crappy way of showing it."

His face flushed, and he nodded in agreement. "I know I do," he admitted. "And I will regret that for the rest of my life. But you know why I treated you so badly. I was trying to protect you. I didn't want you doing the dangerous jobs that you've done."

She tensed now. "Done? You think I'm going to quit now that you've proposed to me?"

"No," he hastily assured her. "*You* won't be the one quitting."

She stepped back and bumped into her couch. Her apartment was small—a tiny living room, a tiny galley kitchen and an equally tiny bathroom and bedroom. Spencer made the space seem even smaller.

"You're lying again," she said. "There's no way you're going to quit River City PD, especially now. You're the hero of the hour for taking out Luther Mills." Not hour. Day. Month. Year.

His career with the River City PD would take off even more than it already had.

"I'm thinking I might make a better bodyguard than a detective," he said.

And anger coursed through her. "No! You can't follow me around all day trying to keep me safe! I can't live like that. You're going to make us both crazy."

"Is that why you keep saying no?" he asked. "Is it because you think I'm going to make you quit your job?"

It was because he didn't love her—no matter what he claimed—that she'd said no. He'd already had the great love of his life—with Rebecca. And she...

Nobody had ever loved Keeli—not even her own mother. She wouldn't give her heart to someone who didn't really want it. But she was afraid it was already too late.

"You can't make me do anything," she pointed out. Except love him...

Somehow he'd made her do that.

"I've certainly tried," he admitted with a sigh that sounded as if it was almost regretful.

But she must have been wrong.

Then he said it, "And I'm sorry for how I treated you. I should have respected that you know what you're doing. That you wouldn't deliberately put yourself in danger unless it was to protect someone else."

She narrowed her eyes and studied his handsome face. He had to be lying. But the one thing she'd always counted on from Spencer Dubridge was the truth. He was known for always being brutally honest. "Parker didn't think so back at the airstrip."

"He was wrong," Spencer said. "Just like I was wrong back at the Payne house. I was so scared that I was going to lose you that I overreacted."

"You were afraid I was going to lose the baby."

"That, too," he admitted, and there was the honesty she'd counted on from him. "I love our baby—I love our baby because we made it together. But I love you more."

"Stop saying that," she said, as her heart raced with panic. Because if he kept saying it, she might start to believe him. And if she discovered later that he really was lying, she'd be humiliated and devastated and, worst of all, heartbroken.

He reached out and slid his fingertips along her jaw. "Why won't you believe me?" he asked. "Don't you know how incredible you are?"

She lifted her chin, pulling away from his touch. It was making her skin tingle, her pulse race with desire, as it always did—as he always did. "I know how incredible I am," she said, and maybe she was the one lying now. "But you've certainly never acted like you knew."

"I knew," he said. "I knew from the first day you walked into River City PD. And I wanted you…" His breath came out in a ragged sigh and he stepped close again, his hard body brushing against hers. "And that scared the crap out of me. I didn't want to fall for someone with a dangerous job, with a dangerous life."

"You didn't want to lose someone like you lost Rebecca."

He nodded. "I didn't…"

"But I can take care of myself," she said. "And bad things happen to people no matter what. Even soccer moms…"

He nodded again. "I know. I was overreacting, but the way I feel about you—" he leaned down and pressed his forehead against hers "—it makes me crazy. *You* make me crazy."

She chuckled. "Don't blame me for that." Her heart was beginning to lift with hope. Could he really care about her? Could he actually love her? She stared into his eyes, and finally she saw the truth—and the love.

"Can you forgive me for being such an idiot?" he asked.

She smiled and leaned closer, pressing her lips to his. She kissed him gently before replying, "Yes…"

"Can you love me?" he asked gruffly.

And her smile stretched her mouth wider. "I already do…"

Now he stared at her incredulously. "You do?"

"Why is that so hard to believe?" she asked him.

"Because I've been a complete ass to you," he said. "And I don't deserve your forgiveness, let alone your love."

"You saved my life today," she reminded him.

He shrugged. "So what? You saved my life many more times." He touched his lips to hers in a gentle kiss. "And from more than Luther Mills or his crew.

You saved my life by making me fall for you, by making me risk my heart again."

"I'm sorry about Rebecca," she whispered. And she felt a twinge of jealousy and fear that he would never love her like he had his high school sweetheart.

He stared deeply into her eyes, as if he was trying to read her mind. "She was special," he said. "And I loved her. But it was more the love of friendship than what I feel for you, than what we have."

She sighed. "No. You and I have never been friends."

"That was my fault," he said. "I didn't want to let you close. I didn't want to risk getting hurt if you got hurt. I don't just love you, Keeli. I am *in love* with you—so deeply, hopelessly in love with you."

Warmth flooded her heart as she finally let that love in; he really did feel that way about her. She believed him now. And she wanted him to believe her.

"You are a jerk," she said.

And his brow puckered with confusion.

"You're also the hardest-working lawman I know," she said. "You stuck with it—you wouldn't give up—until you brought Luther down."

"You didn't give up, either," he said. "I was a fool for ever accusing you and the others of having done that. You found a way to protect people before they got hurt. I was just trying to get justice after they already had been hurt."

"And that's noble and necessary." She looked him square in the eye. "You can quit if you want—if you think you would be a better bodyguard. But I've always thought you were an amazing detective. And when I learned about Rebecca…" From Luther Mills of all people. "...I understood why you gave me such a hard time, that you were worried I would get hurt."

"I should have trusted you," he admitted. "I know how damn good you are at what you do. I should have known you could take care of yourself."

"I needed you today," she reminded him. "Luther would have killed me if not for you."

He shrugged. "I don't know. I think you would have figured a way to get yourself out of that, like you have every other dangerous situation you've been in. I trust you to keep you and our baby safe. The only reason I want to marry you is because I love you and want to be with you—always."

Tears stung her eyes, and she blinked furiously. But a tear escaped, slipping through her lashes to run down her face.

"Pregnancy hormones?" he asked, as he wiped her cheek.

She shook her head. "I don't blame the baby," she said. "I blame you."

He sucked in a breath. "I know I've been an ass, but I never wanted to make you cry."

"These are happy tears," she assured him. "Because you've made me happy. I love you."

"So you'll marry me?"

"Yes!"

He swung her up in his arms then and carried her into the bedroom. They made love slowly and gently this time—because they knew they had all the time in the world. They had the rest of their lives.

And a lifetime of love...